ALSO BY BUD SHRAKE

NOVELS

Blood Reckoning
But Not for Love
Blessed McGill
Peter Arbiter
Limo (with Dan Jenkins)
Strange Peaches
Night Never Falls
The Borderland

NONFICTION

Willie (with Willie Nelson)
Bootlegger's Boy (with Barry Switzer)

WITH HARVEY PENICK

Harvey Penick's Little Red Book
And If You Play Golf, You're My Friend
For All Who Love the Game
The Game for a Lifetime
The Wisdom of Harvey Penick

BILLY BOY

A NOVEL

Bud Shrake

SCRIBNER PAPERBACK FICTION
PUBLISHED BY SIMON & SCHUSTER

NEW YORK   LONDON   TORONTO   SYDNEY   SINGAPORE

SCRIBNER PAPERBACK FICTION
Simon & Schuster, Inc.
Rockefeller Center
1230 Avenue of the Americas
New York, NY 10020

This book is a work of fiction. Names, characters,
places, and incidents either are products of the
author's imagination or are used fictitiously. Any
resemblance to actual events or locales or persons,
living or dead, is entirely coincidental.

First Scribner Paperback Fiction edition 2002

SCRIBNER PAPERBACK FICTION and design are trademarks
of Macmillan Library Reference USA, Inc., used under license
by Simon & Schuster, the publisher of this work.

For information regarding special discounts for bulk purchases,
please contact Simon & Schuster Special Sales at 1-800-456-6798
or *business@simonandschuster.com*

Manufactured in the United States of America

10   9   8   7   6   5   4   3   2   1

The Library of Congress has cataloged
the Simon & Schuster edition as follows:
Shrake, Edwin.
   Billy Boy : a novel / by Bud Shrake.
       p.   cm.
     1. Teenage boys—Fiction. 2. Golfers—Fiction.
3. Texas—Fiction. I. Title.
PS3569.H735 B55 2001
813'.54—dc21   2001042633

ISBN 0-7432-2480-9
0-7432-2748-4 (Pbk)

DEDICATED WITH LOVE TO HELEN PENICK

Special thanks to Frances Trimble, former director of the Texas Golf Hall of Fame, for the facts about John Bredemus and to Bob Townsend for capturing Captain Tanaka's notebook.

DEDICATED WITH LOVE TO HELEN PENICK

Special thanks to Frances Trimble, former director of the Texas Golf Hall of Fame, for the facts about John Bredemus and to Bob Townsend for capturing Captain Tanaka's notebook.

BILLY
BOY

T One

HE BOY AWOKE to the snuffles of a woman softly sobbing in the bed across the room near the open window. For a moment he thought he was dreaming of his dead mother. Then he heard snoring and saw his father's undershirted back turned toward the woman, who was whimpering, "Where am I? Oh God, what has happened to me?"

She looked at the boy, surprised to see him. He rolled off his foldaway cot already dressed in Levi's and a white cotton polo shirt and white socks. He kept his eyes away from her as he tied the laces of his black tennis shoes and combed his hair with his fingers. The room stunk of whiskey and cigarettes.

"Who are you?" she said. "Where am I?"

"You came here with him," the boy said. "He's my daddy."

"He's too young to have a son your age. Why are you here?"

"This is our room," the boy said.

"I've never done anything like this before."

The boy nodded. He had pretended to be asleep when his father brought her to their hotel room after the saloons closed. A half bottle of bourbon lay on the floor on top of her white cotton dress and her earrings and her white gumsole shoes. The boy figured she was a waitress or a nurse. A cool breeze blew across his father, who slept nearest the window. They heard from down below a street-sweeping machine blasting water into the gutters.

"Please tell me you wasn't laying there watching me all night," the woman said.

"I was asleep."

"You promise?"

"We drove all night and all day and into the night again to get here. I was tired."

"Your daddy wasn't tired."

"He didn't do the driving."

With a snort, the boy's father slapped at a fly on his face, sat up and opened his eyes. He had the look of a cowboy, wide shouldered, lean, blond hair rumpled, firm jaw that needed a shave. He licked his lips and wiped his mouth with the back of a golden hairy wrist. He shook a cigarette out of a pack of Camels on the windowsill. Using the lucky Zippo he had carried through France and Germany during World War Two with his old artillery unit, he lit the cigarette and inhaled. He coughed.

"Billy Boy. Where you going in the middle of the night?" he said.

"The sun'll be up in a few minutes."

"You don't need to clear out because of her. She's leaving."

"You filthy rat, you got me drunk," the woman said.

"Billy Boy, I'm truly sorry about this. I didn't set out last night to bring a woman to the room."

The woman clutched the sheet tighter around her breasts and began weeping again, weakly. "I don't know your name," she said. "What's your damn name?"

"I'm Tyrone, remember? You said I look like Tyrone Power with a bleach job."

"Please, Jesus, I'll never drink again," the woman said. "What is your name, really?"

"Troy."

The woman looked around at the greasy wallpaper with faded roses on it.

"This room is trashy. What hotel is this?"

"The Half Moon," said Troy.

"You told me you kept a suite downtown at the Blackstone," she said.

"I'm liable to say most anything, Marie."

Hearing him speak her name, the woman looked at Troy with interest, seeing anew his opaque blue eyes that could frighten a person, his hair, crushed by the pillow, with yellow curls around his ears and forehead, streams of cigarette smoke coming from his nose and drifting around his lips. She dried her tears on the sheet and reached for Troy's cigarette to share it. She looked at the boy and frowned.

"What are you staring at?" she said.

"I'm leaving."

"You going to try for a bag at Colonial?" asked Troy.

"Yes sir."

"Not much chance for a new boy at a place like that."

"I'll try, though."

"They'll be rough on you," Troy said.

"I expect they will."

"Maybe you'll see Ben Hogan," Troy said.

"Hope so."

"Tell Ben I said 'hidy.' "

"More of your bull," the woman said. "You don't know Ben Hogan. Do you?"

"There was a time I could beat him."

"Sure there was. Two years ago when he was three-quarters dead and lay crippled in the hospital after a bus run head-on into his car," the woman said. "If he give you enough strokes, you might of beat him while he was unconscious in a cast. But now he's back on his feet, nobody can beat him."

"A golf expert, are you, Marie?" Troy said.

"My sister's husband plays every Saturday and Sunday at Rockwood Park on the Jacksboro Highway."

Troy smiled and tickled the woman's ear with a forefinger.

"I need the car today to scout around for business prospects. I'll set up a bank account," said Troy. "We'll have a first-class meal tonight when you come back, Billy Boy. You and me. We'll

3

have two big steaks with French fries and onion rings at the Cattleman's Café. We'll order shrimp cocktails to start. Tomorrow we'll find a place to live. How's that?"

"That sounds great," the boy said.

"Would you please get out of here?" the woman said. "I need to potty."

BILLY WALKED DOWN one flight of stairs and turned into the lobby of the Half Moon Hotel. The head of a steer with an eight-foot spread of horns looked out from the wall through brown glass eyes. An old black man with a mop and a bucket was wetting the white tile floor. He had stacked up three copper spittoons to clean and polish later. The night manager leaned his elbows on the registration desk. A ceiling fan creaked overhead and rustled the sports pages that he was reading in the morning *Star-Telegram*. Billy noticed a front page headline that said REDS DRIVE ON KWANG JI. The boy knew his father was worried about being called back into the Army and sent to Korea. It was five years since Troy had been discharged as a first lieutenant after serving in hard fighting during World War Two, but all commissioned officers remained in the Reserves indefinitely, and a buddy had written in a letter that the Army was getting desperate for Forward Observers in the artillery in the hills of Korea.

"Where is Colonial Country Club at?" Billy asked the night manager.

The night manager looked up from the box scores and took sight of the boy with an amused appraisal from the tennis shoes up to the tangled hair. The boy could have passed for a younger brother, but he was clearly his father's son, the night manager thought. Narrow hips, a cocky way of walking, a tilt of the head. The same blue-gray eyes. A few hours ago a drunken older version of this kid had slipped the night manager two dollars and patted his shoulder and swaggered up the stairs with Marie, who worked at the beauty shop down the block but drank in saloons up and down North Main Street and Exchange Avenue.

"Now why on earth would you want to know something like that?" the night manager said.

"I need to go there," said Billy.

"Hey, Raymond, you hear this? The kid needs to go to Colonial Country Club."

"Well, knock me down and steal my teeth," the old black man said, slapping the tile with his mop.

The night manager looked at Billy. "For what?"

"To find some work."

"What're you? A hubcap thief?"

Billy's tennis shoes squeaked on the tile as he turned abruptly and started toward the door.

"Hey, boy," the night manager said.

Billy stopped and waited.

"Colonial Country Club is on the other side of the river about ten miles south of here."

"And watch out for the po-lice," said Raymond, sloshing his mop in the bucket. "They don't want boys like you walking through the Colonial neighborhood unless you be pushing a lawn mower."

The boy stepped through the open glass-and-wood door of the Half Moon Hotel and onto the sidewalk. The air smelled rich with the odor of cow manure from the huge stockyards nearby. The street-sweeping machine had left the curbs wet and the scent more pungent. There was a hint of hay and hide in the smell, and bits of straw floated among the bugs that darted around the streetlights. The boy noted that the block housed two more walk-up hotels like the Half Moon and three saloons with the streetlights reflected in their windows. On the other side of North Main Street he saw the New Isis Theater, a movie house.

Billy loved movies, but he had been so tired after driving all the way from Albuquerque that he hadn't noticed the theater last night.

Halfway along the block Billy was relieved to find their black and yellow Chevy Bel Air, parked a little too close to the curb, but unharmed. The two-year-old Chevy was their most important possession. Truth be, Billy thought, the Chevy was their only possession other than the clothes on their backs and in their suitcases and the bank draft in his daddy's wallet. The night his daddy had arrived at their adobe house in Albuquerque two years ago in this almost new black and yellow Chevy, Troy had been laughing, looking wild and tough, flashing his big smile, staggering, drinking from a bottle of Wild Turkey. He said he won the engine and the frame of the car playing golf at Santa Fe Country Club, and the body and the tires shooting dice in the back room at El Nito in Tesuque.

Billy remembered that his mother had smiled without humor at the new Chevy and at Troy as he stumbled into the rose and lilac bushes and thumped against the wall. Hours later as Billy sat listening in his bed, smelling the scent of pinion from the log that smoldered in the fireplace, he thought he heard a slap and he seemed to hear his mother crying. Many nights while growing up, Billy had lain in bed or crouched at the door of his room listening to his parents arguing and fighting. He was afraid for his mother's beautiful frail body, angry at his daddy's rough drunken ways, ashamed of himself for not having the strength to rush into their room and make them stop. He had tried several times. At age eleven he had heard her crying and ran into the kitchen and saw blood on his mother's lips. Billy lost himself to rage. He swung a croquet mallet hard at his daddy's head, hoping to crush his skull, to kill him, to bring peace to their home. Troy had dodged the blow and knocked the boy down with an open hand, and Billy's mother ordered him back to bed. He sat in a wooden chair at his window and looked at the Sandia Mountain until the sun appeared over it, and he yearned to be gone from this house, but he was afraid to leave his mother, afraid of what Troy might do to her. Billy kept in his chair at the window until Sandia Mountain was red with light above its crest and he heard soft laughter from his parents' bedroom as they made love.

But the night Troy brought the black and yellow Chevy home, she yelled at her husband and wept loudly, and she slapped him, as she often did. And then their voices became low, solemn, restrained, broken by the dry cough his mother had developed, and about sunrise, Billy fell asleep in his chair looking out at Sandia Mountain. That was when they learned she had cancer. They buried her two weeks ago in Albuquerque and sold their house day before yesterday.

Outside the Half Moon Hotel, a slash of pink began spreading across the eastern sky, and the street lights flipped to dark as Billy was scraping away grasshoppers that had mashed against the Chevy windshield. He realized he must hurry. Golfers would be on the first tee in an hour, and he was ten miles from Colonial and on foot. It was amazing to think the golf course could be ten miles away but still inside the city. He began to understand what an enormous city Fort Worth was, and that everything from now on would be new and strange and dangerous.

L Two

LAST NIGHT Billy had noticed a city bus passing south on North Main with a DOWNTOWN sign above its front window. Pausing on the sidewalk in the dawn, Billy dug coins out of the pockets of his jeans. He found three quarters and a dime—eighty-five cents. He wondered if bus fare was a nickel or a dime and if he could make his way across this enormous city to Colonial Country Club by bus in time to catch the early golfers. His stomach rumbled with hunger. He rapped on the window of a diner until a woman with a kind face unlocked the door and sold him a Coca-Cola and four fresh hot sugar-glazed donuts in a paper bag for twenty-five cents.

Billy left the diner running, munching a donut and carrying the paper bag, swigging from the Coke with his other hand. As he arrived at the end of the block, he almost collided with a blue Chevy police car that swerved in front of him with a squealing of brakes.

"What you running from?" asked the cop sitting on the passenger side.

"I bought these donuts. I paid the woman for them," Billy said.

"Maudie don't open for half an hour yet."

"I knocked on her window."

"You mean you busted her window and stole them donuts."

"I bought them. Honest."

The cop on the driver's side got out of the car and walked around the trunk until he could see through the window of the diner. He looked at Maudie moving behind the counter. The cop was well over six feet tall, chest and biceps straining at a tailored starched blue uniform shirt. With a thumb he pushed back the bill of his soft cap, the kind of cap Billy had seen photographs of war aviators wearing, with the fifty-mission crush.

"You gonna hog them donuts?" the big cop asked.

"This is my breakfast," Billy said.

"One of them donuts would sure hit the spot with me," said the big cop. He had a square face and a blunt nose and was showing a trace of a scowl.

Billy opened his paper bag and handed each of the cops a donut, then quickly jammed the remaining one into his mouth.

"You're new in town," said the cop who leaned his head out the window.

"Yes sir."

"Well, let me tell you how it is here in Fort Worth. You don't steal nothing here. Understand? You don't burgle no houses. You don't rob nobody. You don't sass no police officers. You walk the straight and narrow path here. You say 'yes sir' and 'no sir' to your elders. You hear what I'm telling you?"

"Yes sir."

"Now if you forget these rules and show bad manners, we will jerk you off the street and beat you into a pee waddlin' squat. You'll pray to God to help you forget you was ever in Fort Worth. You understand?"

"Yes sir."

"If you are the type that feels like you need to make trouble and steal and hold up people, go to Dallas," the cop in the window said.

"Yes sir."

The big cop in the aviator cap said, "Where you heading this morning, boy?"

"To Colonial Country Club," Billy said.

Billy felt their attitude soften. They looked at him in a new and more friendly way, as if he might have decent qualities after all.

"You a caddie?" asked the big cop.

"Yes sir. I hope to work at Colonial."

"Get in the car," said the big cop.

Billy climbed into the back seat. The big cop spoke into the radio. "This is Car Seven. We're out on a personal. Won't be long."

"Ten four, Car Seven," crackled the radio as the big cop spun the wheel and the Chevy shot onto North Main and began speeding south toward the river, then over the bridge to the tall red granite county courthouse with its clock tower.

"We both used to be caddies," said the cop in the passenger seat. He smiled at Billy, his mouth curling up into his plump cheeks, a gap in front from one missing tooth. "That's hard work, kid. But you know what? It makes you feel good. It makes a man out of you."

Looking out the window, Billy saw the courthouse go past and then the huge department stores, one after another, their windows full of dressed-up clothing dummies and furniture and rich rugs, like nothing he had ever seen in Albuquerque.

"How big is this place, anyhow? Sir?" Billy asked.

"Fort Worth? Why it's big, that's all. And getting bigger every day. We got more than two hundred thousand people here now. Only a hundred years ago this was a fort on the frontier against the hostile Indians. Used to be a wildass town. Outlaws and gamblers and gunfighters. You ever hear of Luke Short or Butch Cassidy? Wyatt Earp? Machine Gun Kelly or Pretty Boy Floyd? Well, they were tough guys who operated in Fort Worth over the years and have gone to meet their maker. Now we got cattle and oil and a bomber plant. We are civilized here. Good people live in Fort Worth. The hijackers and thugs and queers and pimps and cons, the safecrackers and white slavers, the killers, we run their butt to Dallas, where they fit right in," said the cop with the plump cheeks.

A black marble and white stone building whizzed past the window.

"That's the city hall and the police station. You want to stay away from there," the big cop said, wheeling the car past six motorcycle officers who were kicking their machines into action, preparing to start their shift. They wore Sam Browne belts, aviator caps, black leather gloves and polished knee-high boots. A couple of them shouted and shook their fists at Car Seven.

South of the city hall they passed a number of small hotels.

"When you get a few bucks, kid, these places are full of whores. They're clean girls. Get regular inspections by doctors."

Billy saw dense stands of trees as the car cut through a park and then went beside what he thought must be the Trinity River. He saw a sign that said they were on University Drive. There was parkland all around, forests, rolling fields of grass.

"We're gonna let you out up here a ways, kid," said the cop with the curling smile. "It wouldn't do your new career as a Colonial caddie no good if you was seen getting out of a police car in front of the club."

"Damn, I wish I was going with you," the big cop behind the wheel said. "I love golf. I wish I'd of stayed with the game. I might have been a professional at some municipal course by now. Hey, here we are. You get out right up here. You'll see greens and fairways pretty quick, but the clubhouse is about a mile to the east. I reckon you can run a mile?"

"Yes sir. Thank you, sir," Billy said.

"Ben Hogan is my hero," the big cop said.

"He's my hero, too," said Billy.

The car stopped.

"Out you go, boy. Good luck to you. Tell Ben Hogan that if there's anybody who's pissing him off that he wants to have beat up or killed, call Car Seven and we'll handle it for him. Burgin, that's him, the driver. I'm Boyle. You got that, or do I have to spell it?"

"I won't forget, sir," Billy said.

The police car sped away the instant Billy leaped out.

He trotted along the street past what by his standards were mansions on his left—large brick homes with green lawns in the early shadows thrown by tall oak trees. To his right was a long hedgerow. Through small gaps in the hedges Billy caught glimpses of sand bunkers and a flag on a green, and he felt a rush of excitement.

A red Chrysler convertible hummed past him, then stopped fifty yards ahead. For a moment he was afraid the owner of one of these mansions was going to order him out of the neighborhood. But he kept running and saw the driver of the convertible was a girl who was looking back at him and smiling.

"Going to the club?" she asked.

"Yes."

"Get in."

Billy opened the door and sat on the first leather seats he had ever seen in an automobile. The girl pressed a shapely bare foot on the gas pedal and the car pulled smoothly away, its automatic transmission shifting. She wore a bathing suit beneath a man's dress shirt. Her short hair blew in the wind. Billy guessed the girl was about his own age. She was so beautiful that he ached to touch her.

"You're kind of cute," she said.

"You're pretty cute yourself."

"Whose guest are you?"

"I'm a caddie."

"Oh damn," she said. She steered the Chrysler to the curb and stopped. "I'm sorry, but you better get out. It's nothing personal, but I can't be seen driving a caddie to the club. I'd never hear the end of it from my grandfather."

12

"I understand," Billy said, getting out of the car. "But you're still awful cute."

"My name is Sandra," she said.

"Billy."

"Maybe I'll see you again, Billy," she said, and drove away.

Billy began running toward the clubhouse, which he could see a few blocks in the distance, a red brick building with white columns in front.

E *Three*

LVIS SPAATZ, assistant pro and caddie master at Colonial Country Club, was walking down the hill from the golf shop, passing the practice putting green and then going between the ninth green and the tenth tee, heading toward the caddie yard off in the woods north of the tenth fairway.

Elvis was reading the list of starting times on his clipboard. He had eleven foursomes going off that morning between 7:30 and noon. The spacing was leisurely, as it should be at a proper club. Now Elvis was on his way to see how many caddies had showed up for work. Elvis was beefy, with a sunburned neck that he protected by turning up the collar of his golf shirt. As a former number-one caddie at Colonial, Elvis had been promoted to junior assistant pro and given the additional duty of caddie master when old Mr. Booley, the caddie master since the Great Depression, had nearly drowned in the Trinity River flood that put the Colonial Country Club golf course under water two years ago.

"Sir."

Startled, Elvis looked up from his clipboard to see standing before him a blond-haired boy with wild blue eyes. The boy was of average height, slender but with sinewy arms.

"Don't leap out at people, kid!" Elvis had grown more nervous in the past week since he had failed his night school classes at TCU and lost his student deferment. He had become 1-A in the draft. Elvis had to decide which was the most dangerous course—to find someone to marry and make pregnant right away, or to take his chances in the Army in Korea.

"Sorry. I'm looking for a bag."

"Where'd you ever caddie before?"

"Albuquerque last summer," the boy said. "The summer before that, I worked for Mr. Hardy Loudermilk at Santa Fe."

"Hardy Loudermilk is the pro at Jal, New Mexico."

"Yes sir, I know. Jal is where my daddy grew up. Mr. Loudermilk spent the summer as pro in Santa Fe two years ago. He hired me to work for him up there."

"Those are the only places you ever caddied?"

"Those are the only places I've ever been until last night."

"Why would Hardy Loudermilk hire you to go to Santa Fe with him?"

"Mr. Loudermilk said I have some talent for the game. He coached me a little. Last summer my mother was sick and I stayed in Albuquerque to be with her."

"What did you come here for?"

"My daddy moved to Fort Worth on business. He buys and sells cattle on commission."

"I mean, why Colonial?"

"This is the best golf course in the world."

"How would you know?"

"It's where Ben Hogan plays."

"Kid, when you see Mr. Hogan, don't even look at him. If anybody catches you looking at him, you're fired."

"So I'm hired then? I can have a bag today?"

"How old are you?"

"Eighteen."

"You ain't eighteen."

"Sixteen, really."

"I'm guessing fifteen." Elvis was nineteen. He had started carrying bags at the age of eleven at Glen Garden Country Club on the east side of town. Elvis saw in the eyes of the boy from New Mexico that air of a lost puppy searching for a home, a feeling known to Elvis, who had found his first real family in the caddie yard at Glen Garden. The boys and men in the caddie yard, of all colors and ages, became his brothers once he proved he was worthy of their affection. Elvis had worked his way through Polytechnical High School on the coins and dollars he had earned as a caddie at Glen Garden. He had crossed town and advanced to assistant professional at Colonial Country Club on the wealthy west side. Elvis was on his way up in the world, if only he didn't get blown up in Korea or dragged down by a fat, lazy wife and a houseful of babies.

"We use lots of coloreds and Mexicans as caddies. That don't bother you?" said Elvis.

"Not me."

"But our number-one caddie is a white boy. Chili McWillie, youngest of the McWillie brothers. I guess you ain't heard of the McWillie brothers?"

"No, I ain't."

"The McWillie brothers have whipped forty tons of butt in this town. There's some people let out a cheer when the oldest one, Booger McWillie, was killed in Korea last month." The thought of Korea struck Elvis with dread. He forced his mind back to his starting sheet. He looked at the blank next to the name of Dr. Ira Sandpaster. Dr. Sandpaster had fired his caddie again yesterday, the fourth in the past week, the seventeenth so far this year and it was barely June. Elvis wrote the new kid's name—Billy—beside the name of Dr. Sandpaster. "Follow me."

Billy walked behind Elvis on the route from the clubhouse to the caddie yard. The boy was astonished at the intense green of the grass that smelled wet and freshly cut and at the blue of the pond in front of the sloping ninth green, guarded by white sand bunkers and oak trees. Billy had been six years old when the United States Open was played here at Colonial Country

Club in 1941, but his daddy had been riding in a rodeo near Fort Worth that week and was in the crowd for the final thirty-six holes on Saturday. Before the war his daddy had been the best golfer ever to come out of Jal. Troy, son of a range boss, was raised on the mighty JAL ranch that spread across the southeastern corner of the state. Troy was a top calf roper and bronc rider in area rodeos by the time he was thirteen, and New Mexico bareback champion at sixteen. But Troy's daddy changed Troy's life by taking him to play golf at the nine-hole Jal course. They wore boots and played through sage and mesquite onto sand greens. The first golf ball Troy ever swung at, he hit squarely on the club face and it went much farther than anyone else's. Troy fell in love with the game. He was a natural. Troy played golf every chance he had, and every night he swung a driver fifty times with a lead weight taped to the head of it. Troy could beat or hold his own with anybody in New Mexico and most of West Texas in the last summer before the war. After that 1941 United States Open—with the big war still six months away—Troy had hurried back to their adobe house in the Old Town area of Albuquerque with roses and lilacs blooming at the front door and described to his son, Billy Boy, the awesome wonders of Colonial Country Club, with fairways lovely as the fields of heaven compared to the goat pastures Troy was accustomed to playing on, with slick curving greens of bent grass, giant oak trees—and the water, such beautiful water, the Trinity River, the ponds. Water was a blessing they saw little of on the West Texas and New Mexico golf courses where Troy had begun making more money gambling than he was earning as a cowboy or as an agent buying cattle and selling them on commission to the meatpackers.

Watching his daddy's excited expression, drawn into the worlds behind those mysterious eyes that squinted through the smoke of the Camel cigarette in his lips, seeing his daddy's thick blond hair mussed and shiny with sweat, smelling of Vitalis   17 tonic, the boy imagined Colonial Country Club as a paradise he must someday reach, impossible though it appeared. This was long before Billy heard of Ben Hogan, who became his idol for the courage Hogan showed putting himself back together and becoming a champion again after his terrible crash into a bus on a highway in West Texas in 1949.

Billy fell in love last year with a *Life* magazine photograph of Hogan, pictured from behind at the finish of a swing that hit a long iron shot onto the final green at Merion and helped him win the U.S. Open. In this photograph Billy saw grace and control and balance and attitude and the force of will that overcame the pain in Hogan's legs. Billy taped the photograph to the wall near his bed and looked at it for long periods. Troy looked at it once and nodded and never looked again.

Only five weeks ago Troy had taken Billy and his mother to see the movie about Hogan called, *Follow the Sun*. Troy hooted at the golf swing of Glenn Ford, the actor who played Hogan. Billy wished they could have gotten Gary Cooper to play the part.

And now Troy had sold their adobe house in Albuquerque in which Billy's mother had died of cancer, and they had moved to Fort Worth to be at the center of the cattle business, where Troy could make a living dealing in beef, and here was Billy, approaching the caddie yard at the fabulous Colonial Country Club. He could hear his blood pounding, his breath coming fast. He knew the law of the yard. A new boy wouldn't get a bag without fighting for it.

"Hey, get your butt in gear," Elvis called.

T Four

HERE WERE FIFTY BOYS and men mingling, squatting, lying on the bare ground in the caddie yard, an area the size of two tennis courts hidden in the forest beyond the practice area west of the ninth fairway. About thirty of the caddies were Negroes, eight were Mexican and the rest white. The groups did not intermingle but gathered among their own for games of coin tossing and mumblety-peg. The air was blue with cigarette smoke. They wore overalls, blue jeans, khakis, their clothes old and mended and reasonably clean. Some wore tennis shoes, others railroad boots or old brogans. Occasionally a person from one group would call out to someone from another, and it would be a remark meant in humor. No racial insults were tolerated. Chili McWillie ran a tight yard. He refused to allow trouble unless he started it.

Foxy Lerner was first to see the new boy approaching the yard with Elvis Spaatz.

"Fresh meat," Foxy said, tugging at the elbow and looking up at the freckled face of Chili McWillie.

"Look at him walk. He looks like a stuck-up sucker to me," said the scrawny Foxy. He had combed his long oily hair into ducktails.

"New boy! Smell a cherry comin'!" yelled Ham T, the tallest and most muscular boy among a group of young blacks. Ham T wore overalls with a green shirt, a brown fedora hat and black tennis shoes. He was smoking a hand-rolled cigarette.

"Belt line! Belt line! Belt line!" The cry went up all over the yard. Men and boys began to pull off their belts and spread about to form a gauntlet.

"You dumb bastards wait a damn minute!"

The voice of Chili McWillie spoke barely above normal but with an edge that stopped the milling caddies.

"I'm the one that calls belt line when it's time to call belt line," Chili McWillie said.

The caddies fell silent and some looked at their feet.

"Am I right, Ham T?" said Chili McWillie.

"You right," Ham T said.

Elvis walked into the yard and straight up to Chili. Elvis had earned respect by having been a number-one caddie at both Glen Garden and Colonial. When it came to confronting one of his peers, Elvis knew no fear. Elvis had faced the McWillie brothers while growing up on the east side. He would rather give orders to Chili McWillie than carry a rifle in Korea, as Booger McWillie had been doing until his abrupt death.

"This here's Billy. This here's Chili. You'll get to know the rest of this bunch if you last long enough. All you need to know now is Chili runs the yard and I run Chili," said Elvis.

Chili pursed his lips in a thin frown but kept quiet.

"No belt line for the new boy," Elvis said.

"Just a damn minute, Elvis. That's yard business. That's for me to decide," Chili said.

"Look here at this starter sheet. I got the new kid bagging for Dr. Sandpaster. It's only fifteen minutes from now. I don't want the new kid showing up with a bloody butt and his shirt tore half off his back."

Chili thought it over.

"Afterwards," Chili said. "We'll whip the new boy's butt after he comes in."

"Yeah, and he's got to bag for crazy old man Sandpaster in between," said Foxy. "New boy, this is gonna be the worst day of your life."

"Stuff you," Billy said.

"Hold it. No fighting," said Chili McWillie.

"Billy, you come on with me. I better introduce you to Dr. Sandpaster. He's a little odd," Elvis said.

"He's a damn lunatic," said Foxy.

Billy fixed his gaze on Foxy for a moment, until Foxy looked away. Billy turned his back on the caddie yard and followed Elvis toward the practice area.

"Afterwards, new boy!" shouted Foxy. "Belt line when you come back! We'll whip the smart off your ass!"

D

Five

R. IRA SANDPASTER, owner and president of Sandpaster Oil & Gas, located in the Petroleum Building downtown, had determined this was the year he would shoot his age—seventy-nine—and it was already June. A mere four months to go before his eightieth birthday, and time flew so fast nowadays. It was a fact that time moved faster the older one became. Dr. Sandpaster, a scientist with a doctorate in petroleum geology and a vast knowledge of how the world was put together, had confirmed this to his own satisfaction. The reason was because as one grew older one's head became more stuffed with information and ideas and communications ranging from important to useless, and since the brain considered only one thing at a time, no matter how little time that took, it was using up time that would in his young days have been allotted to lazing beside a livestock tank or with a cane pole and a coffee can of worms at a blue hole on a creek, cork bobbing for catfish while he waited for an oil well in the East Texas pine forest to blow in. Time passed much slower then, because his head was relatively empty. Catfish tasted better, too, in those days. There wasn't really a damn thing that tasted good anymore, not even hot dogs with chili and cheese and onions. When he had bitten into a chili dog at his most recent Christmas dinner—the others were eating the same old damned turkey they always ate, year after year—and the chili dog bored him, Dr. Ira Sandpaster felt an icy brush with death. Some voice told him if he wanted to shoot his age before he left this earth, he had best get cracking.

Ira had never shot a score below 83 in his life, and he had started playing golf fifty years ago on a trip to Scotland. The first time he shot 83 was the day World War Two ended. He would never forget that day. Only twelve putts on the back nine. He shot an 83 in Costa Rica in 1946 when he served as U.S. Ambassador there for a year. The last time he shot an 83 was just last week—and it could have been a 79 if his caddie hadn't kept making those annoying uh-oh sounds that caused four three-putts and two topped drives.

He had sworn he would break 80 before he turned eighty, and he had never failed to reach a goal he had set for himself. If this quest to score a 79 at the age of seventy-nine were a business proposition like the financing and drilling of an oil well, Dr. Sandpaster could do it easily by hiring smart lawyers and cheating. But this was golf, not business. Dr. Sandpaster swore, drank, sometimes misrepresented oil deals, and had committed adultery. But he had never lost his religion or cheated at golf. He believed people who cheated at golf went screaming on their way to hell.

Using his Tommy Armour blade putter, Dr. Sandpaster was stroking putts on the long, narrow practice green near the first tee when he saw the other members of this morning's foursome arrive. Here came Dr. Arnold Kemp, the proctologist, waddling, fat, red-faced, wearing plaid trousers and a sour bulldog expression that meant he was very hung over.

Onto the practice green behind Dr. Kemp stepped a tall, thin man wearing tortoiseshell eyeglasses and a pencil mustache. His dark hair was parted in the middle and well greased. This was Titus, chief accountant for Sandpaster Oil & Gas. Dr. Sandpaster preferred to keep Titus close and observe his behavior. The doctor believed this was a way of watching his money. All three men had white left hands and white foreheads from wearing golf gloves and visors in the sun.

And here, striding along the path from the clubhouse, wear-

23

ing a white pima cotton polo shirt with the collar turned up, belt-less pressed cotton khaki pants, and brown alligator shoes with spikes, came handsome young Sonny Stonekiller, tan and al-mond-eyed, thick black hair combed straight back from his forehead, swinging his brown arms and giving off an aura of assurance as he walked. This aura was damned irritating to Dr. Sandpaster, but he put up with it because Sonny Stonekiller was already the club champion at age seventeen, the youngest champion ever. Sonny had been the all-district quarterback last year at Arlington Heights High School, and it was thought by many that he would be all-state in his senior year beginning soon. Football playing didn't impress Dr. Sandpaster, who had run on the cross-country team and also high jumped and won three letters at TCU while getting his doctoral degree in geology, writing his thesis on the fossil *Kingena wacoensis*—"tiny things," he called them. But he had seen that the football nonsense, the cheering and rushing about, the young men in tight pants, had an arousing effect on his granddaughter, as it had on most all girls as long as Dr. Sandpaster could remember.

Dr. Sandpaster looked on Sonny Stonekiller as a freak of nature. Sonny's great-grandfather, a Cherokee, had accumulated thousands of acres of cheap, worthless land in Oklahoma that eventually proved to cover an ocean of oil. Dinosaur wine, they said it was. The Cherokees had not been trained in finding oil, had not looked for it or really wanted it. But there it was beneath their feckless feet. Now the old Indian's great-grandson lived with his father and mother in a three-story stone mansion on Medford Court, on a hill above Forest Park and the city's famous zoo, near Colonial Country Club. Without the luck of there being oil under the scrubby, forlorn Oklahoma land, Sonny today would be just another Indian playing football on dirt fields on the reservation. Instead he was club golf champion of Colonial— the best player among club members except for the great Ben Hogan himself—and most people fawned over Sonny. Not Dr.

Sandpaster, though. He had never fawned over anyone once his own personal fortune passed fifty million dollars.

If not for the astounding good luck of owning land with oil under it, Chester Stonekiller, father of Sonny, would never have become a member of Colonial and would sure as hell never serve on the greens committee, in Dr. Sandpaster's view. There were other Colonial members that Dr. Sandpaster disliked—most of them, in fact. But cigar-smoking Chester Stonekiller with his big brown face was at the top of the list. For years Chester Stonekiller had asked the committe to chop down the giant pecan tree called Big Annie that guarded the left approach to the seventeenth green. Big Annie did not fit Chester's game, which was a slice that he called his "cut shot." Dr. Sandpaster, however, loved and found solace in Big Annie and defended her with passion. But he was willing to disregard some of his objections to the Stonekiller family while Sonny was a long-hitting club champion. As club champion, Sonny was allowed, even encouraged, to go to dances and on other dates with Dr. Sandpaster's grandaughter, Sandra.

Dr. Sandpaster hoped that this summer of friendship with Sonny would help him to shoot a score of 79, the theory being that Sonny's smooth tempo and solid strikes and awesome distance off the tee—Sonny was believed to drive the ball farther than Hogan, but Hogan would never consent to play with him—would cause a psychological benefit for Dr. Sandpaster's own game, would inspire him to dig up the personal best that was deep inside his soul.

"HE DOESN'T LOOK CRAZY to me. What's crazy about him?" Billy asked Foxy Lerner. Billy was carrying Dr. Sandpaster's big black leather golf bag toward the practice green. Foxy struggled under the weight of the proctologist's golf bag, and Ham T ambled along carrying the enormous green bag of Mr. Titus as though it was light as a pillow. Elvis Spaatz walked ahead of them. Billy nudged Foxy and said, "Why won't you answer my question? What's crazy about Dr. Sandpaster?"

"I don't talk to a new boy until you've had your butt whipped," Foxy said.

"What've you got it in for me for?"

"Foxy was the new boy until you showed up," said Ham T. "Oh my, did we whip his little pink butt? Did he cry like a girl?"

"Shut up. I did not," Foxy said.

Ham T laughed and walked on toward Mr. Titus, the leather bag creaking like a saddle.

Foxy and Ham T had worked for Dr. Kemp and Mr. Titus before, and the men waved at the caddies and started toward the first tee. Sonny Stonekiller stroked two six-foot putts into the cup and picked up his white canvas bag and slung it over his shoulder and followed. Billy liked hearing the sounds of their spikes on the walkway.

"Dr. Sandpaster, this here is your new caddie," said Elvis. "His name is Billy. He comes highly recommended to us by Mr. Hardy Loudermilk out in New Mexico. I hope he fits the bill. You gentlemen are next on the tee. Play well. Excuse me now."

Billy looked up at a gaunt man with narrow shoulders and a face that had been baked leathery and wrinkled by a life spent outdoors in all sorts of weather. Dr. Sandpaster peered back at the boy through prescription dark glasses that gave the world a purple hue. Nice enough looking lad, the doctor thought. Has a brightness of the eye that indicates the possibility of intelligence.

"Son, before we start down this path together, I will explain the purpose of life to you," said Dr. Sandpaster. Billy was impressed by his large yellow dentures. "I live for one thing. Well, I live for three or four things, but as far as you are involved I live for one thing. I live to shoot a 79 from the regular tees here at Colonial. I have four months to do it."

"Are you sick?"

"Certainly not. I am strong as French mustard. But I am on the verge of turning eighty years of age. I must shoot a 79 while I am seventy-nine. You, Billy, are now my partner in this quest."

"Hey, come on, Ira! You're up!" shouted Dr. Kemp from the tee.

"Wait a moment," Dr. Sandpaster yelled. He stared down at Billy through his purple glasses. Strings of sandy hair fell across the doctor's forehead. "Billy, all you need to do is carry my clubs and find my ball. I do not want advice. I know which club to hit on every shot. I know every yardage. I know how hard the wind is blowing. In fact, I know more about the golf swing than anyone at this club, including Ben Hogan. They say Hogan has learned the secret to the golf swing. Nonsense. Hogan works harder than the other professionals, that's his secret. Watch me today and you will see the real secret of the golf swing."

"Why is it so important for you to shoot your age, sir?" asked Billy.

"Ah, a child philosopher. You don't yet realize that inside every older person is a young person wondering what the hell happened to the time. You know that speech from *Richard II?* He says, 'I wasted time, now time doth waste me.' Oh, you wouldn't know it. It's a play by Shakespeare."

"I have seen *Richard II,*" Billy said.

"Surely not."

"My mama taught English at the University of New Mexico. She took me to the big plays they did in the drama department."

Dr. Sandpaster clapped his palms together. "Excellent. We're going to get along. I feel confident in you already."

Billy carried Dr. Sandpaster's bag off to the right side of the tee box. Billy noticed Sonny Stonekiller staring at him curiously, judging him with dark eyes. The three men put on golf visors and pulled golf gloves onto their left hands. Sonny Stonekiller remained hatless, his long black hair swept back from his forehead, and his bare hands fondled the cord grips of his new driver. Sonny's hands looked strong but surprisingly delicate. They fit well on the club.

"You hit first, Sonny," said Dr. Sandpaster. "I'm not cosmically prepared. I must do my five deep breaths and my three snorts."

"What's the game?" asked Sonny. "Same as usual?"

"Five dollar Nassau each to each. Automatic one down presses. Full handicaps for us," Dr. Sandpaster said. "That's eighteen for Dr. Kemp, fourteen for Titus and sixteen for me. Grownups play from the regular tees. Sonny, you play the back tees at scratch. Titus, you keep score."

Sonny showed them a new ball marked SS with black ink. He stepped back to the championship tee, which made the hole play thirty-five yards longer. He teed up the ball, looking graceful and confident. Glanced down the long fairway of the par-five first hole. Widened his stance. Waggled once, then swung the club with effortless rhythm—and *crack!* A noise like a gunshot. The white ball flew high against the sky and cleared a large oak tree that stood in the fairway 250 yards from the tee. The ball came down nearly 300 yards away. Billy gasped, and Sonny gave him a small smirk.

"Brassie," Dr. Sandpaster said.

Billy removed the leather cover from a gleaming No. 2 wood and put the club into Dr. Sandpaster's hand.

"I'm going to play my wind shot," said the doctor.

Billy felt only a tiny breeze against his cheek. Dr. Sandpaster settled into a crouching stance, cocked his wrists in what Billy thought was the start of a chop, and then suddenly swung the club. The doctor hit a waist-high line drive that bounced into the rough short of the big tree.

"So far, so bueno." Dr. Sandpaster grinned at Billy. "Come on, boy. Don't let me beat you to the ball."

As they strode down the fairway, Dr. Sandpaster said, "Did
you see it?"

"Sir?"

"The secret of the golf swing. I showed it to you."

"No sir. I didn't see it."

"Watch more closely next shot." Dr. Sandpaster threw back his head and spread out his arms and sucked in a full belly of air. "You're in for a treat today, Billy. Your first walk around our wonderful golf course. It's a thrill you will always remember. Seven thousand yards carved from nature by that genius, that strange man, that loner, that artist. I am talking about John Bredemus, the father of Texas golf. The Johnny Appleseed of Texas golf. I suppose your mother taught you about Johnny Appleseed, who planted apple trees everywhere he went? John Bredemus built golf courses everywhere he went. He built nearly one hundred golf courses in Texas, many in places where they had never heard of golf and didn't realize they wanted it. People came to see what golf is about, and they still play his courses to this day and always will. He built five golf courses here in Fort Worth—Colonial, Worth Hills, Rockwood, Ridglea and Z. Boaz—and he remodeled Meadowbrook and the famous old Glen Garden, where Hogan and Byron Nelson were common caddies like you. Bredemus never got rich because he didn't own the courses. He just built them and moved on. He traveled in an old car with a bag of books, a checkerboard and a sock of checkers, one satchel of clothes and a canvas golf bag with seven clubs in it."

Billy found Dr. Sandpaster's ball in two inches of grass thirty yards short of the big tree. The other players were scattered left and right. Sonny Stonekiller stood seventy yards ahead of them in the fairway, leaning against his canvas bag.

"Bredemus was very mysterious," Dr. Sandpaster continued. "Educated at both Princeton and Dartmouth, football all-American at both universities. A track and field star. Finished second to Jim Thorpe in the decathalon at the Olympics. Posed for the naked statue of the athlete in the lobby of Union Station in Washington, D.C. I never knew where he was born, or why he went to universities back East, or why he came to Texas, or where he went afterward. But he built us this masterpiece we call Colonial. I love this place, Billy."

"Hit the damn ball, Ira!" shouted Titus. "Kemp and I are already laying two."

"Wind shot again. Give me my brassie," Dr. Sandpaster said.

"Brassie? From this high grass?"

"Do I hear an offer of advice?"

"No sir."

The doctor crouched over the ball, which he could barely see down in the grass, cocked his wrists fully backward and up so that his club shaft was sticking straight up in the air when his arms were extended waist-high parallel to the ground, and then he swung and the brassie head cut through the grass and another hip-high liner sang beneath the tree limbs and rolled 200 yards down the middle of the fairway.

"Did you see it?" asked Dr. Sandpaster.

"It's in the fairway."

"I mean the secret of the golf swing?"

"No sir."

"It's the wrists. I cock my wrists to start and then I never uncock them throughout the swing. They uncock themselves, of course, because of the dynamics of the swinging clubhead. But I never consciously uncock them. How else could I have socked a brassie out of that tall grass?"

The game continued with the men walking briskly. Dr. Sandpaster was one over par on the fifth tee and was feeling expansive. "It's this new boy. He is bringing me luck." Titus did the arithmetic on the bets with his mental calculator and told the players how they stood. Foxy Lerner and Ham T had gone on down the fairway to watch the drives land on this world renowned par-four hole that had the Trinity River along its right side, and a ditch shaded by a row of trees along the left.

"You guys are beating the hell out of your handicaps today. You're hot," said Sonny, who listened to Titus and realized he was losing money. "I double press every bet."

"Throwing money away comes natural to your people," Dr. Sandpaster said.

Sonny's eyes widened and his lips turned down. "I'll play you for another hundred starting now, Dr. Sandpaster."

"Done and done," howled Dr. Sandpaster. "You run ahead, Billy, down along the riverbank. I am going to unleash the power of the universe from within me through this beautifully carved block of persimmon wood that is the head of my driver."

"Just last week I was looking up Ira's ass with a flashlight, and if what I saw is the power of the universe, you don't want to know about God," Dr. Kemp said.

Billy found a spot under a tree about two hundred yards from the tee. He saw several small bass swimming in the clear water of the Trinity and smelled the wildflowers. A turtle slid off a rock and plopped into the water. Foxy and Ham T waited in the shade on the other side of the fairway, expecting their men to hook. Even from his distance Billy recognized the distinctive crack of a Sonny Stonekiller drive. Then he heard a shout of "Damn," from the tee. Billy looked into the fairway, waiting for Sonny's drive to come down. He sensed rather than actually saw something pass over his head and he heard a splash and thought he saw a white object disappear into a deep pool of the river.

Moments later Dr. Sandpaster's ball bounded into the light rough a few yards from Billy. As he heaved the big leather bag onto his shoulder, Billy saw Sonny come past, walking very fast. Sonny drifted into the trees along the bank. Waiting for Dr. Sandpaster, Billy saw Sonny bend down near a clump of grass, reach into it as if looking for a ball, then rise and walk on.

"Lost, are you, Sonny?" cried Dr. Sandpaster.

"It's right in here someplace. I marked it with that stump," Sonny said.

Dr. Sandpaster walked into the rough and began kicking the grass. Sonny took out an iron club and swept along the bank. Billy laid his bag on the ground and walked straight to the clump of grass where he had seen Sonny kneeling. "Here's a ball," Billy said. "It has SS on it."

"Hey, your boy found my ball," Sonny said.

"Well, I found this ball here," said Billy.

"What do you mean by that? It's clearly my ball," Sonny said.

Looking into Sonny's eyes, Billy was fairly sure the club champion had palmed that ball and tucked it into this clump of grass so he could come back and find it.

"Lucky for you Billy has sharp eyes," said Dr. Sandpaster.

"Yeah," Sonny said. He stared at Billy, waiting.

"Come on, Billy. Let's go hit my shot," said Dr. Sandpaster. "Leave the Indian boy in his native foliage."

Sonny whacked the ball out of the clump of grass with a wedge, hit a 5-iron onto the green, made his putt for a par and won the hole from all three men, despite it being a one-stroke handicap hole for them. Walking to the sixth tee, Sonny veered close to Billy.

"Thanks for nothing," Sonny drawled a warning.

Three hours later they stood on the eighteenth tee, looking down the sloping fairway toward the clubhouse, a stream along the right side, a cluster of large trees on the left and a long blue pond stretching beside the green.

"Beautiful, isn't it, Billy?" said Dr. Sandpaster. "I wish John Bredemus could be here with us at this moment. I would give him a big hug and kiss. I wonder whatever happened to him?"

"For God's sake, Ira, save that crap for the bar," Dr. Kemp said.

"Please do play on, Ira," said Titus, looking at his watch.

Dr. Sandpaster had one-putted five consecutive holes on the

back nine and was ten over par on the eighteenth tee. He needed a birdie for his 79. But he discovered he was not nervous, not anxious. He was relishing this. This was golf, by God. He had found a lucky boy today. Something primal told him that a score of 79 soon would be his—if not today, then soon.

Even when he three-putted for a double-bogey six and an 82, Dr. Sandpaster was delighted with life, thrilled with the game, full of hope that the next few weeks would produce a 79. There was energy coming from this new boy, Billy, that was enhancing the doctor's muscles and his mind and heart.

Dr. Sandpaster was so full of joy that before the players went into the men's grill to tote up the bets, he called Billy aside and tipped him with a ten-dollar bill. This was Dr. Sandpaster's most extravagant tip in the history of Colonial.

"You be here in the morning at 8:50, Billy," Dr. Sandpaster said. "We're on a quest, my boy."

"Yes sir. Thank you," said Billy.

Climbing the hill to the clubhouse where the clubs would be stored, Sonny Stonekiller fell into step with Billy.

"What did you mean back there on five? You accusing me of something?"

"I think your ball went into the river," Billy said.

"Why didn't you say so back there?"

"I wasn't sure," Billy said. "Now I'm sure."

"Are you going to make a stink about it?"

"I'm not a snitch," Billy said.

"If you mention this, I'll whip your butt."

Billy glanced at Foxy Lerner and Ham T, who were turning their bags in at the storage room.

"Get in line behind Foxy," Billy said.

"You better not start a rumor is what I'm saying."

"Kiss my ass," Billy said.

Billy checked the black leather bag in with the attendant and watched Sonny go into the clubhouse. Billy hadn't been able to keep up with the bets, but he knew Sonny was a big loser and Dr. Sandpaster was a big winner, and he smiled.

"We'll take that smile off your face, new boy," said Foxy.

The belt line gauntlet looked much worse than Billy had expected. At Albuquerque, he'd had to fight the biggest kid near to his own age to gain acceptance to the yard. In Santa Fe they had stuffed him inside a barrel and rolled him down a hill. But he had never seen this many caddies, twenty-five on either side of a tunnel he would have to run through. Each man and boy had a belt or a rope or a bag strap to slash him.

"Ready?" called Chili McWillie.

"I'm ready," Billy said.

And Billy hurled himself into the tunnel.

He fell three times and staggered up and ran on, covering his head with his hands and arms as blows tore at his legs, his buttocks, his back. He felt a belt buckle rip into his shirt. He lurched out of the end of the gauntlet and dizzily heard Chili McWillie shout, "Again! Run it again!"

Billy plunged back into the tunnel. The blows were fewer and less vicious this time. Billy noticed that Ham T held back from flailing him with a strap, but Foxy caught him a sharp cutting smack across the small of his back with a knotted rope.

Billy stumbled out of the end of the tunnel again and fell to his knees. Chili McWillie walked up to him. "You had enough?" Chili said.

"I'm done."

"Wrong."

Chili kicked him in the stomach and Billy flopped over backwards. Stunning and painful as the kick felt, it was not as devastating to Billy as the warm wetness he felt oozing onto his thighs.

"He pissed his pants!" Foxy yelled. "The new boy pissed his pants."

• • •

BILLY TRIED TO SLIP DOWN Colonial Parkway without acting suspicious and drawing attention to himself, while he pulled his torn and blood-spotted polo shirt down tightly between his legs with both hands to cover the telltale stain in his jeans. It was not just the stain but also the odor. He could smell his urine, still warm. To him it smelled orange, which he feared might mean he was bleeding from the penis. He had the ten-dollar tip in his pocket, plus the two dollars he had earned for carrying the bag, but he would not get on a bus smelling like this. Anyone who came close to him could tell he had pissed his pants. He must run the ten miles back to the Half Moon Hotel and clean himself up before eating a steak and onion rings for dinner with his daddy. Billy hadn't eaten since the two donuts early this morning.

The familiar red Chrysler convertible pulled up beside him.

"Hey, Billy, hop in," said the prettiest girl he had ever seen.

"I better not."

He kept trotting.

"Are you hurt?"

"I fell down. I'm all right."

The car cruised alongside. "It's okay. You caddied for my grandfather today. He really likes you. I can give you a ride. Get in."

"No thanks," Billy said, continuing to trot.

"What? What did you say? I can't believe what I'm hearing," asked the girl, shocked.

"I better not ride with you," Billy said.

"Well! I never! You are insulting me."

"I don't mean to insult you, but you just go on ahead without me."

"My grandfather may like you, but you are a stupid redneck. You can go to hell," she said and jammed her foot on the gas pedal. Billy heard that smooth automatic transmission shifting gears, and the red Chrysler convertible sped around the corner onto University Drive.

Billy picked up his pace. He ran with his arms swinging free now, ignoring the wet stain at his crotch, breathing and running smoothly as he had done running the mile on the track team at Albuquerque High. But this afternoon, it was nine more miles to the Half Moon Hotel.

T
Six

ROY SAT AT A BOOTH beside the window so he could watch for his son to cross Exchange Avenue and enter the Cattleman's Café. Troy wore a new white linen double-breasted suit with a blue soft cotton shirt the color of his eyes and a red silk necktie and new black and white wingtip shoes with black silk stockings.

A paper sack containing a fifth of Wild Turkey lay on the table beside an open pack of Camels and Troy's silver Zippo. A cigarette smoldered in the ashtray. Troy swallowed from his glass of bourbon and water and said to the waitress, "Bring me another setup, please, darlin'. Little lighter on the ice."

"You drinking your dinner, handsome?" said the waitress.

"I'm waiting on my son. What time do you get off?"

"My husband picks me up at eleven. He's a sheriff's deputy."

"Nice to know," Troy said.

"I've seen you in here before, but you was a cowboy, not a slicker," she said.

"Hon, I am pure cowboy to the bone. But I been around the world and back, and sometimes I like to dress up like a Frenchman."

"I got to admit you do look strong in that white suit. You could pass for a big time gigolo," she said.

"You real sure you got a husband?"

"I'm thinking about it," she said.

Troy watched her hips swish in her yellow uniform, and her dark hair was long but pinned up. He imagined stripping her naked and taking down her hair. He should feel guilty to have sex on his mind with his poor lovely wife, wasted by cancer to eighty pounds, only two weeks in her coffin. But he couldn't help it when the urge came over him.

Troy sipped his bourbon and saw Billy coming across the street, dodging between truckloads of bawling cattle. Troy had left word with the desk clerk where he would be. As Billy entered the cafe, Troy saw bruises and scratches on his son's face. Billy glanced in his direction, looked away, then suddenly looked back again. Billy's eyes widened. He was accustomed to seeing his father in boots, jeans, a big rodeo belt buckle, a t-shirt with a pack of Camels rolled up in one sleeve, or in a dress shirt with pearl snaps, and always a wide-brimmed Stetson felt or straw hat on his head out in public.

"Sit down, son. Tell me about it," Troy said.

Billy eased into the booth, pain running along his ribs and searing from the welts on his back and buttocks.

"Where'd you get that outfit?" Billy asked.

"Stripling's Department Store downtown. Like it?"

"You don't look like yourself," Billy said.

"I'm not just a cowboy now. I'm a businessman. I got to look like a businessman."

"But you deal cows."

Troy flipped the lid on his Zippo.

"I also deal cards and shoot dice in a very professional way," Troy said. "You ain't walked in my boots, Billy Boy. There's lots you don't know."

The waitress put a pitcher of water and a pitcher of ice on the table. Billy read her name tag: Wanda. Troy pulled his Wild Turkey bottle out of the sack and began unscrewing the top.

"I can see this is your son," Wanda said.

"Yes. This is Billy Boy."

"Billy Boy. You been in a fight?" asked Wanda.

"Sort of," Billy said.

"Then you need a big steak right away. How about an eighteen-ounce Porterhouse?" said Wanda.

"Two of them. And two orders of French fries and onion rings," Troy said.

"And two shrimp cocktails to start," said Billy.

"How you want those steaks cooked?" Wanda asked.

"Darlin', you ever hear of a cowboy ordering rare meat? Make ours well done. Burn those screwworms," said Troy.

When Wanda left the table, Troy poured two inches of bourbon in his glass, added an ice cube and a splash of water. The sweet smell of the whiskey made Billy turn away, feeling sick in his stomach. Troy was already a little drunk. The jukebox was playing a western swing number by Bob Wills. Billy looked around the restaurant. A few of the men customers wore suits and ties but most were in western clothes. Every man but Troy was wearing boots.

"I apologize about bringing that woman to the room last night," Troy said. "I am truly sorry. I loved your mother, and I miss her dearly. I didn't aim to insult her memory. I just got a little too much juice, and my natural impulses took over."

"If you loved her, why did you two fight so much?" Billy asked. His pain from running the belt line, his weariness from running ten miles back to the Half Moon, and his disappointment at seeing Troy well along toward being drunk again, moved him to blurt out the question that had haunted him for years.

"I loved her, Billy Boy. I really did," Troy said, gazing at his son.

"Then why did you hit her?"

Wanda appeared at the table with their shrimp cocktails. Each was six large shrimps on ice with small bowls of red sauce.

"That's a pretty ugly bruise you got on your eye," Wanda said. "How does the other kid look?"

"We'll call the hospital and ask," said Troy.

Billy dipped a shrimp into the bowl of red sauce, stirred it carefully around, and then plopped the dripping red end into his mouth. Billy had heard of shrimp cocktails being served at Albuquerque Country Club, but he had never seen one. He didn't know if a shrimp would taste like fish or like some kind of bird. He found it to be rubbery and tasteless except for the red sauce that burned his tongue. He scooped up a second shrimp and noticed Troy had pushed his bowl aside and lit another cigarette.

"I don't know why I ever hit her," Troy said. "I'm sorry as hell about it. I was mad a lot of the time. I took things out on her that wasn't her fault. I truly do regret it."

"Are you going to eat that shrimp cocktail?" asked Billy.

Troy pushed the bowl across the table to his son.

"I know I haven't been a great father," Troy said. "I swear I'll try real hard from now on. You've got to remember, Billy Boy, that your mama and I were both sixteen years old—the same age you are now—when you were born. It was the middle of the Great Depression. We didn't know what to do with a baby. Suppose you woke up tomorrow and found a baby in your room and you were his father? What would you do? Your mama and I dealt with life from day to day. We did the best we could. We loved you, Billy Boy, and we tried hard. You may not believe that about me, but you know your mama tried hard."

Wanda placed two wicker baskets of fried onion rings on the table and then the two steaks, sizzling hot, with a mound of golden French fries beside each.

"Make your daddy eat his supper, Billy Boy," Wanda said.

Troy picked up the steak knife and sliced into the beef. He chewed, and Billy noticed tears in his daddy's eyes. Troy wiped his face with a napkin, took another drag off his cigarette and another swallow of bourbon. His face brightened.

"Look here," Troy said. He reached into the inside pocket of his white suit coat and pulled out a wad of money with a rubber band around it. Troy rolled down the rubber band and peeled five twenty-dollar bills off the roll. He tossed the twenties to Billy and put the roll back into his inside pocket. "For you."

"What's this?" Billy said. "What are you doing?"

"I deposited the twelve-thousand dollar check we got for the old house and two acres," Troy said. "Safe and sound in the Fort Worth National Bank. I didn't get around to finding us a place to live yet. We can do that tomorrow. I'll look for an office in the Livestock Exchange Building tomorrow, too."

Billy picked up the five twenty-dollar bills and studied them with a twinge of foreboding.

"Where did this money come from? Did you make a sale today?"

"Well, I actually deposited eleven thousand dollars of our check and kept back one thousand in cash," said Troy. "For expenses. Walking around money. Food. Gasoline. And a couple of hundred for a shrewd investment I aim to make after supper. Oh yeah, and I bought this suit and these wingtip shoes. What do you think?"

Billy shrugged and kept chewing. He had eaten his basket of onion rings and was halfway through his steak and French fries. It was the juiciest, tastiest steak he had ever put on his tongue. Troy had eaten two bites that Billy saw, and one onion ring, but had kept smoking his cigarette and drinking bourbon.

"How bad did they beat you up?" Troy said.

"I could take it all right."

"You get a bag?"

"A rich oil man. He said he knows the secret of the golf swing," said Billy.

Troy laughed.

"Did you see Ben Hogan?"

"No. I heard one of the men say he is coming to town tonight. Aren't you going to eat your steak?"

"Your stomach is a bottomless pit. I remember when I was that way," Troy said.

He cut one more bite of his steak and pushed the platter over to Billy.

"Why did you quit playing golf?" Billy asked.

"Oh, I haven't quit. I still play if anybody wants to bet me I can't. You see, I really do know the secret of the golf swing." Troy grinned.

"I mean, you used to be really good. What happened?"

"One more little tiny drunk and then I'll cool it with the booze," Troy said, pouring bourbon into his glass. "Did I say 'drunk?' That's funny. What would your mother call it—some kind of a slip?"

"You used to could beat Ben Hogan. I heard them say so in Albuquerque and Santa Fe and Jal."

"I never met Ben Hogan."

"I know, but they used to say you could beat him if you met him. You said so yourself. So what happened? How come he's a champion and you're . . . well . . ." Billy paused. Never had he spoken so frankly to his father. He wondered if Troy would hit him. Troy squinted hard at his son, thinking, then blew out two strings of smoke.

"One afternoon six years ago, in 1945, I was up in the bell tower of a church in a village in France," Troy said. Billy leaned forward and stopped chewing. Troy had never talked about the war in front of his son. "We had walked across France in the snow and mud and were getting ready to walk into Germany. We got shot at every day and plenty of us got killed. This one particular day in the bell tower I had a radio operator with me instead of carrying my own radio. What a Forward Observer does, Billy Boy, is go find a vantage point where he can see the enemy and then direct artillery fire onto their ass. I was real good at it. I could estimate a range like nobody else. I blew up thousands and thousands of Germans. I enjoyed it. It was like going hunting. Go ahead and finish my steak, Billy Boy. I'm having one final little nip."

Troy leaned back in the booth and looked at the ceiling, seeing something Billy could never understand.

"Half of the hunt is the Germans try to find out where the Forward Observers are, and kill us soon as possible. It ain't too hard to figure out where a Forward Observer is gonna be at. Look for the most prominent vantage point and you found him. The Germans would shoot artillery at us and send patrols to kill us. We had to be quick. Well, this one day in France, in the bell tower, I caught a German infantry division in the open and hammered them to pieces. I mean I really nailed em. Laid 155 howitzers, high explosives and air bursts right in their lunch kit. It was such good shooting that I stayed in the tower a few minutes too long. A German patrol came through the door of the church as we came down from the tower. They shot my radio man in half with submachine guns. I dived behind the altar and they tore it up with bullets and I heard them running toward me. I remember thinking, well, I never did know if I believed in God, but I better come out right then as a true believer because I was about to find out if God exists, and if He did, I sure as hell didn't want to be on the wrong side."

Troy lowered his eyes and looked at his son.

"Some damn fool two miles away in a 155 battery got my co-ordinates wrong and dumped three high explosive shells onto that church. There was such a bang that everything turned white. I woke up with, I swear, a statue of Jesus laid over me in the rubble. I was the only living person left in the church. The roof was gone. The Germans was all dead. I kissed that statue and said, 'Thank you, Jesus.' Then I got myself out of that church at a dead run until I found my own unit. I went to the damn fool that fired the short rounds and I punched him in the mouth. Knocked out his front teeth. Yeah, he had saved my life, but what if the Germans hadn't showed up? He would of killed me."

Without announcing it or seeming to notice, Troy poured another slosh of bourbon into his glass.

"I lost my nerve," Troy said.

"What do you mean?" Billy said. He would have been hard pressed to name a person who had more nerve than Troy.

"You asked why I don't play much golf? Why I'm not a champion? I believe the truth is I lost my nerve in the church in France that day. I don't know why I feel so strong about that church. I was in plenty of rough spots before that day and plenty more after that day. Lots more killing. But I remember that church, in some way I can't explain, as the place where I lost my nerve. I never told anybody this, except your mama, but always in my mind there's a picture of that white wooden statue of Jesus with bullet holes in it. Ain't that spooky?"

"I saw you ride bucking horses at the rodeo in Albuquerque three months ago. Mama and I saw you. You ain't lost your nerve," Billy said.

"For golf I have," said Troy. "After I came home from the war, my golf swing was as sweet as ever—you never lose your golf swing if you were born gifted with one, like I was and you were but most people aren't—and I looked like the same guy that had robbed everybody on every golf course in New Mexico and West Texas before the war. But the difference was that before the war, I was shooting 65s at places where after the war I was shooting 71s. A 71 is a terrible score for a gambler to shoot on the golf course. You're playing just well enough to lose your ass. It's like holding a straight at the poker table and staring at a flush. I went up on top of Sandia Mountain one morning and sat there and prayed to Jesus and said I sure was sorry I'd gotten his statue shot up and please don't take it out on my golf game. Please punish me some other way. I don't know if it come from Jesus, but I did get this sudden revelation about my golf game.

The reason I was shooting 71 and will never shoot 65 again is *because I had lost my nerve for golf.*"

Troy lit another cigarette although one was burning in the ashtray.

"Riding a bucking horse takes courage and skill," Troy said. "You're in combat against what the horse does. Like when I played football at New Mexico State. You run and knock the other guy down. That takes courage and skill. But golf takes nerve. You're alone with yourself on every stroke. The ball don't give a damn. Shooting a 65 under pressure takes nerve and skill. Shooting a 71 takes skill, not nerve. Before the war I knew I could hit any kind of shot I wanted. After the war, I was no longer sure. That doubt is the difference in a 65 and a 71. So that's what I mean when I say I lost my nerve for golf. I don't know where my nerve came from in the first place, and I don't know where it went, but it's gone."

Billy had eaten his steak and half of Troy's and most of the French fries and onion rings. He felt his usually tight stomach pressing against the waist of his clean jeans. He had washed his soiled pair in the bathtub and hung them on the shower curtain rod.

"I'm tired," Billy said. "I'm ready for a good night's sleep."

"I want you to drive me someplace and wait for me and bring me home," Troy said.

"Why?" Billy said.

"Because I've had a few pops of booze. And I'll probably have a few more before I'm ready to come home. We don't want me thrown in jail for drunk driving, do we?"

Billy remembered Burgin and Boyle, the cops who had picked him up that morning. He knew Burgin and Boyle would not tolerate a drunken Troy. Billy imagined them hitting his daddy with their big black flashlights and their slapjacks.

"I told you I am gonna make an investment tonight," Troy said. "I have put aside three hundred dollars. I can turn this three

45

hundred into five hundred or a thousand tonight in two or three hours shooting dice and playing cards at the 2222 Club on the Jacksboro Highway. Hey, Wanda, hon, bring us a check, please?" said Troy, pulling out his wad of money.

But it wasn't really Troy's money, Billy thought. It was *their* money.

B Seven

ILLY LIKED THE SOUND of the tires whining on the asphalt as he drove the black and yellow Chevy along the Jacksboro Highway northwest of downtown Fort Worth. The dash lights glowed green, and he saw the speedometer hit fifty-five. On the radio, Nat King Cole was singing, *"They tried to tell us we're too young . . ."*

"Slow down some. The 2222 is pretty close," said Troy.

"I wish you wouldn't do this," Billy said.

"Don't worry about nothing, Billy Boy. Your old man is real sharp at cards and dice. I never lost my nerve or my touch with cards and dice. How you think we been making a living since I got out of the Army?"

"With mama teaching at the university," said Billy.

"Yeah, bless her heart, she did work hard and was a steady provider. But I brought in money, too. I bought and sold cows and did all right. I gambled at golf with guys who could beat me unless I made the right bets, but when I got to the dice game or sat down to gin rummy, I won. Did I ever tell you I won this car?"

"You told me," Billy said.

"Well, I damn sure did win it."

"Daddy, you're drunk."

"I am feeling very lucky," said Troy.

In the headlights they saw the small white sign that said 2222 at the entrance to a long driveway hidden by trees.

"This is the place. Turn here," Troy said.

Their black and yellow Chevy cruised along the driveway

through a tunnel of trees toward a large white frame house with its windows lit up. They could see a dozen cars parked on the grass near the house.

"Stop worrying, Billy. The most we got at stake here is three hundred dollars. Listen, it hurts me that you might think I didn't love your mama. I did love her and I still do. You know I love you, too, don't you, Billy Boy?"

"I guess."

"You guess? You guess? My old man would never use that word to me, but I am using it on you, and all you can say is 'I guess?' "

"You're too drunk to gamble," Billy said.

"Stop here and let me out."

Billy stopped the car at the end of a row of shiny Cadillacs and pickup trucks. Troy opened his door and got out. He straightened his tie and squared his shoulders.

"Do I look like a businessman who means business?" Troy said.

"Daddy, please leave the rest of our cash money with me. Just take the three hundred."

Troy leaned down and looked in the window into Billy's face.

"Ben Hogan used to deal cards for the house right here at the 2222 Club before he made it in golf. Cut me some slack, will you, Billy Boy? Give me a chance to show what I can do. I'm going to make you proud of me tonight."

Troy turned and walked toward the front door of the club. He had taken in a lot of whiskey, but he was handling it well. He walked with grace and balance in his white suit and wingtip shoes, looking blond and rugged in the pale lamps from the trees, not a man to be taken for granted.

Billy couldn't play the radio because it would run down the battery. He got into the back seat and lay down and tried to

48

sleep. He spent two or three fitful hours, exhausted and dozing but jerked to life by the pains in his ribs and back and buttocks. Their black and yellow Chevy was no longer first in the back row but now was on a full row three from the back. As the night grew later, more people kept arriving. Billy peeked at them. Nearly all were men, wearing Stetson hats and business suits. A few were swarthy and slope shouldered and wore fedora hats like gangsters Billy had seen in the movies. He saw one man in a western suit he thought at first was old Elmo, who dug postholes at the JAL. But the man lit a fat cigar and his finger showed a diamond ring. Must be a big cattle dealer or a rancher or an oilman.

Close to midnight, by Billy's reckoning, he was awakened by a car door slamming. More people arriving at the 2222. Billy got out of the Chevy and crept between the rows of automobiles toward the corner of the house, where he saw a lighted window beside a stand of hedges. Edging up to the window, Billy peered inside and saw a large room full of men and women who were lifting drinks from trays carried by black waiters and who were crowding around several poker and dice tables. He saw Troy, conspicuous in his white suit, far across the room, surrounded by gamblers at a dice table. Troy clenched a cigar between his teeth and shook the dice with his right hand. Billy could see a fistful of money in his daddy's left hand, and there was a wildness, an arrogance about his bearing, as if he had just ridden the world champion bucking Brahma bull.

"Hey, kid, what the hell are you up to?"

Billy turned and saw a large man in a gray double-breasted suit scowling at him and tapping a blackjack against his left palm.

"I'm looking for my daddy."

"How'd you get in here?"

"Drove my daddy here. I'm waiting to drive him home."

"Nobody stopped you at the front entrance?"

"No sir."

"That damn Snuffy. I'll kick his ass," the big man said. "Who's your daddy?"

"The cowboy in the white suit."

"Okay." The man slipped the blackjack into his belt. "Go back and wait in your car."

"Would you tell my daddy it's late and I need to go?"

"Kid, the cowboy in the white suit is busting everybody at the dice table. You better get back in your car. I expect he won't come out until he's ready."

Billy returned to the driver's seat and sat with his forehead leaning against the steering wheel. He could barely hold his eyes open, but he felt a peace come over him, a delight that eased his pains. His daddy was winning big money. Troy was as good as he said he was. For a moment Billy was sorry he had doubted his old man. Maybe he shouldn't have blamed Troy for everything bad at home. Billy thought of Dr. Sandpaster, who would be waiting for him on the first tee at Colonial Country Club in a few hours. Billy smiled as he slid into a deep sleep. He dreamed of Sandra Sandpaster's bare legs in her red Chrysler convertible.

"MOVE OVER, KID," said the big man in the gray suit. He wore a grey fedora hat with the brim turned up in front. The big man opened the driver's door.

"I'm driving," Billy said.

"Your license is no good in this county. Move over."

Billy saw two men carrying, half-dragging, Troy between them. Troy's head fell onto his chest, his blond hair streaked with blood. There were spots of blood on the white suit, and one coat pocket was torn and flapped. The two men tossed Troy into the back seat. Troy's limbs sprawled. The two men pushed his arm inside and slammed the door.

"You need me to go with you, Puny?" asked one of the men.

"Naw, I can handle this," said Puny, the big man. "Where you staying, kid?"

"What happened to my daddy?" Billy said. He saw blood oozing from Troy's eyebrow. "What have you done to him?"

"I just give him a gentle tap. His problem is he is passed out drunk. Where you staying?"

"The Half Moon Hotel on North Main," Billy said.

As the black and yellow Chevy spun along the Jacksboro Highway, Puny glanced sideways at Billy and said, "Your old man is a real jerk, kid. I'm sorry about that."

"My daddy has some great qualities," Billy said.

"Hey, calm down. My old man was a real jerk, too. I know how it is. Having a jerk for an old man is like swimming with a big rock tied to your leg."

"How much did daddy win?" Billy asked.

Puny shook his head. "He busted out."

"He lost all three hundred dollars?"

"He lost every penny he had on him."

"But you said he was winning big."

"True. He was. But his luck turned."

"He lost it all?"

Troy groaned and flopped onto the floor of the back seat.

"All. And he give us an IOU for eleven thousand dollars, which he is supposed to have on deposit at the Fort Worth National Bank. That money damn sure better be there. I'll put a bullet in this blond-headed Romeo where it hurts the worst."

Stunned, Billy leaned back against the seat and watched the lights go by.

"Are you sure he lost all the money in the bank?"

"Yep. Tell him I'll be by at 8:45 in the morning to take him to the bank soon as they unlock the doors, and don't get no ideas about skipping town."

"But he was drunk. You took advantage of him. That isn't fair," Billy said.

51

"He's a jerk. What else can I tell you?"

Puny steered the black and yellow Chevy to a halt at the curb in front of the Half Moon and honked the horn until the night manager stuck his head out the door. The big man yelled, "Hey! Give this kid a hand getting his old man to his room."

"Oh, Puny, it's you," the night manager said. "What did you do to him?"

"He done it to himself. Tripped and fell. Too much booze."

Billy and the night manager dragged Troy out of the car. Troy's knees sagged, and he nearly fell to the sidewalk.

"Don't forget. Tell him I'm picking his country ass up at a quarter of nine," Puny said, moving down behind the wheel again.

"Hey, the car!" Billy shouted. "That's our car!"

"Not no more it ain't," said Puny. "The jerk lost it at the dice table."

Billy watched the red and yellow taillights as the Chevy pulled onto North Main and then did a U turn. The big man, his hat brim turned up, smiled and waved at Billy as he drove away.

Billy and the night manager draped Troy's arms over their shoulders and struggled up the stairs, with Troy almost a dead weight between them. He managed to catch a few steps with his scuffed wingtips and push himself upward a little. He seemed to be regaining his senses.

They dragged him to the bed by the open window and then let him fall. He lay across the bedspread with his arms outflung, a silly grin on his face, his eyes fluttering.

"Thanks," Billy said to the night manager.

"The clientele we attract, I have to do this quite a bit," the night manager said. "Did you see Ben Hogan out at Colonial?"

"He wasn't there."

"Pretty crappy day all around," the night manager said.

After the night manager returned to the lobby, Billy took his wet jeans and polo shirt and white socks off the shower curtain rod, wrapped a towel around them and put the clothes into his canvas satchel on top of everything else he owned. He pulled the zipper shut, and the sound apparently awoke his daddy. Troy sat up on his elbows on the bed and looked at his son. Billy picked up his satchel.

"What are you doing, Billy Boy?" Troy said in a hoarse voice.

"I'm leaving."

Troy wiped his mouth with a hand, feeling sick. He shook his head and ran his fingers through his blond hair. He tried to focus his smoky blue eyes on his son, but the boy's figure was in shadow.

"Turn on the light," Troy said.

"I'd rather not."

"I'm sorry. We were rich for a while until the dice went cold. I'll win it back and more. Put your bag down."

Billy pulled two twenty dollar bills out of his jeans and tossed them onto the bed.

"This is to pay the hotel. I'm keeping the rest of our money, all sixty dollars of it. I never want to see you again."

"Hell, I said I'm sorry. What more can I say? I'm doing the best I can, Billy Boy."

"You're pitiful," Billy said. "If this is the best you can do, you're nothing but a jerk. I hate you."

Troy stood up.

"You ungrateful little son of a bitch. Get the hell out of here," Troy said

BILLY LEANED OVER the railing of the bridge on North Main and looked down into the dark water of the Trinity River. The tears he had been holding back surged up from his heart, and he began sobbing. By the clock on the courthouse tower it was two in the morning, so there was no one to see or hear him. He wept from within, gasping for air, his nose pouring, tears flying from his eyes and rolling down his cheeks.

He looked down again into the dark water and the urge to jump came into his mind.

"Mama," he said. "Mama, I need you. Mama, I don't know what to do."

Five minutes went by on the courthouse clock. Gradually Billy stopped crying. He felt there were no more tears left. If there was a heaven, that's where his mother had to be. She couldn't be watching over Billy any more. She was in heaven. He was alone.

He heard a rumbling and a hiss of compressed air. Turning, Billy saw a city bus had stopped in the middle of the bridge and the driver had opened the door.

"You all right, kid?" called the bus driver.

The bus was empty except for the driver, a sturdy man who wore a tweed cap pulled low. The sign above the front window said OUT OF SERVICE.

"I need a place to stay. Cheap," Billy said.

"Get on board then. I can drop you three blocks from the YMCA," the bus driver said.

B Eight

ILLY PAID A WEEK'S RENT of one dollar per night for a small room with a single bed at the YMCA downtown and slept for a few hours. His room had a metal locker in it, and a padlock. He locked away his money, his canvas bag, his one sports coat and his other jeans, which were still damp, and then he walked and trotted to arrive at Colonial Country Club by 7:30 in the morning.

When he thought of his daddy, of that last sight of the drunken, broke and belligerent Troy, red eyed and bellowing in the shabby room at the Half Moon Hotel, Billy felt a hot ball grow inside his breast, felt his fingers tingling and his eyes moistening, and he didn't know whether it was sorrow or anger that he felt the most. But he did know that he never wanted to see Troy again for the rest of his life.

"Hi, Billy. You burning all over?" said Foxy Lerner at the entrance to the caddie yard. Foxy tucked his rat tail comb into the hip pocket of his jeans and touched up a wave of his ducktails with spittle and a little finger.

"You hit me with a knotted rope," Billy said. He saw Chili McWillie walking toward them. "I don't appreciate that."

"Hey, brother, nothing personal. A knotted rope sure stings, don't it?" said Foxy.

"You guys got a beef?" Chili asked. Though the youngest of the McWillie brothers, Chili stood three inches over six feet and was two hundred pounds of freckled muscle. All four McWillie brothers had played football in the line at Poly High. They had never won District, but they had punished the hell out of the fancy boys from Paschal and Arlington Heights.

"No beef," said Foxy. "This guy's my pal."

"That right?" Chili asked, turning his curious pale gaze and red hair toward Billy.

"Sure," said Billy.

"Elvis was here already. You got a different game today. Chester Stonekiller is joining your foursome in place of that butt doctor."

"Hey, crazy old man Sandpaster hates Chester Stonekiller. I heard the old man say he'd like to tie that damn Indian to a log and burn him alive," Foxy said.

"Well, since the butt doctor ain't here, you got Chester Stonekiller's bag today, Foxy."

"Aw Jeez. Does he still carry 100 practice balls in the side pocket?"

Billy looked around the caddie yard. Thirty or forty men and boys stood talking or playing games, and a few slept on the ground. The other caddies paid no attention to Billy. He was accepted now but was still the new boy. Only Ham T waved a black arm of greeting that Billy returned.

A few minutes after eight o'clock, Billy, Foxy and Ham T reported to the storage room to pick up their assigned bags. Dr. Sandpaster didn't believe in hitting practice balls before teeing off—practice putting was the only thing to do, he believed. So the other members of Sandpaster's foursome also practiced their putting, except for Sonny Stonekiller, who slipped off early to the range and hit a shag bag of balls to prepare for a round of golf as it should be played by the club champion.

Dr. Sandpaster broke into a horsey smile, his large yellow dentures clicking with moisture, when he looked through his purple-tinted glasses and saw Billy approaching with the big leather bag over his shoulder.

"I hear you were rude to my granddaughter yesterday, Billy," said Dr. Sandpaster.

"Sir, I'm very sorry about that. It couldn't be helped," Billy said.

"Sorry! Don't be sorry! It's the biggest laugh I've had since Roosevelt died. I've raised that precious girl and her mother ever since my son got blown up flying his bomber over Germany in that stupid war. We were on the wrong side in that war, if you want to know. It's Roosevelt's fault." Billy thought of Troy in the church in France with the high explosive shells falling on him, losing his nerve for golf.

"Come on, Ira. Let's play," said a tall, burly, brown-skinned man wearing plaid beltless slacks, white shoes and a white polo shirt. Billy figured this must be Chester Stonekiller. Billy had grown up among Indians and Mexicans in Albuquerque. He thought Chester looked Navajo, not Cherokee. But Sonny's cheekbones and strong profile were Cherokee. Probably his mother was a Cherokee beauty.

Walking toward the first tee, Dr. Sandpaster said, "I'm pleased with you, Billy, for taking Sandra down a notch. I love her to death, but since she started dating Sonny Stonekiller, she thinks she's a Hollywood princess. I keep telling her, hell, Sonny is just an Indian who can run fast and play good golf. How long can that last? In a few years he'll be an old fat wagon chaser like his father, but she'll be beautiful and well educated and rich. I believe she understood my point that puppy love with Sonny Stonekiller could ruin her life."

Chester Stonekiller lit a large cigar that smelled to Billy like the sizzle of a branding iron against cow flesh. Sonny walked onto the tee a little late, dapper in yellow slacks and a white shirt with the collar turned up and black and white saddle oxfords, his rich black hair combed straight back, his light canvas golf bag hanging from one arm. Sonny caught Billy's eye, questioning whether Billy was going to make trouble. Billy met his gaze but was impassive.

"Last night Sandra told me you really pissed her off, new boy," said Sonny.

"He sure did. Oh, my, did he ever!" Dr. Sandpaster said. He looked at the tall thin Mr. Titus, chief financial officer of Sandpaster Oil & Gas. "Tell them what you saw last night, Titus?"

"I saw Sandra break a plate."

"You saw her break two plates."

"All right. Two plates and three glasses and a bottle of excellent Chateauneuf du Pape."

"Hey, boy, I better never hear of you bothering her again," Sonny said.

"What's it got to do with you?" said Billy.

"Sandra is my girlfriend. I won't have you insulting her," Sonny said. "Don't ever speak to her again if you know what's good for you."

"Shut up! All of you shut up!" cried Dr. Sandpaster. He took three deep breaths and snorted twice to tune with universal energy waves. "It's time for golf, not bickering. Same game as usual. What's your handicap, Chester?"

"Sixteen," Chester said.

"Put feathers in your hair and paint your face, if you plan to massacre us. You're at least a twelve," said Dr. Sandpaster.

"Look on the damn handicap board, you old crank," Chester said.

Dr. Sandpaster looked at Titus, who nodded. "Sixteen."

His Perfect Golf Swing worked like machinery as Dr. Sandpaster parred the first two holes, lipping out what should have been a birdie on the second. The ball hung over the edge of the cup, defying gravity, until Chester shouted time was up. This incident planted a tiny fear in Dr. Sandpaster's wiring. Uncomfortable. Who's to say it wasn't an omen? He pondered the possibility of roaming pockets of reverse gravity. What was it the great teacher Harvey Penick said? "Golfers are gullible." Yet Ira had the Perfect Swing to fall back on. All professionals had what they called a "choke stroke"—a swing they could count on making if the mortgage was riding on it. But Ira didn't need anything but his own Perfect Swing that he had designed through many years of work at the drawing board, using a ruler, a compass and a T-square, feeling very much as da Vinci must have felt when he invented flying, the doctor thought. Einstein wasn't right about everything, but he was damn sure right about gravity being constant. Or was he? It would figure the devil was smarter than Einstein. Ira would like to hear Einstein and the devil go up against the Quiz Kids on the radio. The devil could read the human makeup and find faults the same way Dr. Sandpaster found cracks in the structures on his geological maps.

"Have you gone to sleep up there, Ira? Do you need an ambulance?" yelled Chester from the third tee. Dr. Sandpaster flushed the devil out of his mind with the powers of concentration he had developed as a scientist who could see beneath the ground. He placed the bothersome thoughts on a glass slide beneath his imaginary microscope and then he focused to see beyond them.

The third hole at Colonial—Billy remembered it from yesterday as the hardest hole he had ever seen until he reached the fifth—was a par four that played 476 yards from Sonny's championship tees, and 450 yards from the men's regular tees used by the other three.

Sonny cracked his drive over the large bunker that guarded the fairway at 260 yards, where the hole turned to the left. In the middle of the bunker grew an island of pampas grass, in which Chester's slice landed. Chester let out a howling scream of curses that sounded to Billy like language from the pueblos.

Dr. Sandpaster played two of his wind balls with his brassie, the first down the right side of the fairway and the second a bouncer across the fairway bunker. He was 135 yards from the flag, which was in the center of the raised green. He needed to get his ball into the hole in two to stay even par. But this was, after all, one of the holes he could bogey and still shoot a 79. Counting on a par on this three-handicap hole was statistically a poor risk. In fact, he had not parred the third hole in two years. Yet here he was, only 135 yards from the pin, with an excellent opportunity to be on in three and have a putt at a par.

"Three-iron, Billy. I'm going to cut it in there."

As well as Dr. Sandpaster had been striking the ball, a 3-iron seemed like far too much, but Billy knew better than to speak. He handed the club to the doctor.

"Do I see doubt on your face?" asked Dr. Sandpaster.

"No sir," Billy said.

Billy looked down at the ball as Dr. Sandpaster went into his fully-cocked stance and backswing. What Billy saw was that in the deliberations of distance and breeze and sun and shadow and choices of clubs, the doctor had neglected to attend to his address. He was standing far too close to the ball.

The sound was an ugly clank and the ball flew off to the right for thirty yards in an almost semicircle and landed in two inches of rough.

Shank!

Sandpaster was shocked numb. He hadn't shanked a ball since the day the atomic bomb was dropped on Hiroshima.

He glared at Billy.

"You were thinking something," Dr. Sandpaster said.

"No sir."

"You were thinking something evil. I could detect your lack of confidence. Let's have no more thinking, Billy. Promise me. No more thinking. Thinking is my department. Your department is toting the bag and shutting up."

Dr. Sandpaster recovered for a double bogey six on the third hole and he arrived at the ninth tee still only two over par. This could be the day. His senses were coursing. Except for that one shank—hush, mustn't think of the word—he had hit the ball with solid strikes, as befits a man who knows the Perfect Swing.

Without uncocking his wrists, as near as he felt it, Dr. Sandpaster whacked his ball straight down the middle of the ninth fairway. It was the best drive the doctor had hit since Billy had been caddying for him. The ninth was 355 yards long from the regular tees—391 from Sonny's tees. Billy estimated, Dr. Sandpaster's drive had gone 240 yards. His ball was equidistant between the bunkers on either side of the fairway. Ahead of the doctor, less than one hundred yards from his ball, lay a blue pool, with geysers of water spurting on the right side. Beyond the pond was the green, well bunkered and shaded by oaks. Dr. Sandpaster needed to hit a high shot that would carry 115 to 125 yards into the center of the green. That would leave him two putts for a 37, which would be his personal best for the front nine at Colonial.

Sandpaster pulled a 9-iron, a 5-iron, a 6-iron and an 8-iron, one after the other, studying his shot, making a mental picture of it as Bobby Jones always did, like a photo from a camera.

"Will you hit the damned thing, for God's sake?" shouted Chester Stonekiller, who was in the left greenside bunker in three.

Billy tried to look away, tried to make his mind go blank. But he couldn't avoid noticing that Dr. Sandpaster was again standing far too close to the ball.

The doctor swung his 6-iron down sharply into the smooth grass and shanked the ball.

The ball flew into the right fairway bunker thirty yards short of the pond.

Dr. Sandpaster glared at Billy.

"What are you thinking?" asked the doctor.

"It's in the bunker. You only lay two. You can knock it on the green and make a four."

Billy hurried on. Dr. Sandpaster muttered to himself. That

was his second shank in one day. Incredible. His swing was shank-proof. Where had the shanks come from? Was it this new kid, Billy, putting a hex on him with those intense blue eyes? Yesterday Billy had seemed sent from heaven. But that's how devils arrive. They don't come with red tails and foul breath. Devils appear as sympathetic children who make your heart move, make you want to help them. That's why it was wise to avoid the poor.

From the bunker short of the pond, Dr. Sandpaster shanked a pitching wedge that carried the water, turned hard right, bounced off a tree trunk and fell into the right greenside bunker.

The doctor walked over calmly, as if nothing were out of order, and stepped into the white sand bunker on the right of the ninth green. He carried his Sarazen sand wedge, with which Sandpaster was adept. The ball had found a level lie in the sand. The pin was only thirty feet away. On sand shots Dr. Sandpaster could look like an expert. In his imagination the doctor saw himself swing and the ball flop onto the green and then the ball roll into the hole for a four and a 37.

What Billy saw, in horror, was that the ball was maybe three inches from Dr. Sandpaster's right foot as the wedge started down with a lurch and a lifting of the head.

The onlookers and other players laughed when Dr. Sandpaster shanked the ball out of the greenside bunker with such force that the ball flew nearly behind him, all the way up the hill to the practice putting green, where voices could be heard yelling, "Who?" and "What's this?"

With his head down, his brain churning, his lungs heaving, Dr. Sandpaster marched up the hill to the practice putting green, passing Foxy who was guarding the green leather bag of a hugely grinning Chester Stonekiller. "What's going on?" Foxy whispered to Billy. "He's standing too close to the ball," Billy said softly. Billy climbed with the big black bag behind the wheezing

Sandpaster. Golfers scattered before them on the practice putting green.

"I may lift my ball off the practice green with no penalty and drop it no closer to the hole. I am shooting five," Dr. Sandpaster said in an even temper.

"Shooting seven, I believe," someone said.

"Shut up. If I need a ruling, the board will convene at a later date," said Dr. Sandpaster. He turned and looked at Billy. "Well? Out with it! What did you say?"

"Nothing."

"Yes, you did. You think I'm old and deaf, but I can hear like a bat. You were saying something about me to that little rat-faced caddie. What did you say?"

"Well . . ."

"Well?"

"It was just an observation. I didn't mean for you to hear."

Dr. Sandpaster pulled off his purple-tinted glasses and blinked his eyes. A few strands of hair fell across his pale forehead, always protected from the sun by a visor.

"What was your observation?" Dr. Sandpaster shouted.

A large group of golfers and caddies were gathering. Elvis Spaatz was squeezing his way through the crowd along the sidewalk toward the putting green.

"I said you were standing too close to the ball when you hit those shank shots," Billy said.

"Why didn't you warn me, then?"

"You told me never to give you advice," Billy said.

Dr. Sandpaster stood at the edge of the practice putting green, where the land fell off toward the ninth green below. The area was filling not only with golfers but with men who pruned the roses and mowed the fairways and trimmed the hedges and manicured the greens into such beauty. For an instant Dr. Sandpaster thought he saw John Bredemus at the edge of the crowd, near the bunker left of the ninth green, but when the doctor looked again he saw a fat man who was president of a bank.

"I have played golf with Gene Sarazen. I have played golf with Walter Hagen [the doctor wondered if his Hagen story was true or if he had dreamed it, but no matter, it was never questioned], Byron Nelson, Dr. Cary Middlecoff, the amateur champion Charlie Coe—all fine gentlemen, each a credit to the game. I have played with generals and admirals and great statesmen in Washington and in Europe and in South and Central America. I have played with captains of industry at Pine Valley and Augusta, Georgia. I played with the sheik of Oman. I played with Dwight D. Eisenhower, for God's sake! And since the first day Colonial Country Club opened its doors, I have played golf here with you men, some of you worthy members and stout comrades, but most of you sadly not quite up to snuff."

Ellis Spaatz moved up and took his elbow. "Dr. Sandpaster, are you feeling all right?"

The tall geologist-oil man turned and looked down his nose at Elvis with an expression that could have passed for sorrow if the doctor's facial muscles had been trained in registering emotion of that sort.

"That caddie, Billy, that I have had for the last day and a half? I want him fired."

"Yes sir. You want him booted clean off the course?"

"No. I have an unfathomable fondness for the little devil. Let him keep his place in the yard. Assign him to the bags of my enemies, but not the enemies I play golf with. Just keep Billy out of my sight. Will you do that, Elvis?"

"Yes sir. What did the boy do to you, sir?"

"He told me I was standing too close to the ball when I hit those shank shots. I played with Tommy Armour. Surely Tommy Armour would have noticed if I stood too close to the ball. But I didn't hear a peep out of the great Tommy Armour. Elvis, I see that boy is still here."

"Billy, you're fired from this bag. Go back to the yard," Elvis said.

Billy laid the big black leather bag at Dr. Sandpaster's feet. "Sir," Billy said, "you are shooting five. I hope you sink it."

"I am so disappointed in you, Billy. I thought we had a special comradeship developing between us. I should have realized a boy who had seen *Richard II* would prove a wretched caddie."

Nine

O N HIS WAY DOWN the hill Billy passed Foxy Lerner, who said, "I told you the old man is crazy."

Billy walked on past the tenth tee and turned into the woods that hid the caddie yard. He was not surprised to see Chili McWillie come out to greet him. No doubt Billy's indoctrination was not yet finished. Even fired, he might still have to pay the yard for the four shank shots. That's how it was on the football team in Albuquerque. If you dropped three passes, that meant nine licks with a board on your bare butt, even if you had a broken wrist.

"You're in trouble," Chili said.

"What? Do I fight you now? Is that how I escape from this place after I already been fired?"

Chili scratched his knuckles against the bristle on his chin, so that it sounded like brushing a dog.

"Naw, you're a good kid," Chili said. "You got a place here. Your trouble right now is a drunk cowboy who says he's your old man."

"Troy?" Billy was startled.

"Yeah, Troy is his name. He's in the yard now telling how he could beat Ben Hogan before the war. If he gets one of my boys drunk passing around his bourbon, I'm gonna have to knock him out."

"My daddy is one tough cowboy. Look out for yourself."
Chili chuckled.

"It's our favorite sport for me and my brothers to go trolling for drunk cowboys to beat up on Saturday nights after the pro rassling matches at the North Side Coliseum. Besides, I think Elvis has done called the cops."

Wearing his broadbrimmed black 5 X beaver Stetson hat, a blue cowboy shirt that revealed his solid torso, his big silver belt buckle from winning the bareback bronc riding in Cheyenne and his clean pressed Levi's that came down to the heels of his hand-made boots, Troy looked like a teenage boy's dream of a cowboy, except for one item that jarred Billy's eyes—the pint of bourbon in his hip pocket.

"Billy Boy!" Troy said. "Come and give me a hug, Billy Boy!"

Billy ducked away from Troy's clasping arms, from the crooked smile on his daddy's face, from the whiskey smell. It was like a move in the boxing ring, dodging an opponent. The other caddies were watching.

"You've got to get out of here," Billy said.

"That pro shop flunkie is calling the police. Well, the hell with them," Troy said. "What can they do to me now?"

"Let's go outside the yard and talk," Billy said.

Troy stumbled over a rock as they left the caddie yard. He cursed and drank a nip from the hip pocket bottle.

"You're embarrassing me. Please leave. I'm having a hard time. You're making it harder."

Troy pushed back his hat brim with a thumb and lit a Camel with his old silver Zippo. He snapped the lid of the lighter a couple of times, his eyes searching his son's face for some sign of compassion.

"Well, all right then. This is what I did," Troy said, exhaling a long plume of smoke. "This morning I thought about what you said. You're right. I'm a loser. I'm a jerk. So I went over to the U.S. Army this morning and re-upped for another tour of duty. They jacked me up a rank—to captain. Sounds classy, huh? They're happy to have me back. They need me. I'm leaving on a bus for Fort Sill, Oklahoma, in a couple of hours. Short refresher course in how to blow people up from a long distance, and I am off for Korea. Your old man is a captain, an officer and a gentleman. Now do I get a hug?"

"I don't believe you," Billy said. "You're boozed up and you tell lies."

"I am having the Army send you half my salary, Billy Boy. You are my insurance inheritor in case they kill my ass. I told you I'd get that money for the house back for you, and that would do it."

Billy noticed a number of the caddies had followed them out of the yard to hear what they were saying, and he saw Elvis Spaatz coming down the hill with two uniformed cops that Billy recognized as Burgin and Boyle.

"Now, do I get a hug, son?" Troy said.

"Throw away that bottle."

"You don't believe me?"

"You get to feeling regret and remorse and you tell lies to make it all right. You don't fool me anymore. Throw away that bottle."

"Hell, no. I'm trying to say goodbye to you, you little son of a bitch. You won't even let me do that. I devoted half my life to you, and all you can say is you don't believe me, throw away my bottle. This bottle is taking me to Fort Sill."

"Daddy, you are drunk and talking stupid. I'm not falling for it again."

Boyle and Burgin arrived, each at one of Troy's shoulders. Both police officers were armed with pistols and the nightsticks that yesterday they had told Billy they enjoyed using.

"This be the trespasser?" said Burgin, the tall one in the starched shirt.

"Tell these cops I'm your daddy," Troy said.

"Please get my daddy out of here," Billy said.

"He is annoying the members," said Elvis.

The two officers twisted Troy's strong arms behind his back

and handcuffed his wrists. Billy saw Boyle and Burgin glancing around and knew they were hoping for a sight of Ben Hogan.

"I got a taxi waiting," Troy said.

"We'll send the taxi away. It's Car Seven that'll be taking you from here to your next destination," said Boyle, curling his lip to show his gap tooth.

Troy leaned forward and thrust his face toward Billy.

"Give me a hug and a farewell kiss, Billy Boy," Troy said. "I may be gone a long time."

"You're drunk," Billy said. "I'm not going to kiss you."

"I don't know how you got so mean," Troy said. "So long, Billy Boy."

As Billy turned back toward the caddie yard, he heard Troy telling Boyle and Burgin to take him to the bus station, that he was a captain in the U.S. Army and was due at Fort Sill. There was a chance, Billy thought, that Troy might be telling the truth about re-upping in the Army. Didn't sound like Troy though. Nothing Troy had ever said or done would cause Billy to believe he was willing to rejoin the Army, knowing he would be urgently wanted in Korea.

No, this was another fantasy from the booze that had soaked Troy's mind for many years and made him tell lies. Billy heard Troy talking to the two officers as they escorted him to their patrol car, and then he heard the doors slam. Billy hoped they would not be hard on his daddy but would put him on some bus bound for somewhere.

Billy looked up and saw Sonny Stonekiller standing twenty feet away with a glass of ice tea.

"Dr. Sandpaster quit for the day. You spooked him. I don't think he saw your drunk father being carried out by the cops, but he's hearing about it by now," Sonny said.

"All right," Billy said. "You been looking at me funny for two days, even before I caught you cheating. Like you think you're better than I am. Put your hands up. I'm going to whip you."

Sonny smiled, his teeth so white and even. He held up a delicately designed but muscular right hand, the long fingers of an artist.

"Much as I'd like to beat the hell out of you, I'm not going to break a knuckle on a hick from nowhere. These hands are worth millions."

Sonny turned his hand palmside up and thrust up his third finger at Billy and smiled.

"Suck on this, country boy," Sonny said.

Sonny walked away while Billy was considering whether to hit him. That's what Troy would have done—hit him.

IT WAS LATE IN THE AFTERNOON when Billy gave up on getting another bag for this day. Chili had promised him the next spot in line, but members kept turning him down because Dr. Sandpaster had said he was a jinx. None of the caddies had mentioned the scene with Troy, not to Billy's face. Every boy and man in that yard knew what it was like to grow up among drunks.

Billy checked out of work with Chili, who warned him to watch for queers at the YMCA. "And don't take a piss at the library, either." When Billy walked onto Colonial Parkway he heard the familiar engine of the red Chrysler convertible. He turned toward the car, but Sandra lifted the tip of her nose with a forefinger in a gesture that clearly said "snoot," and then, like Sonny, she stuck up her middle finger as the Chrysler disappeared around the corner. Billy had a feeling she must have waited two hours or more to snub him. He didn't believe it was coincidence. How would she know when he might leave the yard and go home? Thinking about Sandra being so furious, so offended, made him smile.

He thought of her bare legs and her cropped hair. She had waited two hours to see him. He liked that.

Instead of going north on University Drive across the Trinity River bridge toward town, Billy cut eastward through Forest Park. He could hear the lions growling in the zoo in the gathering evening and the cries of birds and beasts from their pens. He passed a lighted softball field where two teams in uniforms—one sponsored by a gun shop and the other by an insurance company—played a game of fast pitch, with a small but noisy crowd and coolers of beer.

Billy started up a wooded hill which Foxy Lerner had told him was famous locally as a place to park with your girlfriend. He saw a new Buick, with two couples who were already kissing, turn into a lane. Behind the Buick came a maroon Dodge that looked as if the boy and girl were both driving it.

Listening to the music from the radios of the lovers in their cars, his thoughts drifting to Sandra's bare legs, to his monk's cell at the YMCA, to his future—if he could no longer get a bag at Colonial because of Sandpaster, what would he do?—Billy almost passed by the object lying beside the road.

A flash came from it. A flash of moonlight or a flash from the floodlights at the softball diamond. But there it was, in the weeds, a golf club.

Billy stopped and picked up the club and hefted it. The club had a good springy feeling. It was a 7-iron with a polished steel shaft, not a speck of rust though this was a very old Bobby Jones model. His fingers caressed the leather grips that had been cleaned and lightly oiled and well cared for. Billy wondered where the club came from. Did some kid take it out of his daddy's bag to hit balls in the park and then forget it? Did it fall out of the back of a pickup truck? Did someone get furious at the game of golf and throw the club away? Maybe he would find an entire set scattered along the road up Park Hill toward town.

"Pardon me, son. Is that a 7-iron in your hands?"

The sound frightened Billy. He had heard no one approach. Now he turned and saw an old Ford car, a 1946, had arrived beside the edge of the road. The driver looked like a man of about sixty, wearing a tweed golf cap. Billy couldn't make out his face in the shadows.

"Yes sir," Billy said.

"It's a 7-iron, isn't it? The Bobby Jones model?"

"That's it," Billy said. He walked toward the car holding out the iron. The man leaned forward across the empty passenger seat and took the club. Billy saw more of the man's face now. A craggy nose, powerful jaw, bushy gray eyebrows.

"Still in perfect balance," the man said after hefting the club. "I was afraid falling out the window might throw it off an octave."

"How did it fall out the window?" Billy asked.

"Well. I was listening to opera on my radio and conducting with my 7-iron, and out the window it went. Didn't even realize exactly when. I've been backtracking through the second act of *Don Giovanni.*"

"By Mozart," Billy said.

"You know music," the man said.

"My mother was a university professor."

"Boy, I am very hungry, and I will guess that you could use a meal yourself. We'll go to that cafeteria on Berry Street. Wonderful meats and vegetables. An entire counter of pies of all sort. Get in the car."

"I will pay my own way," Billy said.

"This meal is my reward for you finding my favorite 7-iron. This is my lucky club. It's priceless. Thank the angels in heaven it fell into the right hands."

The man got out and opened the trunk and placed the Bobby Jones 7-iron into the small canvas golf bag with six other clubs, two of them woods, Billy noticed. The trunk held a flowered carpetbag, a net sack of books, and a couple of long argyle socks stuffed with items. A few checkers had fallen out of one sock. Leaning against the back of the trunk was a checkerboard.

"Oh," Billy said.

"You stump your toe?"

"I just realized who you are."

The man was large and athletic and he came back around the car to face Billy, his tweed cap pulled low but sparks of light in his eyes.

"You're John Bredemus. You're the Father of Texas Golf," Billy said.

"How would a young fellow like yourself have heard of old man Bredemus?"

"You have built a hundred golf courses. Dr. Sandpaster told me you travel by yourself in an old car with a few clubs and a bag of books and a sock of checkers."

"It would follow I would have a checkerboard as well, and a carpetbag of clothes, such as you noticed in my trunk?" the man said.

"My name is Billy."

They shook hands.

"I'm John," the man said. "Let's go eat, Billy Boy."

T Ten

HE PICCADILLY CAFETERIA was clean and well lit. Smells of hot food made Billy's lips wet in anticipation. He pushed his tray along shining silver tracks past a banquet of salads, breads, vegetables, meats, fish, soup, cream gravy and biscuits, fruits, and an array of desserts—peach cobblers, coconut cream pies, banana puddings, chocolate cakes, apple pies, ice cream—all of it dished out by women in white uniforms trimmed with green.

Bredemus paid the cashier and carried his tray toward a table. Walking behind him, Billy saw that the legendary golf-course builder was larger than the boy had first thought—broader than Troy—and moved with the assurance and grace of an athlete. Bredemus was tall and solid. He looked more like a football player than a golfer. His head was big, though not oversized for his body. He had a dimpled chin, a confident smile, prominent ears, thin wrinkles at the corners of his eyes from squinting, and deep wrinkles across his forehead as if he were pondering a riddle. His hair was short and thick, showing strings of gray among the bushy brown, and his sideburns were cleanly shaved above the ears.

For all his physical power, Bredemus's manner was gentle, his voice soft, as he placed his tray on a table, pulled out a chair and grinned, looking at the plates and bowls Billy was unloading.

"Is that cream gravy I see poured over your biscuits and your mashed potatoes and meat loaf and also over that slice of cantaloupe?" the man asked.

"I love cream gravy," Billy said. "My mama made the best. Sausage and biscuits and scrambled eggs with cream gravy on top of everything. I never tried it on cantaloupe before, but it's pretty good."

Billy noticed that Bredemus had several plates and bowls—roast beef and creamed potatoes and green beans and cornbread but no gravy or dessert.

"I would have thought that growing up in Albuquerque, you would have been weaned on *huevos rancheros* and refried beans and tortillas and green chile salsa," said Bredemus.

"My mama grew up in Lubbock," Billy said. "Hey, how do you know I'm from Albuquerque?"

"Why, you mentioned it driving over here. Your mother taught English at the University of New Mexico."

Billy remembered he had mentioned that his mother had made him familiar with opera, but he didn't remember talking about Albuquerque or saying his mother taught English there. But maybe he did. Bredemus had played the radio loud and had shouted remarks Billy could hardly hear, and perhaps, in his hunger and his exhaustion from the events of the day, Billy had forgotten what he had said.

"By the way, Billy Boy," said Bredemus, sipping his coffee, "you must not tell anyone you have seen me. You have never met me. You don't know me. It's very important to me that my presence here is just between you and me. Promise?"

"My daddy is the only one ever called me Billy Boy."

"I'm surprised more people don't call you that. It's such an easy, rhythmical name, it just slips out that way," Bredemus said. "Please, especially, do not mention me to anyone at Colonial."

Billy dug into his meat loaf and gravy with a spoon.

"How do you know I'm working at Colonial?"

"I saw you through the trees this morning. You were carrying Ira Sandpaster's bag."

"I didn't see you."

"I didn't intend that you should," said Bredemus.

"Dr. Sandpaster fired me for telling him he was standing too close to the ball when he shanked it."

Bredemus laughed.

"Ira never takes advice from anyone who has less money than he has, so he is unaccustomed to advice," said Bredemus.

"How come you would go to Colonial today if you don't want them to know you are here? They're bound to see you."

"Billy Boy, it has been fifteen years since I finished my work at Colonial and moved on. They don't remember me anymore."

"Dr. Sandpaster remembers you. He said you are a genius."

Billy admired the way Bredemus had of talking while he ate but never showing food in his mouth or spilling anything on his blue and white striped dress shirt, which he wore with the collar open and no necktie. It seemed to the boy that Bredemus came from a different class than Billy had ever encountered.

"Ira approached me one day in 1936 when Colonial was playable but not finished. I was walking the seventeenth, trying to decide if the Lord really intended for Big Annie to be beside the green, and Ira hailed me down," Bredemus said. "Ira fancies himself a philosopher. He had been in the grill at lunch arguing a point that he wanted my opinion on. He wanted to know if golf is a sport or is it a game?"

"What did you tell him?"

"Golf is a jackass in a hailstorm," Bredemus said. "Golf is whatever you want to make of it."

"I don't understand," Billy said.

"Golf is a sport if you are trying to beat somebody. It's a game if you're playing for fun. Golf is a business, if that's what you want to make it. The mysterious aspects of golf fill up enough books every year to fill a library, all of them written by experts who are trying to top each other. The range for metaphysical or philosophical debate about golf is enormous because golf is elusive. That's the main reason golf has been popular for centuries—one day you've got the answer, and the next day it's gone."

"My daddy said that's how he lost his nerve for golf," said Billy. "One day it was gone."

Billy was starting on his hot apple pie with ice cream. He tried to eat it in the manner of Bredemus, but he felt a trickling down his chin.

"Your daddy must be a good player, because only good players are good enough to lose their nerve. The ordinary dub doesn't know what nerve is."

Billy thought of Troy. If his daddy had been telling the truth about joining the Army, he should be in Oklahoma by now. He wondered how soon Troy would be sent to Korea. He knew he should care, but he realized he didn't.

"Let me explain my need for secrecy," Bredemus said. He had finished his dinner, though his plates and bowls were not scraped and licked clean, as Billy's were. "I am constantly and anonymously touring the golf courses I have built to see what changes are being made. What happens, Billy Boy, is I build a wonderful golf course. Then others come in and build a grand, expensive clubhouse, and charge a lot of money to join. Golfers play on my course until they get quite good, and that gives them the privilege to demand changes be made, bunkers moved, trees cut down, greens flattened, and so on. These golf clubs organize committees to listen to critiques and come up with notions of their own. Soon the course is being systematically ruined."

"Is Colonial ruined?"

"Oh, my, no, I trust not," said Bredemus. "Colonial was so grand in the beginning, it will be difficult to ruin. But I haven't really walked the course in years. I only took a quick peek today."

"Why have you built all these golf courses if you know people are going to come along and ruin them?" Billy asked.

"Well, they're not all ruined. Intelligent changes are made from time to time. Now and then I am able to influence a player or a greens committee chairman by subtle methods. But even so, yes, I have spent more than half my life building golf courses in Texas. Other than my love of the game and the outdoors, there are two reasons. Golf courses inspire community. And open spaces are the lungs that allow the communities to breathe."

"Dr. Sandpaster said you should have gotten rich, but you worked cheap and just kept moving on and never owned anything," Billy said.

"Bless your heart, Billy Boy, money does not bring satisfaction." Two large hands pushed Bredemus in his chair away from the table. "A full belly and a good sleep followed by a world-class bowel movement, that is satisfaction. Finish that pie and let's be out of here. It's late for an old man like me."

"You keep calling yourself an old man. You don't look it. How old are you?"

"Precisely between yesterday and tomorrow, that's my age." Bredemus yawned and stood up and placed his Scottish-style tweed cap on his head, pulling the brim down low and at an angle and squinting out from underneath. He looked as if he might be on his way to a rugby scrum. "I'll drop you home. Where are you staying?"

"The YMCA."

"Ah, happy coincidence. So am I."

AT FIRST THEY COULDN'T HEAR the siren above the sound of the car radio. Then Billy saw a motorcycle officer appear beside the driver's window and motion for Bredemus to pull the old Ford over to the side on University Drive.

"I'm sorry, officer. I had no idea I was speeding," Bredemus said.

The officer was young and wore black boots. He climbed off his big Harley.

78   "Let's see your driver's license, Pop," he said.

Bredemus found his wallet and began looking for his license.

"How fast was I going?"

"You were closer to going too slow than to going too fast. But your left taillight is out."

Bredemus handed the officer his driver's license. The officer shined a flashlight on it, studied it, looked back and forth from the license to Bredemus.

"I mean your current license, Pop."

"That is it," said Bredemus.

"This license is dated 1946."

"Really? Has it been so long?"

The officer leaned in the window.

"Hey, kid. You got a driver's license?"

"Yes sir." Billy dug it out of his jeans. "It's a New Mexico license."

The officer examined Billy's license and handed it back.

"You get behind the wheel and drive," the officer said. He looked at Bredemus and produced his book of tickets. "I was going to let you go with a warning, Pop, but a five-year-old driver's license is too much. I'll write you up, you get your license renewed, and they'll drop the charge. Get that taillight fixed. Please don't make me have to come to court and spend three or four hours on this."

"Thank you, officer," Bredemus said, getting out of the car to change places with Billy.

The officer was impressed by Bredemus's size and demeanor and took note of the tweed cap.

"Are you a football coach?"

"No."

"You look like Knute Rockne or somebody famous. Are you famous?"

"I'm afraid not," Bredemus said.

"Well, get a taillight and get that license renewed, Pop, before you run into serious trouble. Drive safe, kid. I'm off work in five minutes. I don't want to see you again tonight."

Billy started the engine and steered the old Ford onto University Drive as the motorcycle officer roared past them, heading back to the station for his shift change.

"Nice fellow," said Bredemus.

Billy found a space around the corner from the front door of the YMCA and parked the Ford. Bredemus got out and opened the trunk.

"Wait a moment, Billy Boy," Bredemus said.

Bredemus pulled the Bobby Jones 7-iron out of his golf bag and handed the club to Billy.

"Take this with you to Colonial in the morning. It's a lucky club."

"What am I supposed to do with it?" Billy asked.

"Just carry it. We'll see what happens. It is a very lucky club."

"Okay. Thanks," Billy said.

"But remember. When they ask you where you got this club, tell the truth and no more. You found it in the weeds beside the road in the park. Never mention my name. Agreed?"

"Agreed."

"Shake on it."

Bredemus's hand felt like the gnarled and calloused hands of cowboys Billy had known.

BEleven

ILLY SPENT FOUR HOURS in the caddie yard the next morning without getting a bag. Elvis Spaatz told Chili McWillie that Dr. Sandpaster had spread the word that Billy was a jinx. Dr. Sandpaster went onto the course later than his usual hour, using a caddie named Fonda, a slender white boy who could walk all day, summer or winter, toting a sixty-pound bag and never saying a word. Some of the caddies said Fonda was too dumb to talk, but others said he was too smart to talk.

As the number-one caddie, Chili McWillie could have any bag he wanted, but he preferred to hang out in the yard and keep order. Chili took half a dozen golf balls out of a paper sack and organized a game of chipping toward a hole in the ground. A hole in one was worth a nickel from each of the other players. Billy chipped it in on his first three shots with the lucky 7-iron and was staying comfortably ahead.

"You banging old Ira's granddaughter?" Chili asked.

"Why? Is she the kind that bangs everybody?"

"Naw, she don't bang nobody that I know. Sonny Stonekiller wants people to think he does it with her, but I don't believe him. That girl thinks she is too good for banging. I'd like to be the one that teaches her different. Hey!"

Chili chipped one into the hole and collected nickels.

"Then why would you ask if I'm banging her? Don't seem very likely, does it?"

"Don't seem likely at all, new boy," Chili said. "But you got old Ira furious at you, and Sonny Stonekiller told his football player pals he'd like to see you get the snot kicked out of you. So I figured the girl is behind it."

"She won't speak to me."

"That's a come on," Chili said. "In my neighborhood, when a girl won't speak to you she is begging for a banging. I hear you challenged Sonny Stonekiller to a fistfight and he backed down."

"Yeah," said Billy.

"You a good boy," Chili said. "I like you. You got grit."

"Why can't I get a bag?" said Billy.

Billy chipped another ball into the hole.

"Hey, you'd be losing money bagging. You make more chipping with that old 7-iron you found."

"Good Lord God Awmighty!"

The caddies looked around from their games and sat up from their naps.

Ben Hogan stood at the entrance of the caddie yard, studying them with those eyes that led other players to call him the Hawk. He wore a flat white cap, a white cotton golf shirt, a black leather belt, gray pleated gabardine slacks and gleaming black shoes that were spit shined. Sunlight fell upon him and glowed from him in the imaginations of the stunned caddies.

Elvis Spaatz rushed up to Hogan's side.

"Mr. Hogan, I'm sorry your man got food poisoning. Those deviled eggs should have been thrown away. I will carry your bag myself," Elvis said.

"No," Hogan said.

"Oh, I consider it a real honor, sir, something I can tell my children about someday."

"No," Hogan said. He looked at Billy. "Hey, kid. You with the golf club. Come here."

Billy knew from photographs that Hogan was a handsome man, who resembled a shorter, fiercer Gary Cooper, but the closer the boy approached the more Billy realized he and Hogan were the same height and build.

Hogan took the cigarette out of his mouth and mashed it under his right shoe.

"Let me see that club," Hogan said.

Billy handed him the club. Hogan wrapped his fingers around the leather grip, waggled the club a few times, held it in front of him at a forty-five-degree angle as if checking the straightness of the shaft. Hogan looked at the clubhead, read the name Bobby Jones and ran his fingers along the grooves.

"I've seen this club before," Hogan said.

Billy became aware that his mouth was hanging slack, that he must look like an idiot, but he was lost in the thrill of standing in the presence of the greatest golfer in the world, a true hero. A feeling of strength radiated from the champion like electric current. It struck Billy that he was feeling the power of Hogan's will.

"Where did you get this 7-iron?" Hogan asked.

"I found it in the weeds beside the road in the park," said Billy.

"When?"

"Yesterday afternoon."

Hogan waggled the club again.

"What's your name?" Hogan asked.

"His name is Billy, sir. Hardy Loudermilk sent him to us," Elvis said.

Hogan held the Bobby Jones 7-iron under his right arm as he lit another cigarette. He looked at Billy.

"Are you the boy who told Ira Sandpaster he was standing too close to his ball?"

"Billy is awful raw, Mr. Hogan. He wouldn't do that again," said Elvis.

"So you're the boy who Ira Sandpaster says is the jinx who made him shank it four times?"

"Yes sir," Billy said.

A light came into Hogan's eyes. He smiled like Gary Cooper. The smile was fascinating at the core of force that surrounded him. He dragged on his cigarette, considering, and then blew a stream of smoke and laughed out loud.

Hogan laughed until he started coughing.

"I wish I had seen that," Hogan said.

"It was pretty ugly, sir," said Billy.

"Yeah. That's what I mean."

Hogan inspected the 7-iron once more and then gave it back to Billy.

"I'm getting ready to play the back nine. You want to carry my bag?" Hogan said.

"Yes sir!" said Billy.

"I'll meet you on the tenth tee in five minutes. Be sure to bring that 7-iron with you," Hogan said.

D Twelve

R. ARNOLD KEMP, proctologist, was lining up his bogey putt on the ninth green when the word went around that Ben Hogan was heading toward the tenth tee and would be playing alone, cutting in ahead of the Sandpaster foursome.

The accountant Titus, Dr. Ira Sandpaster and Sonny Stonekiller urged Dr. Kemp, who was down on his knees in his beltless plaid slacks, searching for the grain in the green—grain being the direction the grass is growing, which Dr. Kemp had never in his golfing life been able to detect—to hurry up and putt his ball. They were eager to go to the tenth tee and watch Hogan. Already, a dozen club members had gathered around the tenth tee, waiting. Sonny Stonekiller, four under par through nine, saw Hogan come out of the clubhouse and stride through the crowd, looking straight ahead, not acknowledging any of them. Sonny had a sudden hope that Hogan might notice him and invite him, as club champion, to join him on the back nine, just the two of them.

When he saw who was standing beside Ben Hogan's bag as caddie, Dr. Sandpaster felt a pain stabbing his chest. He feared his heart was exploding. He reeled backward, prevented from falling by the hands of Titus and Dr. Kemp and others standing near. Oh no, Ira thought, not heart failure, not now, when I am still stuck on 82. It was said one never knew whom Hogan might take a liking to, what kind of a stray dog. Hogan had once befriended an ugly little mongrel named Duffer.

"What the hell is that new kid doing there?" Sonny Stonekiller said.

Billy had thought he would be scared, but he felt a calm falling over him as he stood in the aura of Hogan. Billy saw Dr. Sandpaster and Sonny Stonekiller join the crowd at the back of the tee. Although he enjoyed the stricken expressions on their faces, Billy kept his own face emotionless, like the face of his hero, Hogan, who was squinting down the fairway of the 404-yard tenth hole. There was a ravine in front of the tee box and a deep swale 300 yards away, in front of the green. Billy touched the cover of Hogan's 3-wood but quickly withdrew his hand. Billy saw his old 7-iron nestled in the bag with Hogan's irons.

With his canvas bag slung across his back, Sonny Stonekiller stepped onto the tee.

"I'd like to play the back nine with you, Mr. Hogan," Sonny said.

"No," said Hogan.

"But I'm four under so far today. I can keep up," Sonny said.

Hogan ignored him.

"Elvis," Hogan said to the assistant pro who had accompanied them to the tee, "I want you to keep the Sandpaster group ten minutes behind me." Hogan looked at Dr. Sandpaster. "That's all right with you, Ira?"

"Anything, Ben. Anything. We'll quit right here," croaked Dr. Sandpaster.

Hogan lit a cigarette and addressed the crowd. Billy noticed Chili McWillie and some of the boys from the yard had gathered at the back.

"Fellas," Hogan said, "I'm working on some things today. I don't want a gallery. I would consider it a favor if you fellas would keep your distance."

"Sure, Ben. Of course," voices said.

Hogan glanced again at Dr. Ira Sandpaster, whose normally white forehead had become very red. Hogan turned so that no one else could see his face and winked at Billy.

"What club do you think I should use, Billy?" Hogan asked in a loud voice.

"Three wood, Mr. Hogan."

"Fine." Hogan nodded and took the 3-wood Billy pulled for him. With his cigarette in his lips, Hogan settled into his stance, waggled the clubhead and hit the ball with a sound that only Hogan's shots made. The ball flew so fast it was invisible for the first 200 yards. Then they saw it land and roll to a spot 280 yards down the fairway, favoring the right side.

Hogan walked forward with the 3-wood still in his hands. He held the club at a forty-five-degree angle in front of him and waggled it, caressing it with his fingers, as he strode ahead. Billy hefted Hogan's bag and chased after him.

"Does the Stonekiller kid hit his 3-wood this far?" Hogan asked.

"I believe he does," Billy said as they arrived at the ball.

"Huh," Hogan said. Hogan turned his head to the left as if listening to something. He dug a finger into his right ear. "You hear a radio someplace?"

"No sir," Billy said.

Hogan shook his head as if clearing his thoughts. He stood with his arms folded, the cigarette in his mouth, studying the shot to the green.

"Give me the seven," Hogan said.

Billy looked surprised.

"You think seven is too much?" Hogan said.

"Yes sir."

"How far do you judge it to be to the hole?"

"About 125 yards."

"Billy, I almost never ask a caddie for yardage," Hogan said. "But if I ever ask you again, I don't want to hear it is 'about' anything. I want to hear the exact distance."

Hogan took the 7-iron, tossed his cigarette aside and hit a

soft high shot that fell from left to right and dug into the green near the flagstick.

"The pin is on a ridge at the back of the green, 128 yards, two feet," Hogan said.

Hogan walked forward on the fairway, this time holding his 7-iron in front of him at a forty-five-degree angle and waggling it for a few steps, communicating with it. Rushing along beside Hogan, Billy counted his paces. He made it 129 yards to the pin.

The five-foot birdie putt stopped on the lip of the cup. Hogan walked on to the eleventh tee. Billy scooped up the ball, replaced the flagstick and hurried to catch up. As he arrived at the tee, Billy got the impression Hogan was talking to someone. But there was no one.

Hogan and Billy stared down the narrow fairway of the par-five eleventh hole. A wooded creek ran all along the right side. Along the left were trees and sand bunkers. Billy could barely see the green, 609 yards away, with the fairway bending slightly to the right.

"Give me the 7-iron," Hogan said.

Not knowing what Hogan wanted with it, Billy handed him the 7-iron that he had hit to the tenth green. Hogan took a practice swing at a slow speed, watching the arc of the club. Then Hogan spread his feet wider apart and turned his grip so far to the right that Billy could see the top of his left hand. It reminded Billy of Troy's grip.

Hogan hit a low ball that started toward the creek, then hooked and bounded down the fairway a great distance. Billy reached for the 7-iron, but Hogan kept it and walked forward. Hogan tapped his right hand against his ear. He shook his head. He made a grunting sound in the back of his throat.

When they arrived at the ball, Billy had counted they had walked 239 yards.

Hogan lit another cigarette. He addressed the ball again with the 7-iron and spread his feet wide and ripped another head-high liner down the center. Approaching this second shot, Billy counted that the ball had gone 210 yards. They were 449 yards from the tee, with 160 yards remaining to the green. Hogan resumed his normal stance and hit the 7-iron five feet from the cup. Using the 7-iron as a putter, Hogan rapped the ball one-handed into the hole for a birdie four.

"You see what I mean about clubs and distance?" Hogan asked.

Billy wasn't sure what Hogan meant but he knew he had seen phenomenal golf. Before the boy could answer, Hogan gave him the 7-iron and walked on toward the twelfth tee.

When faced with any unexpected turn of fate, old Elmo, a cowboy at the JAL, used to say, "Life sure does paint a funny-looking picture, don't it?" Billy remembered Elmo's saying as he trotted along with Hogan's golf bag. The boy could hardly have imagined this incredible event, him and Ben Hogan alone together on the back nine at Colonial Country Club. On one hand Billy was stunned by the suddenness of this unforeseen chain of events that began with finding the lucky 7-iron, but on the other he felt invigorated, his cares drifting away like the smoke from Hogan's cigarettes. He glanced down at the bag as he placed it on the twelfth tee and saw the Bobby Jones 7-iron inside. Bredemus had called it a lucky club. But it was more than that to Billy. It had magic that had attracted Ben Hogan. Billy thought for a moment of his daddy, Troy, who might be refreshing his deadly skill as a Forward Observer at Fort Sill at this moment. Billy wished Troy could see him with Ben Hogan, or at least know about it. But he forgot Troy again when Hogan asked for his 3-wood at the twelfth tee.

Hogan hit a long ball that drew from right to left. He walked down the fairway holding the club in front again, waggling it and testing its weight and massaging the handle with his fingers.

The champion appeared to have forgotten Billy but seemed to be having an internal conversation, and once Hogan's thoughts grew louder than his surroundings and he clearly said, "That's a crazy idea." But he was not addressing Billy, who kept quiet except for deep breathing.

"Six," Hogan said.

Taking the 6-iron from Billy, Hogan waggled once and struck a high second shot that came to a stop ten feet from the flag on this 433-yard par-four hole. Hogan studied his putt, missed it, tried again and made it. He handed Billy his putter to put back into the bag and went on to the tee box of the 178-yard, par three thirteenth, where he faced a long carry over water. Hogan lit another cigarette, squinted, grunted in the back of his throat. "Three iron," he said.

Sonny Stonekiller had hit a 5-iron from this tee, but Billy didn't argue with the most recent U.S. Open and Masters champion. Hogan's 3-iron shot carried twenty feet past the pin, hopped once and stopped. He turned to Billy and said, "Go pick it up."

"You don't want to putt?" Billy asked.

But Hogan had already started walking toward the fourteenth tee. He shook his head as if something were rattling inside, and twice he jerked his left shoulder up and scratched his armpit.

The fourteenth was a 426-yard par four. Off the tee Hogan smote his driver a distance that Billy walked off as 290 yards. The boy was trying to guess what club Hogan might request for his next shot of 136 yards. Billy had learned that the champion's concept of distance did not fit the manufactured loft of the club but instead the club conformed to Hogan's imagination.

Hogan chose a 5-iron and hit the ball onto the back of the green. He began walking forward again. After a few moments, Hogan stopped. "Why the hell not?" he said.

"Sir?"

"Nothing. How far is it to the pin from here?"

"One hundred and thirty-two yards," Billy said.

"Throw a ball down. Take out that old 7-iron you found and knock the ball onto the green."

Billy froze.

"Me?"

"You see anybody else?"

Billy carefully pulled out Bredemus's lucky Bobby Jones 7-iron and laid Hogan's bag down. The boy felt that he was trembling with fear, but he saw that his hands were not shaking. He was transported, somehow, seemed to be looking down at this scene that was so unreal it could not be happening. To hit a golf ball under the gaze of Ben Hogan?

Billy made two practice swings, sucked in a lungful of air and breathed out slowly to relax, as Troy had taught him. This was a supreme moment in Billy's life. He looked at the green, looked down at the ball—and swung the lucky 7-iron.

The ball landed a few yards short of the green and rolled into the fringe on the right of the putting surface.

"Hit another," Hogan said.

Billy did it again. This shot was pin high but even farther to the right.

"Slash, slash, chop, chop," Hogan said and walked forward.

Hogan sank his birdie putt and proceeded to the fifteenth tee. The fifteenth was a 430-yard par four that had big trees just to the left of the tee box, creating a narrow chute for the drive, which needed to carry a hillside and come down between the slope and a large bunker. Hogan hit his driver past the trees and over the slope into the fairway. The fairway bent to the left at this point, and Billy could see the green on a rise tucked among trees at what the boy judged to be 150 yards away. Hogan hit a 7-iron onto the green and walked forward ten paces and stopped.

"Throw down a ball and take out that old 7-iron," Hogan said.

When Billy had done so, Hogan asked, "Who taught you how to swing a club?"

"My daddy and Mr. Hardy Loudermilk," said Billy.

"What did Hardy tell you?"

"He said to turn back until my club is behind me and pointing to the target, and then turn forward until I wrap the club around my head. He said when I do that, I've got a golf swing."

"Yeah." Hogan nodded. "And what did your daddy tell you?"

"My daddy said to act like I was walking down a road with a stick in my hand and I came to a tin can and decided to knock it over the fence and then just to swing the stick and knock the tin can over the fence, except it's a golf ball."

"Well." Hogan peeled a bit of tobacco off his upper lip. "I guess you know who Ted Williams is."

"Yes sir."

"You ever see him hit a home run?"

"In the newsreels at the movies."

"You can't describe a golf swing any more than you can describe a kid throwing a rock, but your daddy is real close," Hogan said.

Hogan took the Bobby Jones 7-iron from the boy. He looked at the club for a moment, as if he almost remembered where he had seen it before. Then he arranged himself in a baseball hitter's stance, with his hands cocked behind his right ear, waggled his wrists, and swung the club like a baseball bat. He swung the club four times, lowering the swing each time. The fourth swing brushed the clubhead through the grass.

"Except for Ted Williams being lefthanded, this is the swing," Hogan said. "This is how to hit a ball. Baseball or golf ball, it depends on whether you swing level in the air or whether you swing at that tin can on the ground that you want to knock over the fence. You swing your club like Ted Williams swings his bat. You've seen him do it. Now you go ahead and do it."

Billy settled over the ball.

"Practice it first," Hogan said. "Swing level in the air like it's a baseball bat and then lower your swing like I did."

Billy took four practice swings from shoulder high down to brushing through the grass. He settled over the ball again.

"Start your swing with a waggle," Hogan said.

Billy saw a divot appear in the ground, and the clubhead swished through the ball with a lightness such as he had never felt before, an airiness, and his club was moving fast and effortlessly. He felt the ball leaving the clubface, and he knew the exhilaration of having struck a near to perfect shot.

The club whipped against his back on his follow through. Billy looked up to see his ball falling onto the green from what seemed a great height. At the same time, Billy saw a blur of colors behind the green and around the sixteenth tee, and he realized a crowd of members was back there, watching Hogan, watching Billy as well.

Hogan grunted in the back of his throat and chuckled and walked forward.

"All right. All right. Are you satisfied?" Hogan said, speaking to someone but not to Billy.

When they reached the green, Billy recognized Dr. Ira Sandpaster, Sonny Stonekiller, Mr. Titus, Dr. Kemp, Elvis Spaatz and others standing up around the sixteenth tee among fifty people who were watching this remarkable exhibition taking place before them. Billy saw the freckled face of Chili McWillie and the pompadour of furtive little Foxy Lerner and the dark skin of Ham T among other caddies at the rear edge of the crowd.

Billy tried to ignore them, to wrap Hogan and himself inside their own world. Billy's ball was eight feet from the cup. He hoped Hogan would tell him to putt it, but Hogan knocked both his and Billy's balls aside and proceeded to the next tee.

The sixteenth was a 188-yard par three with water in front of the green. Billy had seen Sonny Stonekiller hit a 4-iron there, into a light breeze. It was a 3-wood for Dr. Sandpaster from the regular tees.

"Seven," Hogan said loud enough for the crowd to hear.

There was muttering among the onlookers. Hogan silenced them with a glance. He turned his hands to the right on his grip, spread his feet, waggled once and fired a low shot that cleared the water and rolled pin high.

"Hit your 7-iron," Hogan said to Billy.

"I can't hit it that far," Billy said.

"Give it a try."

Frightened and nervous with the crowd watching, Billy swung hard and topped the ball into the water.

"Chop, chop, slash, slash," Hogan said. "Try it again.".

Billy tried to picture the ball as a tin can and himself as Ted Williams. He breathed in and out to calm his nerves. He told himself to make a smooth swing. On his downswing, Billy realized with horror that his head was moving forward of the ball, and he hit a thin shot that skipped along the surface of the pond for a few feet before it sank.

"Nothing divided by nothing is nothing," Hogan said.

Hogan was walking toward the green before the ripples from Billy's ball stilled in the pond.

Billy saw Dr. Sandpaster moving with the crowd to get a vantage point above the green and beside the seventeenth tee. Billy caught Sonny Stonekiller's eye for a moment. Sonny laughed and drew a finger across his throat.

Hogan took two putts on the slick, slanting sixteenth green and moved on to the next tee. The crowd backed up away from Hogan's glare. The seventeenth hole was 383 yards from an elevated tee, with rough and a bunker to the left and trees to the right and a swale in front of the green, with the giant pecan tree called Big Annie guarding the approach from the left. Hogan hit a 2-iron off the tee and then a 6-iron to the green. He did not tell Billy to hit another shot.

The crowd held back from following them down the seventeenth fairway but moved over to the eighteenth green to wait.

Billy wondered as he pulled the flagstick out of the cup on

seventeen if Hogan had been disgusted by the two water balls and had decided the boy was not worth more of his time. If so, it still had been an experience that Billy would cherish and, though Billy couldn't think of it in those terms, an exhibition that had thrown a shock through the Colonial membership that would change lives. Ben Hogan urging his caddie to hit golf shots? Extraordinary, fantastic, revolutionary, almost anarchistic.

Hogan cracked a driver off the tee of the 427-yard par-four eighteenth and resumed his familiar march down the fairway, holding his driver out in front at a forty-five-degree angle, waggling the club for the first twenty yards. Billy marveled at the strength in Hogan's hands and forearms. Each time Billy had pulled the driver out of Hogan's bag, he had been surprised anew at how heavy the club was, how thick and stiff the shaft with its rough cord grip.

At 277 yards from the tee, by Billy's count, Hogan stopped beside his ball and asked for his 8-iron. Hogan hit a high fading shot that came down lightly near the pin, 150 yards away. Hogan gave the 8-iron back to Billy, paced off ten steps closer to the green, and then said, "Okay. Hit that 7-iron from this spot. Don't do a fox trot down below. Just stand and hit it. Don't move your right knee. Show all those monkeys around the green what you can do."

Billy was comfortable with the 7-iron at this distance. He felt calm, like he had felt on the fifteenth. As with all who play golf, Billy knew there were moments in the game that approached divinity. A serenity invaded him, a sense of being at ease, a feeling that swinging the golf club was a simple and natural thing to do. Ted Williams, he thought. Knock the tin can over the fence.

Billy's shot with the lucky Bobby Jones 7-iron struck the flagstick and bounced four feet from the hole.

From above the green near the clubhouse, Dr. Ira Sandpaster shouted, "Great shot, Billy! Great shot! That's my boy!"

On the green Hogan asked, "Want to putt it?"

"Yes sir," Billy said.

Hogan handed the boy his putter, and Billy rolled the ball into the hole. Many in the crowd applauded. Billy saw Sonny Stonekiller staring at him with hatred.

The crowd cleared a lane for them as Billy carried Hogan's bag up the hill toward the locker room. Several hands reached out and touched Billy, as though he were a religious icon rather than a caddie who had been in disrepute that very morning. He heard Sonny Stonekiller say, "Little butt sucker." He heard Chili McWillie say, "You are some kind of hell, Billy."

Then Billy and his hero were standing beside the pro shop and Hogan was talking to a lean man of middle age who wore a cap like Hogan's and had puffy flesh under his eyes, a brown and wrinkled face with a glint of humor in his eyes and a smile that showed gentleness and kindness.

"Come here, kid," Hogan said. "Bring me that old 7-iron of yours."

Billy fetched the lucky 7-iron from Hogan's bag.

"You ever see this club before, Harvey?" Hogan asked.

Before looking at the club, the man smiled at Billy and said, "I'm Mr. Penick's son, Harvey. What's your name?"

Billy knew the name of Harvey Penick, who looked like a photo of an old Scottish golf pro. He had heard Hardy Loudermilk speak often of the revered golf teacher from Austin Country Club in Austin, Texas.

"Billy."

"Let me see that club, Billy," said Penick.

Billy noted the way the older man placed his hands on the grip of the golf club, tenderly and gracefully. Penick waggled the club twice and then looked at the clubface.

"Where did you get this club?" asked Penick.

"I found it in the weeds beside the road in the park," Billy said.

"You know this club, Harvey?" asked Hogan.

"I sure do," Penick said. "This club belonged to John Brede-mus."

"Yeah. John Bredemus. I knew I'd seen it before," said Hogan.

"You found it beside the road?" Penick asked Billy.

"Yes sir."

"I wonder how it got there," said Penick.

"His family didn't claim his belongings, as I recall," Hogan said.

"No. Nobody from his family showed up," said Penick.

"What's it been? Four years?" Hogan asked.

"It's been five years since John died," said Penick.

"Died?" Billy said.

"John Bredemus was a great fellow and a good friend," said Penick. "A terrible loss to us all."

"But John Bredemus is not dead. He couldn't be dead," Billy said.

"Oh, I'm afraid he is, Billy," said Penick. "I went to his funeral. I saw them put my friend John under the ground at the cemetery in Big Spring in May of 1946."

W Thirteen

HO WAS THIS IMPOSTER who claimed to be John Bredemus, the father of Texas golf?

Billy had surprised Ben Hogan, Harvey Penick and the others—including Dr. Ira Sandpaster—crowded around the Colonial Country Club pro shop by stammering excuses and abruptly turning with the Bobby Jones lucky 7-iron in his hands and running around the corner of the clubhouse and into the street.

The questions humming in Billy's mind drowned out the profound experience of the nine holes he had just spent with his hero.

Who was this imposter? How did he get Bredemus's 7-iron? How had the imposter known Billy was from Albuquerque or that his mother had taught English at the University of New Mexico? How had the man known to call him Billy Boy? Why was he carrying a five-year-old driver's license that had the name of John Bredemus on it?

Billy had run two blocks when he heard the familiar hum of the Chrysler, and a girl's voice said, "Hey, Billy!"

He stopped, and Sandra Sandpaster pulled up beside him in the red convertible. He felt a sudden shortness of breath, inexplicable for someone in such good physical condition. She was tan and smiling, her short brown hair windblown, cherry red polish on her fingernails on the steering wheel. Her big brown eyes appraised him in a way that would have been regarded as brazen if she had been a poor girl.

"Hey," he said.

"Well? Can I give you a ride?"

He got into the car, placed the Bobby Jones 7-iron between his knees, felt the plushness of the leather upholstery.

"I need to go to the YMCA," he said.

He glanced down at her bare foot on the accelerator. Her toenails were cherry red. The Chrysler leaped forward.

"The Y?" she said. "You're so cute. You're not one of those homos, are you?"

"I don't know any homos."

"Well, I heard they hang out at the YMCA, and since you're so cute, I thought maybe . . ."

"Is that how you judge everything? By how cute it is?"

She looked at him and frowned as she swung the car onto University Drive.

"I ought to make you get out," she said.

"Please," Billy said. "I really need this ride."

"If cute is all a boy has got, he's not for me," she said. "If he's cute and has lots of money, forget it. Boring. Cute with interesting character, that's what I like."

"You think I'm interesting?"

"You made my grandfather blow up three times in different directions. He loved you one day, hated you the next, and now he loves you again. I never saw anyone but President Truman do that to him. Sonny hates you, and ordinarily he never notices someone as far beneath him as he thinks you are. Got a cigarette?"

"No."

"There's a pack of Chesterfields in the glove compartment. Light one for me," she said.

Billy passed her a cigarette from the pack and pushed in the lighter on the dashboard. She smiled. "Are you opposed to smoking?"

"I need my lungs," he said.

The lighter popped out and she lit her cigarette as she passed a pickup truck.

"And most of all, Billy, you played golf with Ben Hogan today. That makes you the hottest, most interesting character in town."

"I caddied for him."

"But you hit some golf shots with him? Right?"

"Yeah, I did."

"No wonder Sonny hates you so much."

"I hear Sonny is your boyfriend."

"Who told you that?"

"Sonny did."

She double-parked beside the YMCA building and raised her right arm onto the back of her seat. He saw her breasts swell under her man's shirt as she changed into that position. She poked his leg with a bare toe.

"Do you want to go to a movie tonight?" she asked.

"Can I call you in an hour?"

"No. Make up your mind right now," she said.

"I'm sorry. There's something I have to do."

She found a paper napkin that had fallen between the seats and wrote her phone number on it.

"One hour. I will wait not one minute longer."

He got out of the car and looked around for the imposter's black 1946 Ford but didn't see it parked nearby.

"What if Dr. Sandpaster answers?" Billy said.

"If he answers he will talk for hours about golf and Ben Hogan and that old guy who built Colonial," she said. "But he won't answer. This is my private number. It only rings in my bedroom."

AT THE FRONT DESK, Billy retrieved his room key from its hook while the clerk hardly looked up from his comic book. The imposter's key was gone from its hook. He must be in his room on the third floor. The black Ford must be parked around the corner. Billy raced up the stairs and ran down the hall, his heart thumping, He was anxious about what he might find, and curious about the imposter, and angry that he had been made a fool of. Except, why should Billy feel foolish? The lucky 7-iron had led him into hitting golf shots with Ben Hogan. That was nothing to be angry about.

Billy knocked on the door. No answer. He knocked again. After a minute or two, he turned the knob and the door opened. The bed was made, but the room was empty. The first thing Billy thought was that the imposter had cleared out. But he had left Billy his lucky Bobby Jones club. What for? Who could this man be who claimed to be John Bredemus?

"Why, how de do, Billy Boy."

The imposter was coming down the hall carrying a bag of groceries, his flowered carpetbag, his radio, and a bag of books. He was rolling from side to side a bit as he walked, as if he was thinking about dancing. His eyes squinted from under the Scottish wool cap. He was enormously powerfully built, Billy realized again.

"Can't you speak to me?" said the imposter, pushing past Billy and noticing the door to his room was open. "What have you been looking for in my room?"

"Who are you?" Billy asked.

"A most peculiar and difficult question." The man entered the room and began laying out books and a box of crackers, a loaf of wheat bread and a jar of peanut butter and a bottle of orange drink. "If this is a philosophical inquiry, you might say I am a swirling, ever-changing mass of sensations, with an eternal spirit at the core." The man smiled. "Or do you merely want me to repeat my name?"

"I want to know who you are."

"You know very well who I am."

He plugged in his radio and tuned to the classical station.

"John Bredemus is dead," Billy said.

"Do I look dead to you?"

"No."

"I asked you not to mention my name to anyone," said the man.

"Harvey Penick recognized your lucky 7-iron. Then Ben Hogan said you are dead. Then Mr. Penick said he went to your funeral. So who are you? And what do you want?"

"Harvey has made so many golf clubs with his own hands that he never forgets one. I hadn't considered that Harvey might be in town."

"Mr. Penick saw John Bredemus dead in a coffin that was put in the ground. Now, who are you? I'm not going to call the police or anything or turn you in to anybody. But if I'm going to keep a secret, I have a right to know what secret I am keeping."

"Sit down, Billy Boy. Want a peanut butter sandwich?"

Billy shook his head and sat on the room's only chair at a small desk. The man unscrewed the lid of the peanut butter jar and began to unfold the blade from a pocket knife.

"Five years ago I was driving through Big Spring in a sleet storm. I was on my way to El Paso. I saw a poor, freezing wretch walking along the road, and I picked him up. He'd had a very tough time of things. I stopped at the tourist court in Big Spring and rented the unfortunate fellow a room for a week, paid for it and signed the ledger, gave him a few dollars, and went on my way again in the sleet storm."

The man spread the peanut butter on a piece of whole wheat bread.

"I get low blood sugar in the afternoons and need a pick-me-up snack. You sure you don't want a sandwich? I've seen that appetite of yours in action."

"I just want to know who you are," Billy said.

The man placed the second piece of bread atop the peanut butter and sat on his bed. Billy noticed the thick muscles in his thighs.

"Well, the fact of it is that when I arrived in El Paso I heard over the radio that I was dead. A natural gas explosion had wiped out that tourist court. The poor fellow I had befriended was blown to bits. So was the manager. In the ruins the police found the register, and there was my name in room number seven. There is no coroner in Big Spring. The police assumed the scattered bits were me. So I left it that way."

"You didn't even tell your family that you were alive?"

"I lost track of my family many years ago. When I was killed, they refused to claim my body. The Texas Professional Golfers Association took up a collection to bury me. Closed casket funeral, since there were only pieces to bury. I sent them a large donation for myself—anonymously, of course. In my will I left inheritances to my nieces and nephews. It's very tidy."

"But your friends," Billy said. "Like Mr. Penick."

"Harvey, bless his heart, is a good friend and a saintly man. It's a saint's calling to sacrifice for a greater good, in this case for me to go underground, to disappear. It was merely time that Harvey lost by attending my funeral, and believe me, time is an illusion. I'm still his friend. I whisper to him in the middle of the night."

"You promise me that John Bredemus is not dead and you're him?"

The man took a step toward Billy, flexed his right bicep and said, "Feel that?" Billy touched it with his fingers. "In my youth I was well known for my physique. I posed for classical sculptures. Does that feel like a dead man's arm?"

"It feels like a bar of iron," Billy said.

"I swear to you that I am John Bredemus. You are the only person who knows. Do you swear to keep my secret?"

"But why?"

"I desire it this way. In my underground life I am not constantly being asked to build golf courses for rich people, organize golf tournaments, put on golf clinics, give golf lessons, write golf columns in the newspapers, make speeches promoting golf at Rotary Clubs. Remember when I said golf is what you make of it? Well, I realized I was making it a continual busyness that threatened to become a genuine business. People called me a loner, but I began to feel like there was a crowd around me all the time. I would go down to River Oaks and sit under the trees and play checkers with my old friend Jack Burke, and inevitably people would gather around and ask me why I put a certain bunker someplace or what I think of Pine Valley or the Old Course. First thing you knew I would be in conversation with all these people, and I started feeling like a salesman pushing a product. Now my life contains none of that pressure. Now I have serenity. That's the truth. Do you believe me, Billy Boy?"

Billy looked at the rugged face with the furrowed forehead, at the clear blue eyes, at the wide mouth into which a peanut butter sandwich was disappearing without a crumb being spilt.

"Yes. I believe you," Billy said.

Bredemus sat on his bed again. Billy saw through the window that the sun was going down, and he wondered how much of an hour had gone by.

"I appreciate your faith in me," said Bredemus. "Now tell me what happened at Colonial today. What luck did the 7-iron bring you?"

Billy told him about Hogan, every detail. When he mentioned Hogan's curious quirk of speaking to someone who wasn't there, of shaking his head and digging his finger into his ear, Bredemus nodded.

"Ben has a guardian angel," Bredemus said. "That's who he was talking to."

"An angel?"

"Well, yes. Or you could say a spirit or whatever. He's a little man who perches on Ben's shoulders, hopping from one to the other. Ben calls the little man Hennie Bogan. Sometimes when people think Ben is concentrating so hard that he doesn't see them or is not even aware that his opponent has made a hole in one, what Ben is really doing is holding a conversation with Hennie Bogan. Ben will argue, but he usually does what Hennie tells him."

"How do you know?" Billy asked.

"Oh, it's not really a secret. Ben's closest friends know he believes Hennie Bogan is sitting on his shoulders and has been there most of Ben's life, at least since the caddie yard at Glen Garden. Some wondered why Hennie didn't warn Ben and Valerie that a bus was coming before the crash, but Hennie is a guardian angel, not an oracle. Hennie had no control over the bus, only an influence on how Ben reacted."

"Does Mr. Hogan talk to this little man all the time?" Billy asked.

"Yes, Ben and Hennie discuss everything—but rarely out loud. They must have been having quite a powwow about you. Go ahead and tell me about today. What else happened?"

"This guardian angel came to him in the caddie yard?" Billy said.

"I believe the truth is Hennie Bogan came the day six-year-old Ben Hogan saw his father shoot himself to death in their home."

"I didn't know about that," Billy said.

"Now go on. Tell me what happened today."

"He had me hit some shots with your 7-iron."

"Ha!" Bredemus said. "Now we're getting down to it."

"He showed me how to swing the club." 105

Bredemus leaped up.

"The world is full of people who would pay a rajah's fortune to do what you did—have Ben Hogan show you how to swing a club!"

"He told me to swing like Ted Williams."

"There you have it, then."

"Start it with a waggle."

"That's all there is to swinging a golf club."

"He said for me to stand and hit it," Billy said. "And don't move my right knee."

"Power comes from the earth. You must grip with your feet. Ben has an extra spike on his right shoe for that reason."

"I hit some good shots. Well, two good shots," Billy said.

"You must never reveal a word Hogan said."

"But he didn't tell me much."

"Yes, he did," Bredemus said. "One day you'll realize what he told you. Meanwhile, keep it to yourself. Hogan would be very angry if he heard you were telling anyone the knowledge he shared with you. Ben has showed you how to swing a club. I will show you more about the game, if you want to learn.

"Sure, I want to learn," Billy said.

"I'll show you tonight."

"What time is it?" Billy asked.

Bredemus pulled a gold watch out of his watch pocket and opened the case and told him. Billy had three minutes left before the deadline to call Sandra.

"Not tonight," Billy said. "I've got a date with Sandra Sandpaster."

Bredemus smiled and his eyes crinkled at the corners.

"She must have been about one year old when I last saw her. Charming child. We'll talk golf another night. Tonight is made for romance."

Billy ducked his head, thinking about Sandra.

"Give me back my 7-iron before you leave, Billy Boy. You've had enough luck for one day," Bredemus said.

Billy leaned the Bobby Jones 7-iron against the chair.

"And remember, Billy Boy. This is our secret," said Bredemus. "Please do not mention me to Miss Sandpaster."

S Fourteen

HE ENCHANTED HIM.

As she drove her Chrysler away from the YMCA building downtown and onto West Seventh Street, the radio was playing a song called "Nature Boy," and she sang along, " . . . *the greatest thing you'll ever learn is just to love and be loved in return . . .*"

"I wonder if that's true?" she asked when the song had ended. She looked around for a moment at Billy. He had scrubbed himself in the communal showers at the YMCA and had put on his cleanest shirt and his jeans and his cowboy boots. He has taken on a different look, she was thinking. She had seen him in tennis shoes, but now he was in cowboy boots worn with the jeans coming down to the heels and laying across the bridge of the boot, as she had seen real cowboys dress at the rodeo. She liked his cowboy look. He was very cute as a caddie, but he was even cuter as a cowboy.

Billy took a couple of breaths while he thought up an answer. He was afraid he might blurt out his love for her and make a fool of himself. She wore a white peasant blouse, pulled down low to reveal her shoulders and chest to the exquisite place where her breasts began, and a peasant skirt that swirled around her legs. She smelled like the lilacs that had grown outside the adobe house in Albuquerque. The breeze of a June evening poured through the open convertible and he saw a sparkle on her lips.

"Well? Is it true? Is love the greatest thing you'll ever learn?" she asked.

"I wouldn't know," he said.

"Have you ever been in love?"

"No."

"Me neither. I've been in like, but not in love."

"Are you in like with Sonny Stonekiller?" Billy asked.

"Some of the time."

She drove another few blocks while he gazed at her profile and felt his heart turning flips.

"I hope you like this movie," she said.

"Oh, I will."

"You like this kind of movie, then? You're not kidding?"

"Sure."

She found a parking space in the lot near the Seventh Street Theater. It was a clear blue evening with stars already bright and the wind smelling clean, so she decided to leave the top down while they were inside. "I'll buy the tickets," Billy said as they walked toward the theater.

"All right. But I buy the popcorn and the Cokes," she said.

With a proprietary feeling, proud that she was with him and everyone could see it, Billy stepped in his boots to the window and bought two tickets with a twenty-dollar bill. Clutching two big bags of popcorn and two Coca-Colas in paper cups, they found seats on the aisle in the middle section. Billy was fascinated with her presence, with the way she chomped the popcorn and sucked on the straw. "We're just in time," she said.

The house lights went down and the screen lit up. Billy saw people wearing dresses, some of them apparently men with long swords, and a strange string of chicken scratches appeared across the screen. Billy did not know the name of this movie. He had not even looked at the marquee. He heard sharp shouts and grunts and Oriental speaking, and then he at last saw a word in English letters:

RASHOMON.

"*The Dallas Morning News* says this is Akira Kurosawa's greatest work," Sandra whispered.

Billy noticed the subtitles that summed up the shouts and grunts and long gabbling speeches on the screen. He began to catch on that this was a story about liars. His mother had taken him to French and Italian and Swedish films on the New Mexico campus, so he was comfortable with subtitles. He had seen American movies that he thought would have been better if they'd had subtitles to explain what the actors were talking about.

Billy's left shoulder touched Sandra's right shoulder, and he felt electrified. He tried to judge whether he had leaned against her or she had leaned against him. She had leaned against him, he believed.

"This is so wonderful," Sandra said, staring at the screen.

Inside a crumbling public monument named Rashomon, two witnesses to a rape and a murder were telling their conflicting recollections to a third man, who kept demanding they dig deeper for more truthful explanations. The murder victim, a samurai, appeared as a spirit and recounted his version of how he had been killed and his wife raped, and even his story was called a lie.

They had finished their popcorn and Billy was wondering if he dared put his arm on the back of her seat. He tried to make it seem casual. But his hand touched her bare shoulder, and her skin felt hot despite the air conditioning.

On the screen one of the main characters, who seemed to be some sort of judge, said, "Men are men. They can't tell the truth even to themselves." Billy's thumb, as if by its own will, stroked Sandra's shoulder. She kept looking at the screen, entranced. The man on the screen dismissed the others and walked away, saying, "You just can't live today unless you're what you call selfish."

110   THE END appeared on the screen and the house lights came

up. Billy removed his arm from her chair and scratched his left ear as if that was all he had been intending to do.

"Did you like it?" Sandra asked as they walked up the aisle.

"Yeah," Billy said.

"Are you just humoring me?"

"I kept thinking of it as a western," he said.

She laughed and took his hand, swinging it as they crossed the lobby. "Who do you see playing the Commoner in your western?"

"The who?"

"The man who kept demanding more truth."

"Gary Cooper."

"Gary Cooper would have been the samurai," she said.

"No, he wouldn't. The samurai was dead and not the big part, anyhow. Gary Cooper would have the big part."

"Do you believe there's such a thing as the truth? The rock bottom truth?" she said.

"Sure. I guess. Don't you?"

"I don't know."

They came to the convertible and got in. Billy noticed she had left a pair of sunglasses on the dashboard with no fear of them being stolen.

"Are you a cowboy?" she asked.

"I worked on the JAL ranch in New Mexico."

"You ever ride a bucking horse?"

"Sure."

"You ever brand a calf?"

"No, but I helped rope them and hold them down."

"It must hurt them terribly. I don't see how you could do that."

"It's just nature," Billy said.

The convertible thumped along the bricks that paved Camp Bowie Boulevard.

"What do you feel like doing?" she asked.

111

He wanted to go to the lover's lane in the park near where he had found the lucky 7-iron, but he said, "Anything you want to do."

"I want a frosted root beer," she said.

IT SEEMED TO BILLY that there were more people, mostly teenage kids, in or out of their cars, in the parking lot of the Triple X Root Beer at 9:30 at night than there had been people in all of downtown Albuquerque at noon.

Sandra drove slowly down a lane between cars. She waved and called out to several kids who had yelled to her. She and Billy knew they all were wondering who was that guy in the car with Sandra Sandpaster?

"Is this where your high school bunch hangs out?" Billy said.

"No, everybody in town comes here for the root beer. Look, you can see the downtown buildings right there to the east. At Arlington Heights we have a couple of hangout drive-ins in our own part of town. The other schools do the same, I guess. I never go on the east side unless I'm driving through to Dallas, and I only pass through the north side on my way out to the Lake Worth Casino or the Boat Club at Eagle Mountain Lake, so I really wouldn't know."

She found a place to park. A carhop attached a tray to Sandra's window. Sandra ordered a frosted root beer. Billy ordered a root beer with a scoop of vanilla ice cream in it. He was very happy to be with Sandra in her convertible and felt flush with the change from a twenty in his jeans. Sandra was growing steadily more attracted to this cute cowboy caddie who seemed to speak his mind, and very well, too. She could understand why her grandfather had been drawn to this boy and also had been repulsed by him. Billy had an independent sort of attitude that her grandfather tolerated in very few adults and in no youngsters other than Sandra herself and, for the time being, Sonny Stone-killer.

"Where are you going to high school? Heights or Paschal?" Sandra asked.

"I want to go where you are."

"Is there room for you and Sonny at the same school?"

"We'll find out," Billy said.

"I was kidding." Sandra smiled and licked the lip of her root beer mug. "Isn't that what they say in western movies? 'There ain't room in this town for both of us?' "

"There's room for us at Colonial."

"I doubt it. Even if you obey the rules and stay among your own class, Sonny will find a way to provoke them into getting rid of you. Sonny has a very mean streak."

"What do you mean, my 'own class'?"

"Well, you're a caddie, and Sonny is a rich member and the club champion. That's what I mean. Do they invite you inside for a sandwich? That's what I mean. What does your father do for a living?"

"He's a captain in the Army in Korea," Billy said. He had his doubts, but that sounded better than, "He's a cowboy and a gambler, and he's probably drunk someplace."

"I'm impressed. You're the son of an Army officer. My grandfather will like that."

Billy spooned out the last of his ice cream.

"My grandfather thinks you are the son of a bum who had to be thrown out of the club by the police."

A black Cadillac passed them, and Sonny looked out the driver's window. Billy saw three more boys in Sonny's car.

"Never mind them," Sandra said. "They come here a lot. Tell me, Billy, what are you going to be? A cowboy? A soldier? My grandfather could write a letter and get you into West Point."

A pickup truck went by. Billy saw three crewcut heads in

the front seat, looking around at him. The truck parked beside Sonny's Cadillac. The three boys got out and leaned down to talk to Sonny in his car. They kept looking toward Billy and Sandra.

"Do you know those guys?" Billy asked.

"They're football players. Sonny is their quarterback. He's really good, you know. Lots of big colleges have already offered him scholarships. His mother wants him to go to Yale. But his father wants him to go to Oklahoma."

Sonny and his three passengers got out of his Cadillac. With Sonny in the middle in the front, the seven boys started walking slowly down the lane toward Sandra's car. Three of the boys wore t-shirts with writing stenciled on the chests. Billy knew the writing would say, "Prop. AHHS Athletic Dept." Billy felt fear rush up from his stomach. It was the same fear he had felt each time he had climbed into the chute and mounted a bucking horse. The fear shook him from head to foot like a big dog shaking a bone, and then it left and he felt cold and calm and very much aware of everything.

Sonny looked formidable. He was a little taller than Billy and looked dark and handsome in the drive-in lights, his black hair slicked back. As his group approached Sandra's car, Sonny began pulling on a pair of black leather gloves. They were a tight fit.

"Hello, Sandra," Sonny said. His comrades gathered at Billy's side of the car. Sonny was the smallest of them. He wore jeans and an athletic department t-shirt and white sneakers with no socks.

"What do you want, Sonny?" she said.

"You're trying to make a fool out of me, and I don't like it. You picked up this white trash. I'm going to get rid of it," Sonny said.

Billy looked into Sonny's dark eyes.

"You and me, Sonny," said Billy. "One on one."

114 "However you want it," Sonny said.

Billy hurled the door open so fast that it struck one of the larger boys in the knee and made him howl with pain.

"Stop this!" shouted Sandra.

She jumped out of the car and ran around the front of it. A football player grabbed her and held her. She yelled, "Sonny, you guys get out of here! I'm not fooling with you! I'll ruin you! You know I will!"

People were emerging from their cars and forming a large circle.

Billy faced Sonny. Troy had been in many situations like this. He had taught Billy that most fights were won by the guy who threw the first punch if it connected. Billy's eyes flicked at Sonny's black leather fists. Billy decided to hit Sonny in the middle of his nose and break it. Billy felt that would end the fight and would also make Sonny less handsome.

Four pairs of hands clamped Billy's arms. Billy struggled, but these were strong hands. Billy felt a fifth pair of hands clutch him around the neck from behind.

"I knew it," Billy said. "You're chicken."

"I'm not chicken and I'm not stupid, either," Sonny said.

"You better stop this, Sonny! I'm warning you!" shouted Sandra.

Billy knew from Sonny's eyes to expect a blow to the stomach first. He tightened his abdomen.

"Hey!" roared a familiar voice. "You all want some of our asses?"

From between two cars came the three McWillie brothers. Chili was in the lead, followed by Brutus and then by Lester. Lester was the biggest and the most flamboyant, with a mass of curly blond hair in the style of Gorgeous George, the wrestler. But Brutus was said to be the meanest. Brutus wore steel-toed boots.

"Evening, Sonny," Chili said, looking down at the wealthy quarterback and club champion.

"Hi, Chili," said Sonny, aware he was truly in danger unless the rules of class held.

"You boys turn loose of Billy," Chili said.

"This is a personal matter," said Sonny.

"Sonny, don't make this hard on me. Billy is one of my best boys," Chili said. "I let him go nine holes with Ben Hogan today. You saw that, Sonny. Why don't you get in your car and go someplace else? I can't have these football players beating up my best caddie."

"You McWillie brothers are phonies," said a tall, muscular boy in a t-shirt who was holding Billy's right arm.

"What did he say?" asked Lester.

"I've heard about you guys all my life. You don't look like you could whip Shirley Temple," the tall boy said.

"What was that?" asked Lester, cupping a hand to his cauliflower ear.

"He said we ain't all we're cracked up to be," Brutus said.

"I'll put the crab on him," said Lester.

Suddenly the tall boy at Billy's right was yanked away. He went up into the air. Lester had one arm between the boy's legs and the other around his neck. Billy realized he was free. The football players had let him go. The boy in the air was screaming.

"Put him in the whirlycoopter, little brother," Brutus said.

Lester spun the boy round and round in the air.

"Now crash his ass and I'll dance on him," said Brutus.

"I want to spin him some more," Lester said. "It makes me dizzy and I get high."

"Make him stop," Sandra said.

"Sorry, Miss Sandpaster. Nobody can make Lester stop once he starts spinning," said Chili. "Now, Sonny, you go to your car. I'm not sure what might happen here. But I don't want you to get hurt."

Billy stepped away from the football players and confronted Sonny.

"Next time, it's just you and me, Sonny," Billy said.

"There won't be no next time," said Chili. "You're a yard boy, Billy. You obey my rules. If you beat up our club champion, I will drown you in the river."

They heard a siren and saw flashing red lights. A police car careened into the parking lot, and out jumped Burgin and Boyle.

"Lester, put that boy down," Burgin shouted.

Lester staggered a bit but continued whirling his victim.

"We'll take you brothers to the station and give you a bad whipping," Boyle said to Chili.

"How could you do that, Boyle? There's only you and Burgin."

"The whole third platoon is on the way," said Boyle.

Lester let the football player fly. The boy landed on Sandra's hood. Lester staggered backwards and sat down, a silly grin on his face. "I am high as a white wing dove," he said.

Boyle grinned, showing the gap in his teeth. He saw a peaceable ending possible.

"Billy, you and Miss Sandpaster get back in her car," Boyle said. As Billy brushed past him, Boyle said, "You're a real mover, kid."

"I let him caddie for Ben Hogan today," Chili said.

"Is that a fact, Billy?" said Burgin.

"Yes sir," Billy said.

"Did you give him our message? That Car Seven can handle any problems that might come up?"

"No sir, but I will."

Boyle turned to look at Chili. It was obvious by his dazed grin that Lester was satisfied. Brutus looked as if he could go either way—a bloody brawl or a frosted root beer. The football player crawled off the hood of the red convertible, leaving a large dent and complaining that his ribs were broken.

"Chili, my life is so much more pleasant when you and your brothers stay on the east side," said Boyle.

"We come over here because we heard some football players wanted to hurt my boy," Chili said.

Burgin said, "Miss Sandpaster, would you please drive Billy off to somewhere else while we hold this bunch here?"

"I will not," said Sandra.

"Why not?" Boyle said.

"Billy and I were here first. Make the rest of them leave, and then we'll go."

"You heard the little lady, boys," said Burgin. "You football players get the hell out of here before I call your mothers. Chili, are you willing to leave?"

"Good night, Miss Sandpaster," Chili said. "Good night, Billy. Good night Burgin. Good night, Boyle. Good night, Son . . . hey, where did Sonny go?"

Sonny had almost reached his Cadillac.

"Good night, Sonny!" shouted Chili.

The four doors of the Cadillac slammed and the car turned right and went out of the lot, followed by the pickup truck.

"I hope he heard me," Chili said. "I like my job."

"Good night, Chili," said Sandra.

The McWillie brothers trooped in a line between a row of cars and disappeared. Burgin and Boyle shooed the crowd back to their cars and the carhops back to work. Then the two police officers came to the convertible and stood for a moment as if wondering how to ask something.

"We'll leave," Sandra said.

Billy pulled two dollars out of his jeans and put them on the car hop's tray.

"Thanks again," Billy said to the two officers.

Then Burgin asked the question that was on their minds.

"Did you learn Hogan's secret?"

"I'm not allowed to say."

"I keep telling you," Boyle said. "Hogan ain't got a secret.

That's like thinking Doak Walker has got a secret. He's just better than everybody else."

RATHER THAN DRIVING BILLY straight back to the YMCA, Sandra turned onto University Drive and went in the direction of Colonial Country Club.

"What do you intend to do with your life, Billy?" she asked.

"You keep asking. Why?"

"I wonder if it's anything like what I want to do."

"What do you want to do?"

Sandra leaned her head back and gazed at the stars, the wind rippling her hair.

"I want to win the Nobel Prize. You know what that is?"

"Sure, I do." His mother used to recite the Nobel Prize winners in literature, including the strange ones she had never read. "What do you want to win it in?"

"Poetry, I think. Or maybe chemistry. Or maybe anthropology. Or maybe something else. I haven't decided."

"I wouldn't mind winning the Nobel Prize," Billy said.

"In what field?"

"Ornithology," he said. It was the first big word that came to mind.

"You're trying to snow me. They don't give a Nobel Prize for ornithology."

"Okay, then. Philosophy," he said.

"Do they give a Nobel Prize for philosophy?"

"If they don't, they should," he said.

He realized she was steering the convertible into the lover's lane in the park near where he had found the lucky 7-iron.

Billy looked at her, and as she had affected him before, he forgot to breathe. He saw several cars parked in the woods. There was discernible movement inside two of the cars. Sandra pulled her convertible onto a patch of grass that was hidden from the lane by an oak tree. To the west they could see the lights of the city far below and far to the west.

"No hands below the waist, Billy," she said.

She leaned forward and they kissed.

When they pulled back from the kiss, he saw that her eyes had gone out of focus. Or maybe it was his own eyes that were blurred.

"I love you," he said.

"Don't say that," she said.

She pressed the button that raised the top of the convertible and hid them from sight.

E

Fifteen

ARLY THE NEXT MORNING John Bredemus drove Billy to the Paris Coffee Shop for breakfast. Bredemus ordered black coffee and a slice of melon. He smiled as he watched Billy devour scrambled eggs, sausage, hash brown potatoes, biscuits and cream gravy. The boy talked about the Japanese movie he had seen with Sandra, and he told about the confrontation at the Triple X Root Beer drive-in. Billy did not mention going to lovers lane with Sandra, but his face glowed with the excitement of young love, and he was eager to return to the caddie yard at Colonial Country Club.

"A word of caution, Billy Boy," said Bredemus. "You will be the most sought after caddie at the club. Every member who hires you will want to know what Hogan told you about swinging the golf club. Let them think of you as the boy who knows Hogan's secret."

In the 1946 black Ford with the broken taillight, Bredemus took Billy to the Trinity River bridge on University Drive near Colonial and let him out. Bredemus explained that he did not wish to be seen near the club, but he was off to visit a couple of his courses in West Texas and would return in a few days.

"We've got to get that taillight fixed," Billy said. "Please, don't be driving at night. My daddy told me those West Texas cops can get mean."

"Why, thank you. I'll be careful. My blessings on you, Billy Boy."

As Bredemus had predicted, more than a hundred requests

for Billy's services as a caddie had been phoned in or delivered in person to Elvis Spaatz between yesterday afternoon and the time Billy ran down the first fairway and cut across in front of the ninth green and reported to the yard.

Elvis showed Billy the list of members who had asked for Billy as a caddie. Chester Stonekiller was at the head of the list. But nowhere on it was the name of Dr. Ira Sandpaster.

"I never heard of anything like this. A hundred members wanting the same caddie," said Chili McWillie. "I knew it was a good thing for me and my brothers to keep those boys from stomping your ass last night."

"I appreciate it," Billy said.

"I do wish we had beat up them football players," said Chili. "We'll catch em sometime when Sonny ain't around. But you watch out for yourself, Billy. The whole world saw you in that car with Sandra Sandpaster. There's lots of people will never forgive you for going where a caddie don't belong. Hey, by the way, did you get some?"

"Sandra's not that kind of girl," Billy said.

"You didn't get any, huh? Well, hell."

Billy carried Chester Stonekiller's bag that first morning of his new fame. Though they were playing for high stakes, the Stonekiller foursome was jovial. Billy heard them say on the first tee they were playing Nassau for five "units" each of three ways with automatic one-down presses. This impressed Billy as being an awful lot of money to be wagered by four middle-aged men who had handicaps of fourteen and up. Going down the first fairway, after Chester had sliced his opening drive into the street and had taken the customary first tee mulligan, Billy asked Foxy Lerner what a "unit" was.

"A hundred bucks in this game," Foxy said, humping along with the leather bag of a portly dentist on his back.

"You're kidding."

"Hey, these guys are rich, and they like to gamble. Old Chief Wahoo there," Foxy said, nodding toward Chester Stonekiller, "he'll gamble on anything. He is one crazy Indian."

"You think all the members are crazy," Billy said.

"Tell me I'm wrong."

On the fifth hole, while they were searching for his drive in the right rough along the river, Chester lit one of his foul-smelling cigars, spat into the weeds and in a casual tone said, "What was it Hogan told you yesterday?"

"Sir?" said Billy.

"About how to swing a golf club. I saw him telling you something on the fifteenth fairway. What was it?"

"I can't say," Billy said.

"It's a secret?"

"Yes sir."

"Hogan told you to keep it secret?"

"He wouldn't like it if I told," Billy said.

"How about if I stick ten one hundred dollar bills in your jeans?"

"No sir," Billy said. "I can't do that."

"Name your price."

"I'd tell you for nothing if I could, but I can't, and I won't," Billy said.

"Everybody's got a price."

"Give it up, Mr. Stonekiller. Here's your ball. Let's don't talk about Mr. Hogan anymore," said Billy.

After the round, Chester ordered Billy to carry his bag up to the Cadillac waiting in the driveway in front of the clubhouse. Chester would be playing tomorrow at River Crest Country Club, a few miles northwest of Colonial. "They're the richest, snootiest bunch in town, and they bring out the wild Indian in me," Chester said. "I hate River Crest, and those bastards hate me. It's gone out of style to bash their heads in, but I can grab their wallets every time. You know why? I've learned to beat my handicap. Those old money anglos at River Crest don't know what a real handicap is."

"Are you a Navajo?" said Billy.

"Matter of fact, I was born at the pueblo in Taos. How'd you guess?"

"I grew up in New Mexico."

As they approached the waiting Cadillac, Billy saw a woman in a white dress smiling at them. Her shiny black hair hung to her shoulders. She had classical features, strong cheekbones, a straight nose.

"This woman is the reason I'm standing here today," Chester said. He kissed her on the cheek. Looking at her, Billy knew she was a Cherokee. The oil in Oklahoma was on her land. "Honey, I want you to say hello to Billy. He's the boy who played golf with Ben Hogan."

"I've heard about you, Billy," she said and extended her hand. He didn't know what to do, so he shook her fingers gently.

"How do, Mrs. Stonekiller."

"My name is Lowatha Bird Stonekiller. You call me Lowatha Bird."

"Yes ma'am."

"You look like a nice boy."

"Thank you." Billy looked at Chester, who stood grinning, his fat cheeks puffed out with cigar smoke, the key to the trunk lid in his fingers. Chester wasn't quite ready to open the trunk yet.

"What is this quarrel between you and Sonny?" asked Lowatha Bird.

"It's nothing," Billy said. "Hey, Mr. Stonekiller, you want your clubs in the trunk?"

"If it's over the Sandpaster girl, please don't let her break your heart. I should warn you that Sandra is spoken for."

"Thank you, ma'am." Billy hefted the bag around to the trunk, and Chester popped the lid.

"I mean her dance card is full," Lowatha Bird said.

Lifting the bag to place it in the trunk on top of the spare tire and among a dozen golf clubs, at least one hundred golf balls, hundreds of tees, discarded golf gloves, two umbrellas, three pairs of shoes, a bottle of aspirin, a jar of Vaseline, a shoehorn, two sweaters and an Arlington Heights High School pennant, Billy saw Sonny Stonekiller coming out the front door of the clubhouse.

"Sandra and Sonny are about to start going steady," said Lowatha Bird. "She is going to wear his little gold football on a gold chain around her neck."

"Hi, mama. What are you all talking about?" Sonny said.

Billy slammed the trunk shut.

"Your mother says you and Sandra are going steady," Billy said.

"We plan to do that right away," said Sonny.

Once again Billy found himself feeling like the son of Troy—or like Troy himself. Hot anger took hold of him.

"You're a liar," Billy said.

"Hey, now!" shouted Chester.

"Don't you dare talk like that," Lowatha Bird said.

"If it wasn't for Chili McWillie, you know what I'd do to you?" Sonny said.

"You'd run."

"Someday I'm going to get you, new boy. Count on it," Sonny said.

Sonny slid behind the wheel of the Cadillac. Lowatha Bird stared at Billy and said, "I've seen plenty of your kind. Rude white boys." She got into the back seat and shut the door. Chester brushed past Billy on his way to the passenger seat, barely touching Billy's chest but feeling sparks fly off it.

"You better straighten up your behavior, kid. Don't let this Hogan stuff go to your head. You're just a few minutes of Hogan's life. He won't know you next time he sees you. But I'll know you for as long as I live, and I'll make you miserable if you don't straighten up. You're the son of a bitch on the reservation now, not me."

THAT EVENING SANDRA picked him up on the corner beside the YMCA, and they went to a Doris Day movie downtown at the Worth Theater. Billy wore his cowboy boots and jeans again, and he added a big silver belt buckle that Troy had won at Cheyenne. Sandra snuggled her head against his shoulder during the movie, and his left arm hugged her.

The movie had a song sung by Doris Day, and it put Billy and Sandra in a very romantic mood. They sang the song to each other as she was driving. It became their song. Instead of stopping at a drive-in, Sandra drove directly to the lover's lane, and they began hugging and kissing with a heavenly passion.

When they had gone as far as they could go without violating the no hands below the waist rule, an hour had passed and it was time for her to take him home. She rearranged her clothing and brushed her hair.

"I met Sonny's mother today," Billy said, watching her.

"Isn't she beautiful? That wonderful black hair."

"She told me you and Sonny will be going steady pretty soon, that it's all arranged. She said you'll wear his little gold football on a chain around your neck."

"Well. I don't know."

"Do you mean it's possible?"

He was shocked.

She stowed her hairbrush in the glove compartment, rubbing her breasts across Billy's arm, and then she kissed him.

"You know how my grandfather is," she said.

"Not really. It's hard to tell how he is."

Sandra took both of Billy's hands and held them, feeling their roughness.

"My grandfather rules my life, Billy. He has ordered me to start going steady with Sonny. My grandfather hates the Stonekillers, but he believes he can get something out of Sonny that he wants very badly. Something to do with shooting his age."

"He can't make you go steady with Sonny if you don't want to. Your grandfather said you don't do anything you don't want to," Billy said.

"My grandfather will jerk me out of Fort Worth tonight and send me to a boarding school in Switzerland if I make him really angry."

Billy felt dizzy. Partly it was from hunger, as he'd had no dinner, but mostly it was the confusing passions he was experiencing. She saw the pain and uncertainty in his face, and she kissed him again.

"You swear you don't want to go steady with Sonny?" he said.

"Billy, listen to me. I can't swear I don't want to go steady with Sonny. Sonny is great looking, great body, a star athlete, a great dancer, and he's fun to be with. Being forced to go steady with Sonny is not what most girls would call punishment."

"But I love you," Billy said.

"I told you not to say that."

"Have you seen Sonny lately?" Billy asked.

"We had lunch today at the club."

"And Sonny asked you to go steady?"

"Yes."

"What did you say?"

"Yes. I said yes. But I didn't say when."

She turned the key in the ignition, lowered the convertible top, and backed out from behind the tree onto the lane. They traveled in silence. Sandra felt Billy drawing away from her. She didn't want that to happen. She was powerfully attracted to this cute cowboy with brains.

"I have an idea," she said.

He mumbled and looked out the window.

"One afternoon I'll pick you up at the club and we will go see my grandfather."

Billy sat up.

Sandra said, "He's waiting for you to apologize."

"Apologize for what?"

"I don't know. Something stupid you did on the golf course."

"I didn't do anything stupid. It was him."

"I don't care who it was," she said. "I'm asking you to apologize to my grandfather."

I Sixteen

N THE DAYS THAT HAD PASSED since the time of the four shanked shots, Dr. Ira Sandpaster had worked many hours at his drafting table with his T-square and his compass. He went over his charts again and again, but could find nothing wrong with his theory of the Perfect Swing.

Could it have been a small brain attack that caused the four shanked shots? A tiny clot? A temporary chemical or electrical imperfection that had caused him to overlook a fundamental of the Perfect Swing, which was where to place his feet?

If so, the boy, Billy, had been correct.

But Billy was merely a caddie. A bright kid. He had heard of Shakespeare. A nice-looking lad. But he was at bottom just a damned caddie. He had been at fault when Ira made a fool of himself with the four shanked shots. He was trash. His father was a drunken cowboy who had left Colonial in a police car. This boy, Billy, was a dead end.

Billy had hit golf balls with Ben Hogan, true. Ira had lost control of himself and cheered for the lad. But merely having been an accidental passing fancy of Ben Hogan was not enough. It was said—and Ira, himself, among many others, had seen evidence of it happening—that Hogan had told Billy the secret of the golf swing.

Though Ira was curious what Hogan might have said, he was not impressed the way the rest of the members were. Some were totally agog. They were fools. Hogan did not know the secret of the golf swing. Dr. Ira Sandpaster did.

He poured a tall glass of prune juice and looked out the broad window in his study. He could see a hundred miles to the west. He crossed the room and looked out an opposite window at two acres of mowed green lawn, with a marble cherub spewing water from its mouth into his pond of goldfish. The driveway of red brick ran between trees to a parking circle and a four-car garage. Sandra had told him she would be bringing Billy down this driveway today. The boy was coming to apologize for having evil thoughts.

Beyond Billy's apology, there was this situation with Sonny Stonekiller to be resolved.

Until Billy showed up at Colonial, the fact that Sonny was an Indian disqualified him in Ira's mind as a serious suitor for Sandra. Ira intended to squash the romance between his granddaughter and the Indian boy as soon as Ira shot his age. But now Sandra had been out several times on dates with this Billy, this caddie from nowhere, and she came home looking flushed and wouldn't talk about him. Ira was a realist. Ira had knocked up a girl at Central High School, and she had an abortion in a cheap hotel on East Lancaster. Nobody knew about this except Titus, who was Ira's watchdog. The girl had died at age sixty-eight in her home on the beach in Fort Lauderdale.

Others in the family regarded Ira as a silly old ninny for the obsessive interest he took in Sandra. They said she was only sixteen. Let her date and run around and have fun, they said. Yes, well, Ira was only sixteen when he knocked up the girl at Central High, and she was only fifteen. Two hundred dollars for an abortion was hard to come by in those long ago days, whereas later the bills for her life in Florida went unnoticed by anyone but Titus, who paid them from company funds.

This boy Billy was sixteen. Sonny was seventeen. Their glands were blasting out sex hormones. Ira remembered how powerful sex hormones could be. They could get the best of a saint. It was being reported in medical journals that girls had sex hormones these days. There was no such thing as being too careful. Ira had been named chairman of the interfaith antiabortion committee by the mayor. It would be bad enough if his granddaughter were to get into an awkward condition with an Indian, but Sonny was a very rich Indian and a superb golfer who could feasibly win a USGA Amateur championship. Sonny was a football hero, and girls liked his looks (Ira thought he looked like a Costa Rican gigolo). Sonny was as close to social as an Indian could get. His father was a boob, but his mother was famous for her parties. And Ira must always remember that ocean of oil under the ground in Oklahoma that was owned by the Bird clan.

Sonny was having a beneficial influence on Ira's golf game. It was Sonny's tempo. Smooth and sure. It was rubbing off. Ira knew the movements of the Perfect Swing, but tempo was different than movements. Tempo was like music.

So there were a number of not so awful things that could happen if Sandra were by some prank of nature thrown together more or less seriously with Sonny Stonekiller. Otherwise, Sandra could go steady with Sonny Stonekiller during high school. And then she would leave him and go off to Stanford University and find a smart white boy.

There was nothing good that could come of her dating the caddie.

THE HOUSE LOOKED like the baronial homes Billy had seen in history books. When Sandra wheeled the convertible off Simondale and into the driveway, the vision opened—the great red brick house set on an enormous lawn with flower gardens and trees and a grand vista to the west.

"How many people live here?" Billy said.

"Three. My grandfather, my mother and I."

"Only three? Who keeps the place clean?"

Sandra laughed. "I forgot. There are servants who live on the property. I don't know how many this week. My grandfather hires them from Costa Rica. He was U.S. ambassador down there."

"Will your mother be here?"

"Mother is at our apartment in Manhattan. She is shopping and seeing shows. She loves the theater."

"You have an apartment in New York and this house in Fort Worth, too?"

"My grandfather does," Sandra said. "So will I when I turn twenty-one if he still loves me."

A handsome, dark-skinned maid wearing a black uniform dress with a white apron and white cap met them at the front door, greeted Sandra with a bow of the head and led them down a long hall that had one wall covered with framed landscapes of Scottish links and golf courses painted in oil by master artists and one oil landscape of the eighteenth green at Colonial. Dr. Sandpaster was standing on the green in the painting holding up a golf ball that he has apparently just retrieved from the cup. He is grinning. The painting was titled "Triumph at 79."

Ira heard them coming. He tried to decide where to stand. No, he would sit. Make them stand. He had barely flopped into his leather swivel chair when his darling granddaughter flung herself upon him and hugged him and kissed his cheek and scratched his chest and said, "I love you, paw paw."

"I love you, too, doodlebug."

"I love you more."

"No, I love you more."

Billy watched the old man and the girl throw around the word "love" as if it were light and easy.

"I've brought Billy," she said.

Ira stood up to greet the boy, then realized he had intended to stay seated, so he sat down again. Sandra said, "Paw paw, you be nice to Billy, now. Remember that to forgive is divine."

Sandra went out and shut the study door behind her.

"That's a load of bull, right there," Ira said.

"Sir?"

"To forgive is divine—that's bull. Do you believe it?"

Billy had never considered it before. He thought about Troy. He thought about Sonny Stonekiller. He thought about Dr. Ira Sandpaster.

"I don't think I do. No sir," Billy said.

Ira said, "Some acts, even some thoughts, are unforgivable. That's why we had to invent punishment. Did you read the Bible?"

"Not all of it," Billy said.

"Well, Jesus never said to forgive is divine. Those old left-wing fools made that up. Jesus took his punishment. But he never forgave the bastards that did it to him. Look at what a jam their ass is in today. God does not let you get away with sin. God says you obey the rules, or I'll throw your ass in a flaming lake for eternity."

Ira poured another glass of prune juice. "There's a Coca-Cola in the little refrigerator," he said.

"Thank you, sir."

Billy opened the Coke.

"Sit down in that arm chair," Ira said.

"Thank you, sir."

Ira drummed his fingers on the desk.

"Why do I feel you are being sarcastic? Something in your 'thank you, sir' sounds insincere."

"I don't know," Billy said.

"I'm a scientist. I have discovered that the universe is made up of waves of energy. The waves pass through your body like listening to the radio. The positive waves are God. The devil is in the negative waves. Or call them thoughts rather than waves. God is positive thoughts. Do you follow me?"

"I was wondering," Billy said. "Do you run your oil company by the rules God gave us in the Bible?"

"Did you see anything about the oil business in your reading of the Bible?"

"I was thinking more about the Ten Commandments," Billy said.

"You're insincere. You sit there drinking my Coca-Cola and smiling at me, and your mind is full of negative thoughts about me. This is what caused those four shank shots."

Billy said, "Let me ask you, Dr. Sandpaster. If I had stopped you and corrected your address before that first shank shot, you would have fired me on the spot, wouldn't you?"

"Yes."

"But because I didn't correct you, you fired me anyhow and told everybody at Colonial that I am a jinx."

"That's true." Ira took a fresh look at Billy. There was something appealing about the boy. Ira remembered when he had been sixteen, how full of hope he had been. He remembered giving the two hundred dollars in five- and ten-dollar bills to a small man wearing a straw hat in the alley behind the hotel.

"Has your father always been a worthless drunk?" Ira asked.

"My father was a hero in World War Two. Now he's a captain in the Army in Korea." Billy supposed this might well be true.

"What is he doing over there?"

"Fighting the Communists."

Billy found himself feeling proud of Troy in the face of this old loon. Ira was moved by the idea this lad's father was an Army officer overseas, a commander of men, risking his life in battle against the forces of evil.

"You're from a military family, eh? And your mother was a university professor, I believe. Your father being an officer and a gentleman, that means you as his son may indeed have a future in this city. We'll see," Ira said. He picked up a silver bell on his desk and rang it. "Come in, Sandra."

She had been listening at the door. Sandra bounded into the room.

"Yes, paw paw?"

"Please, doodlebug, don't call me paw paw in front of strangers."

"I feel comfortable with Billy," Sandra said.

"Just the same," said Ira.

"All right, grandfather," she said.

Ira turned to face Billy, who had stood up when Sandra came in.

"I am ready to consider your apology now, Billy," the doctor said.

"What am I apologizing for?"

"Negative thoughts that caused me to hit four shank shots."

"I won't apologize for what I was thinking," Billy said.

"Billy, don't be stupid," said Sandra. "What difference does it make? Apologize to my grandfather."

Sandra was so appealing, so sweet smelling and wonderful looking. He wanted her. But he was thinking about Troy. And Troy would never apologize to a fellow like Ira Sandpaster for something he might be thinking.

"In the game of golf, it's your own fault if you hit a bad shot," Billy said.

"You stubborn fool, apologize to my grandfather," said Sandra.

"I'm sorry, Sandra. I can't do it."

"Do it."

"No."

She raised her hand as if to slap him.

"Don't hurt your sweet fingers, doodlebug," Ira said.

"Are you going to apologize?" asked Sandra. "If I ask you to?"

"No."

"Pretty please?"

"No."

"I'm out of the mood for accepting apologies," Ira said.

"You wasn't about to hear one out of me," said Billy.

"Get out of this house right now, Billy!" Sandra screamed. "Go on! Forget about me! You don't care about me! Walk home! Walk back to the damn YMCA!"

She ran out of the study. They heard her footsteps as she leaped up the stairs that led toward her room.

"Well," Billy said. He couldn't tell whether he felt crushed or angry or merely tired of Sandra and her crazy grandfather. "I guess I'll be going then."

"See you at the club," Ira said.

Billy was surprised at Ira's change of tone.

"Bright and early," Billy said.

"By the way, what was it Hogan told you about the golf swing?"

"I can't tell you," said Billy.

"Was it very different from my Perfect Swing?"

"Yes sir," Billy said.

Ira Sandpaster stood at the window watching Billy walking up the driveway toward Simondale. The boy glanced back a couple of times as if expecting Sandra to rush out to him or call him back. The boy didn't know Sandra very well, if that's what he thought she would do. Ira smiled. This Billy had spirit. And the boy knew Hogan's secret, wrong though Hogan obviously was. But Billy was a goner with Sandra. That problem was solved. No one other than Ira dared defy his granddaughter as this common caddie had done. It was best that she return to dating the Indian boy with the smooth tempo and the Oklahoma oil for her last year in high school. Ira wondered if the young did anything these days for protection against making babies. They didn't have protection against making babies when he was young, not that he heard of. But this was his doodlebug he was worried about.

J Seventeen

OHN BREDEMUS sat at the small table in his room at the YMCA with his left leg crossed over the right, his trousers caught up to reveal a bulging calf that tapered into a collapsed sock. He took a single sheet of notebook paper from his shirt pocket and unfolded it. Nodding with pleasure, he read the paper twice and was starting on a third time when Billy entered.

"I'm glad you're back," Billy said. "I notice that taillight is still busted."

"Good to see you, Billy Boy. Oh, I was careful with my driving. Had a lovely trip. No flat tires. Engine purred right along. Visited two of my courses, which are surviving nicely. They are municipal courses, so they are not threatened by committees of wealthy dubs, only by lack of care from local authorities."

Bredemus showed Billy the sheet of paper.

"I was afraid I had lost this," Bredemus said. "But I found it folded up inside a crease in my bag."

"What is it?"

"Did your mother teach you what a *haiku* is?"

"Some kind of writing?"

"It is an honored form of unrhymed poetry that originated in Japan," said Bredemus. "Poems of three lines that contain five, seven and five syllables. A *haiku* expresses a moment of truth deeper than words alone can do it."

"That's nice," Billy said. He wanted to talk about Sandra and Dr. Sandpaster and the obstacle of Sonny Stonekiller, not about Japanese poetry.

"Perhaps you are not very impressed with poetry," said Bredemus. "But this is a golf story. A friend who was a very good amateur player was in the front lines with the Marines in the South Pacific. He killed a Japanese officer who was leading a suicide charge. In the dead man's breast pocket my friend found a little notebook. Sort of a diary, a rumination. My friend saw a sketch that made him think of golf, so he had the notebook translated. I have one page of it here. Take a look."

Bredemus handed the paper to Billy.

CAPTAIN TANAKA'S GOLF HAIKUS

ON PUTTING

> *Head still, shoulder putt,*
> *Accelerating slightly.*
> *Right palm strikes ball in.*

ON DRIVING

> *To get great distance*
> *Take ten percent off swing and*
> *Add slow hinge at top.*

ON IRONS

> *Eyes seeing divot*
> *Before ball flying greenward.*
> *Keep head behind ball.*

IN GENERAL

> *Backswinging shaft points*
> *At bellybutton causing*
> *One piece takeaway.*

"Lovely, isn't it?" said Bredemus. "I especially like the one on hitting irons. I can see that divot flying with my head behind the   139 ball. Imagine a man who can write these exquisite poems leading a suicide charge."

"Yeah, it's good."

"I have something else to show you. Sit down for a minute."

"Well . . ."

"You have plenty of time. You won't be going to the movies with Sandra Sandpaster tonight."

"How do you know?"

"I can tell by the expression on your face. You and I will go out and have a Mexican dinner in a little while."

"My daddy said Texans don't know how to make good Mexican food."

"I know a place on the west side, somebody's house, really, where they do it New Mexican style, with green chile and mole sauce. But first, see that cigar box on my pillow? Sit down and I'll tell you what's in it."

Billy sat on the bed and put his chin in his hands, elbows on knees. He would rather be talking about his own problems and adventures, but he was fond of the older man. Bredemus had treated the boy with kindness and generosity and had provided the lucky 7-iron that led to the encounter with Ben Hogan. Billy would listen to his story.

Watching as Bredemus paced the small room and gestured with muscular hands, his shoulders thick, Billy remembered Dr. Sandpaster saying Bredemus had been an all-American football player and a track-and-field star at Dartmouth. Then Bredemus transferred to Princeton and broke his nose as all-American halfback for the Tigers while receiving a civil engineering degree. Or so Dr. Sandpaster had said. Billy had come to agree with Foxy Lerner's opinion that Dr. Sandpaster was crazy, but there was in the bearing of Bredemus an authority that demonstrated the athletic part of the story was correct, for certain.

"Have you heard of Jim Thorpe?"

"Sure. The Carlisle Indians. Football, baseball."

"Jim was born on the Sac and Fox reservation in Oklahoma. He is the greatest athlete in history."

"Dr. Sandpaster said you went up against him in the Olympics," Billy said.

"No. I had a pulled hamstring and missed the summer Olympics in Stockholm, where Jim Thorpe won the pentathalon and the decathalon."

Billy said, "Too bad you didn't compete against him."

"But I did. Jim and I met later that year in a showdown at the American championships. There was a great public clamor to see which of us was first among the best. We competed at Celtic Park, Long Island, in the rain and mud. I gave Jim a struggle. But he beat me. He won the gold medals in the pentathalon and in the decathalon. I finished second in both and took the silvers. It was an honor to stand beside such a great man as Jim Thorpe at the awards ceremony. Open that cigar box."

Billy opened the box and saw a velvet pouch inside.

"The following year the Olympic Committee ruled that Jim Thorpe was a professional because he had been paid a few dollars for playing baseball while he was a student at the Carlisle Indian Industrial School in Pennsylvania. If this was a crime, many of our Olympic athletes were guilty. But because Jim was an Indian, the Olympic Committee took his gold medals away from him. Look in that bag."

Billy loosened the drawstring on the velvet pouch and poured the contents into one palm.

"Are these his Olympic medals?" Billy asked.

"Jim's Olympic medals went to a bank in Switzerland. When the Olympic Committee stripped Jim of his medals, our American Athletic Union did the same thing. As second best man, I was offered his American championship medals. I accepted and have carried them in Jim's honor."

"You've carried these medals all this time?" asked Billy.

"I left the cigar box buried under a concrete block in the

maintenance shed in Big Spring in 1946. I swung by and picked it up on this latest trip."

Billy hefted the old medals on their long ribbons.

"These must be very precious," Billy said.

"To those who understand what these medals stand for, they are priceless."

"You left them in a cigar box under a concrete block for six years?"

"They were safe."

Billy thought he remembered Bredemus saying he had not built the golf course in Big Spring, that he was passing through the town when the motor court exploded. But maybe he said he had started on it earlier. Maybe he had built only the maintenance shed. Memories are tricky. Didn't really matter. Billy tried to read the writing on the coins, but they needed polishing. The coins were heavier than he had expected. He imagined them hanging around the neck of Jim Thorpe.

"Put them on," Bredemus said.

Billy draped the two ribbons around his neck and felt the medals dangling against his stomach.

"Feel the magic?" said Bredemus.

Billy did feel a surge of spirit.

"Jim Thorpe's medals. I can't believe it," Billy said. "What do you think I should do with them?"

"He's still alive?"

"He's sixty-three. A proud man. He won't take them back. He trusts me to do the right thing with them. I don't know what that is, but I'll know it at the proper time. Well, what do you think, Billy Boy? Do you feel Jim Thorpe's heart beating?"

"I think I do," Billy said. He felt something beyond the ordinary.

"The same month the AAU gave me Jim Thorpe's medals, I decided no more track and field for me. No more politics. I needed a game I could play by myself, that carried its own chal-

142

lenges and its own reward. I discovered golf at Van Cortlandt Park in the Bronx in New York. Van Cortlandt Park is the first public course built in this country. All sorts of people went there—actors, musicians, journalists, cartoonists, businessmen, laborers. The ninth hole was 700 yards long. Here, let me hold those medals for a moment."

Bredemus juggled the two heavy gold medals in his palms.

"I feel Jim Thorpe's spirit in these medals," said Bredemus. "You said you felt it?"

' "I think I felt it," Billy said.

Bredemus sat in his chair, the gold medals in his hands, staring out the window, lost in reflection.

"What about the golf?" Billy said.

"Pardon?"

"That course in New York where you learned the game of golf."

"Oh, yes." Bredemus seemed to have been listening to faraway music, but he turned his attention back to Billy. "I had the gift. Hitting golf shots came easy for me. I loved the game. Golf is simple but at the same time the most mysterious of games. Before you know it, I was playing in tournaments and using my civil engineering education to help build the Lido Club on Long Island. During that job I realized I had been put on this earth to be a builder of golf courses. There weren't many of us in those days. I followed the sun to Texas. First place I went was Brackenridge Park in San Antonio. That was the only public golf course in Texas at the time. I looked around and I knew that Texas needed me, and I needed Texas."

Bredemus put the medals back into the velvet bag, returned the bag to the cigar box and put it into his locker.

"Let's go have that New Mexican Mexican food, Billy Boy. I want to learn what has happened while I was gone."

They heard a rapping on the doorframe. The door was already open, and a soldier stuck his head inside. The soldier was

143

balding, had two stripes on his arm and a garden of ribbons on his chest. Billy recognized the ribbons for the Purple Heart and the Silver Star medals. Troy had Purple Heart and Silver Star medals in a box someplace, but Billy didn't know where they were. He remembered the weight of Jim Thorpe's gold medals around his neck. If he really had returned to the Army, Troy would be wearing his ribbons now, but Billy resolved to find Troy's medals and keep them safe. They had cost dearly. Troy had lost his nerve for golf to win those medals.

"You named Billy?" said the soldier.

"Yes sir."

"I am Corporal John Dribble of the U.S. Army. I've been looking for you all day. I've got some bad news for you, son."

Dribble glanced at Bredemus, wondering what might be going on in this room, but quickly he became intent on the telegram he produced from the shirt pocket that he was careful to rebutton.

"Your father is dead," Dribble said. "He was killed in an accident on the firing range at Fort Sill this morning."

"He was killed?" Billy said.

This couldn't be true. There must be a mistake.

"That's all I know about the circumstances," said Corporal Dribble.

"What is being done with the captain's body?" Bredemus asked.

Dribble consulted the telegram.

"The captain's remains are being shipped at his request to Jal, New Mexico, for burial. The Army will give the captain a military funeral at the cemetery in Jal."

"When?" said Bredemus.

Dribble looked at the telegram. "Day after tomorrow."

Billy felt numb, unreal.

"I killed him," Billy said.

"Would you sign this paper, son? It says you have been notified and confirms this place as your address. The Army will be sending you more paperwork later."

Using the ballpoint pen offered by the soldier, Billy signed three copies of the document in three places each.

Dribble gave one copy to Billy and then stepped back and said, "This is for your old man."

Dribble saluted. He held his pose smartly for a few seconds and then brought his arm down.

"Sorry, kid," said Dribble.

When the soldier had gone, Billy repeated, "I killed him."

"Put that thought out of your mind, Billy Boy," said Bredemus.

"No, he wouldn't have gone back in the Army if I hadn't shamed him," Billy said.

"He did what he wanted to do. Go throw some clothes in a bag. We must be on our way."

"On our way?" Billy said. He felt heavy and stupid as he absorbed the death of Troy and his own role in it.

"We're driving to Jal, New Mexico, to your father's funeral. Hurry up, now."

As he started for the door, Billy said, "We'll stop and get that taillight fixed first thing. We'll be traveling all night."

T Eighteen

HE OLD BLACK FORD sailed through the night across an endless prairie. Jackrabbits bobbed up in front of the headlights. The car radio could pick up only Spanish-language stations, evangelist preacher stations from the other side of the Rio Grande, a country music station and sometimes the clear channel jazz and big band station from New Orleans.

They listened to Dixieland jazz broadcast from Bourbon Street until static cut in and Bredemus finally turned off the radio. Lightning spread across the sky in the distance. They had not spoken in hours.

"My own father died when I was about your age," Bredemus said at last. "I was at boarding school in New Hampshire when he passed away of kidney disease. I didn't get a chance to say goodbye to him in that life, but I wish I had. I wish I had gotten things straight between me and my father before he was gone. But I thought he would live forever. Well, he does live forever, but you know what I mean."

"I drove him away," Billy said. "He asked me to forgive him."

"Forgive him for what?"

"For being a jerk."

"Your father is a war hero and a champion cowboy and an excellent golfer. Don't you give him credit for those things?"

"The night before I drove him away he got drunk at some gambling club on the Jacksboro Highway and lost our car and all the money we got for our house."

"The 2222 Club," said Bredemus.

"How'd you know?"

"It's a popular club."

"I called him a jerk. I said I never wanted to see him again. I said I hated him. I meant it. Then he came to the caddie yard at the country club and I told the cops to take him away. I wish I had done it different."

"How would you do it?" Bredemus said.

"I don't know. I was awful mad. I hoped he'd go to Korea."

They drove another half hour through the black West Texas night before Billy said, "I think what I'd do different is, I would hug him and kiss him before the cops took him away."

THEY HALTED ONCE DURING THE NIGHT at a truck stop to buy gasoline, hot coffee and apricot fried pies. With Billy at the wheel and Bredemus dozing, they covered the 402 miles from Fort Worth to the New Mexico border in six hours. Billy thought about Sandra and wondered if she had been to the lover's lane with Sonny that night. They stopped again for gas and sweet rolls and Coca-Colas and a walkaround stretch in the Texas town of Kermit, eighteen miles south of Jal. It was just after six in the morning. The air blew brisk and cool on the high plains, three thousand feet above sea level.

While the gas station attendant, who wore overalls with the name Otis stitched on his breast, filled their tank and checked the tires and washed the windows, Bredemus started throwing rocks at a piece of cactus thirty yards away.

"What do you see when you look where I'm throwing?" Bredemus asked.

"I see cactus, mesquite, hard chalky dirt and a cow's skull."

"See where that last rock landed? There's a small swale in there, a contour formed by the dry stream bed that is a natural place to put a green. I can see going back across the road and building a tee over by those mesquites. Say, Otis, how often would water be flowing in that dry bed?"

"Not very much," said Otis. "There ain't a steady flowing stream in 5,000 square miles around here."

"You see a golf course when you look at these miles and miles of nothing?" Billy said. He had put on his new widebrim straw hat that he had bought in Fort Worth and was pulling on his boots. This close to the JAL, he felt the stirring of his cowboy blood.

"When I was a boy we were on a summer vacation in Maryland," said Bredemus. "I suggested we hit golf balls across a spit of water onto an island. My brother asked why would we want to do that? I realized I was seeing what no one else was seeing—a green on that island. I was seeing a golf course. The visions returned when I began playing golf at Van Cortlandt Park. I began picturing golf courses in my mind, rather ghostly images in the beginning, but clearer and clearer as I was drawn into the game. Harvey Penick says a person needs to be an artist to see a golf course in his mind, but he needs to be an engineer to build one."

"Are you a golf professional?" Otis asked.

"I am, indeed," said Bredemus.

Otis screwed the gas tank cap on. He wiped a dipstick on a purple cloth.

"I wish you'd tell me what's so all fired great about golf," Otis said. "I play every other Sunday over at Jal. The guys I play with get mad all the time. I get mad. I don't see it's any fun at all. But there ain't a hell of a lot to do out here."

"May I speak frankly, Otis?"

"I wouldn't expect nothing else."

"Cheerfulness is the greatest essential to enjoying golf," Bredemus said.

"Oh, yeah? You ain't seen them snake cutters and gopher

chasers my pals hit every which direction. I took a lesson from Hardy Loudermilk to cure my slice, but he don't know what the hell he's talking about. It's worse than ever. Now you are telling me to be cheerful about my damn slice?"

"Golf reacts to cheerfulness more than to anything else," said Bredemus. "A happy way of looking at things is invaluable. The man who goes onto the course with good cheer in his heart will soon find himself playing better."

"You got golf clubs in the trunk?" Otis asked.

"Yes."

"I wonder if you'd hit a ball for me?" said Otis.

Bredemus took out his lucky 7-iron and spanked a ball about 145 yards over a creosote bush. Billy walked to fetch the ball. "Well?" said Bredemus.

"I wanted to see if you're just talking or if you can really do it," Otis said. "No offense intended."

"There are mental aspects to the game that are more important than the shot I just now hit," said Bredemus. "Maintaining a cheerful attitude is one. You'll be more at ease. Your shots will come naturally."

"I'll try to remember that next time. Make my damn old self cheerful. You got any more professional tips for me?" Otis produced a greasy notebook and a yellow pencil. "I want to write em down."

"Don't hold onto the last shot you hit, good or bad. The important shot is the present one. Don't underestimate the mental nature of golf. Play with your head as well as your hands. Don't think about any part of your body more than any other part. You're not writing, Otis."

"Keep going."

"Be hopeful and optimistic every moment of the round. Concentrate on your play, but don't confuse lingering memory with concentration. Concentration always implies an element of the present. Be patient. The person who can't control his disposition will never control anything else. Are you going to write this down?"

"Let's hear more," said Otis.

"Don't disregard good advice if it is given in a practical form, as I am doing now, but don't try to follow everybody's advice. Never be tempted to cheat. Never get discouraged. And above all, be cheerful."

"Is that all?" said Otis. "Because I ain't heard a word yet about how to cure my slice."

Bredemus smiled. The slice—the golf instructor's cash cow. He placed the lucky 7-iron in Otis's hands and rolled his grip to the right. He set Otis up with his feet, hips and shoulders a little closed to the line of flight. "Your shoulders were so open you would have to slice to hit the ball at all." Bredemus put the fingers of his right hand against Otis's forehead to keep his head steady and behind the ball. "Now swing."

Otis hit a slice that curled out of sight around the corner behind the gas station.

"See there?" Otis said. "It can't be cured. I'm cursed."

"Have you ever seen Ben Hogan?"

"In the newsreels."

"You notice how sometimes he will walk along holding his club out in front at a forty-five-degree angle and waggling it?"

"No, I never noticed that."

"Well, what Hogan is doing is what you need to do, Otis. Hogan is checking his grip pressure. Grip pressure is vital to the swing. Take that 7-iron and hold it as lightly as you can with the shaft in front of your body and pointing straight at the sky. Got that?"

"I got it," said Otis.

"That grip is too loose," Bredemus said. "Now stick the 7-iron straight out from your belly button, horizontally, and hold it as loosely as you can."

Otis did it.

"That grip is too tight," said Bredemus. "Now hold the club up in front of you at a forty-five-degree angle and grip it as loosely as you can."

"Like this?" Otis said.

"That's right. That is exactly the correct grip pressure. Now keep that pressure the same all the way through your swing and hit another."

Returning from retrieving Bredemus's first shot, Billy saw a ball sail high above his head with a little tail hook on it and come down in a patch of cactus some 130 yards from where Otis had just swung the 7-iron beside the gas pump.

"Hallelujah!" Otis shouted. "Praise be to God, my slice is burning in hell!"

When they drove away they could see Otis standing near his pickup truck with a golf club in his hands, practicing holding it at a forty-five-degree angle and crying, "Mama! Mama come out here!"

On the outskirts of Jal they saw a small sign that said POPU-LATION 1200 and a big sign that said, THE NATURAL GAS CAPITAL OF THE WORLD. They stopped at the Restawee Funeral Parlor. The owner, Mr. Bondini, a pale figure with a black mustache that seemed to drip shoe polish, remembered Troy and Billy. Mr. Bondini expressed his sympathy and said the service was scheduled for 10 A.M. tomorrow, expenses paid by the Army. Troy's remains would arrive by truck from Fort Sill in the morning along with an honor guard. The coffin would be sealed.

During lunch at the Good Eats Café, Bredemus slid down in the booth and kept glancing over his shoulder and hiding his face with a newspaper.

"I'm afraid someone will recognize me," Bredemus said. "Hardy Loudermilk eats in here now and then."

"I want to visit the Jal Country Club this afternoon," Billy said.

"Then you'll be going alone, and you'll not be taking my car or mentioning my name."

First after lunch Billy drove six miles east of town to Monument Draw and rattled over a cattle guard, and they were on the land of the mighty JAL Ranch. Billy drove past the old ranch house where his father Troy had been born and in which Troy's parents had died. Billy saw the cabin where he had lived as a child until his mother decided to return to Albuquerque once and for all, and Troy had more or less followed. A cowboy wearing a tool belt waved at them from the top of a windmill. They passed the rodeo arena where Troy had taught Billy how to ride bucking stock. They passed the loading pens, which were empty on this day but he had seen them crowded with cows all the way to the horizon. The land went on forever and forever, alkaline soil dotted with cactus and mesquite.

Billy drove past a young cowboy who was wearing heavy leather gloves and carrying a wirecutter. The young cowboy's horse was tethered to a fence post. The cowboy had taken off the chaps he wore to protect his legs from thorns and had draped the leather across his loosened saddle. He wore jeans, boots, a big hat and a t-shirt with a tin of chewing tobacco rolled into one sleeve.

"Be back in a minute," Billy said and stopped the car.

The cowboy looked up as Billy approached on foot.

"Is that you, Boo?"

"Billy. I'll be damned."

Boo took off his right glove and shook hands with Billy. Boo's jaw swelled with a lump of tobacco.

"Sorry to hear about your old man," Boo said.

"Thanks." The two boys had grown up together until Billy's mother decided to make a home in Albuquerque. The first few summers after he left the JAL, Billy had returned to work as a cowboy. But then Troy booked him a golf lesson with Hardy Loudermilk, and Billy became a caddie.

"I heard you left Albuquerque," Boo said.

"I'm working at Colonial Country Club in Fort Worth."

"Damn." Boo spat a brown stream. "Fort Worth is too big a town to suit me. I get goosey at the thought of going to Lubbock. What do you do at that country club?"

"I'm a caddie."

"Who's that old man in the Ford?"

"He builds golf courses."

"Can a fellow make a living building golf courses?"

"Sure."

"I never would have believed it."

"How's your folks?"

"Fine," said Boo. "They'll be at the funeral."

Billy looked up at the endless polished sky and filled his lungs with desert air. Boo would spend his life out here.

"I miss this old place," Billy said.

"You could come back."

"I don't guess I'm ready to come back just yet," Billy said.

"The boss has promised me a scholarship at New Mexico A&M if I don't make a grade worse than B this coming year. He wants me to study animal husbandry. I'll be a range boss when I graduate."

"Good for you."

"Yeah. Hell, I might boss the JAL one of these days."

"Could be."

"How do you plan on making a living?" Boo asked.

"In golf."

Until the word golf came out of his mouth, Billy wasn't aware he had decided.

"Are you that good?"

"I don't know."

"I wouldn't care for the suspense of finding out," Boo said.

"I notice you rode your horse down here instead of taking a pickup or a Jeep," Billy said.

"You got to ride a horse to run a fence line, Billy. You know that. Besides, a real cowboy don't belong in a Jeep."

"A real cowboy belongs on a horse."

"You got that right," said Boo.

Billy shook hands again with his childhood comrade and returned to the old Ford. He started the engine and drove back toward town. Billy was growing tired at last. He wanted to rent a room at the Clearview Tourist Court and sleep until tomorrow.

"That boy is an old friend of yours?" said Bredemus.

"Boo? The oldest."

"You call him Boo?"

"He was scared of ghosts."

Bredemus smiled. "A few years ago some fellows in San Antonio invented a handicap system they called the Boo. If your handicap was seventeen, that meant seventeen times during the match your opponent could shout, 'Boo!' at any point during your swing or while you were putting. We had a lot of fun with that game one summer. What's the matter, Billy Boy? Don't you find that amusing?"

"I was thinking about Boo. I could be him. But he couldn't be me."

B Nineteen

ILLY AWOKE EARLY in the Clearview Tourist Court. He had dreamed about Sandra Sandpaster. The other bed appeared not to have been slept in. The boy yawned and went into the bathroom and ran the shower until the water stopped being orange before he stepped beneath the stream. He remembered an early dinner of chicken fried steak with Bredemus at the Good Eats Café. They returned to the room and played checkers. Bredemus talked about his famous checkers matches against the notorious gambler Alvin C. Thomas, better known as Titanic Thompson.

"Alvin can never beat me at checkers, and I won't play him in any other game," Bredemus had said. "If golf professionals played for a million-dollar first prize, Alvin would turn pro and win every major tournment lefthanded one year and righthanded the next." Bredemus won the checkers game in six moves. Billy had not seen the winning jump coming. Resetting the board, Bredemus said, "Alvin won more money off members at River Oaks in a week than Ben Hogan has won in his entire professional career. Alvin is not only a great golfer, he is a mathematical genius. He can figure the odds on any proposition in an instant. He has the nerve to back it up. With his skills, if he had been a Princeton man, he would have gone into investment banking and played high stakes golf and cards at the proper clubs, and he would today be an advisor to presidents and kings. Well, maybe in his next life, huh, Billy Boy?"

That was the last thing Billy remembered before exhaustion overcame him.

Coming out of the bathroom after brushing his teeth, Billy noticed a clean shirt and jeans and his cowboy boots and hat laid out on the chair. On the table, Billy found a note.

HAVE GONE EXPLORING IN THE CAR. TOOK YOUR BAG. HOTEL BILL IS PAID. WILL PICK YOU UP AT HIGHWAY INTERSECTION AFTER THE FUNERAL. KEEP MUM ABOUT ME—

Billy walked four blocks down the road. A row of pickup trucks were parked in front of the Good Eats Café at breakfast time. As he entered the café, a voice called, "Billy. Over here." A wiry man with ruddy, weathered skin slid out of a booth and shook hands with Billy.

"Nice to see you, Mr. Loudermilk," Billy said.

"Have breakfast with me?"

"Thanks."

The waitress brought Billy his favorite order of scrambled eggs, pan-fried sausage, biscuits and gravy with hashbrown potatoes. Loudermilk had already finished a bowl of oatmeal. He sipped his coffee as he watched the boy eat. Loudermilk was thinking what an image of Troy this boy was turning out to be. In some ways that was good, the old pro was thinking, but not in all ways.

"I was very sorry to hear about your mother passing a few weeks ago," Loudermilk said.

"We got your flowers. Thanks."

"And now Troy. So soon. It's not fair."

"No sir."

"How much family have you got?"

"None close."

"How are you going to get by in the world?" Loudermilk asked.

"Golf," said Billy.

He felt good about saying the word, glad he had decided yesterday while talking to Boo. There was a place in the world of golf for Billy. He didn't know what or where the place might be, but he felt sure it was there.

"What part of the game do you have in mind making money at?"

"Right now I'm a caddie at Colonial, and I am doing all right," Billy said.

"If I was a young man with a good natural golf swing like you have, I would be sure to get a good education with a college degree in business. Golf is a big help in doing business. You can get rich out of golf if you use it in business. You sure can't get rich collecting greens fees and teaching lessons."

"Maybe I'll turn out to be a champion player like Ben Hogan," said Billy.

"You sounded like Troy then." Loudermilk grinned.

"Was there ever really a time when my daddy could have beaten Ben Hogan?"

"Well, the year before the Big War, if Troy had met Ben Hogan in a big money match at Odessa or Abilene, I would have bet on your daddy."

An Army lieutenant came in, wearing a khaki uniform that had been creased and starched before his long truck ride from Fort Sill. Two enlisted men—a corporal and a private first class—followed him. They sat at a table and ordered breakfast and coffee. The officer took off his overseas cap. The enlisted men were about to do the same when the officer noticed that the cattlemen and oil field workers kept their hats on indoors, so the lieutenant quickly restored his cap.

"I guess they've got Troy out in that truck," Loudermilk said.

Billy smeared a biscuit in the gravy and snared a piece of sausage for a topping.

"Troy didn't want any church service, huh?" said Loudermilk.

Billy thought about the church with the bell tower in France six years ago. He remembered Troy crouching behind a statue of Jesus while machine-gun bullets tore up the church. Troy had never gone to church after the war that Billy could recall. Before the war, Troy would sometimes go to mass and special ceremonies and talk to his wife and to the priest as if he might convert. But the only time Billy knew Troy had been in church after the war was at Billy's mother's funeral service in Albuquerque.

"I don't think daddy had made plans to die just yet," Billy said.

A thin man wearing a black cowboy hat and lizard skin boots approached the table. Billy noticed his long sideburns. He held a burning cigarette between his lips.

"Howdy, Hardy," the man said.

"Howdy."

The man looked at Billy. "Not hard to tell who you are, son. Damn if you don't look just like your old man. He used to brag about you a lot, you know. Me and Troy played golf and cards together. Me and him cleaned out El Paso Country Club one week, left em screaming for mercy." The man dug a roll of money out of his pocket and peeled off the rubber band. "I owe Troy five hundred dollars from our last gin rummy game. You take it for him."

Billy looked back and forth from the man with the sideburns to the frowning golf pro across the table.

"Take the money, it's only right," the man said.

"Take it, Billy," said Loudermilk.

Billy picked up the money.

"Thanks," he said.

"See you down the road, kid. Look out for yourself," the tall man said. "I'll say a prayer for old Troy. Nice to see you, too, Hardy." He walked toward the cashier to pay his check.

"That's a hustler named Amarillo Slim," said Loudermilk. "I wish Troy had never started running with people like him." The three soldiers stood up. "Time to go, Billy. You need a ride to the cemetery?"

"Please," said Billy.

"How'd you get here?"

"I hitched."

The freshly dug grave was in line with two older graves whose headstones were Billy's grandfather and grandmother. A high plains breeze was blowing a film of dust, but the crowd was in shirt sleeves, except for the son of the owner of the JAL, who wore a western-cut suit and a white Stetson. Troy's former range boss and six JAL cowboys were there, including Old Elmo. Boo came with his mother and father. Boo's mother hugged Billy and wept. Troy's high school English teacher introduced herself to Billy, and she also wept, looking at him, seeing her past. Two attractive women who didn't seem to know each other or anyone else at the cemetery walked past Troy's coffin and rubbed their fingers against the American flag that draped it and held handkerchiefs to their faces.

The son of the owner of the JAL looked to Billy to be about the same age as John Bredemus, who was nowhere to be seen. The rancher took up a position at the head of the grave, facing the crowd.

"Please remove your hats," he said.

As Billy took off his cowboy hat he caught Boo glancing at him. They used to joke that Boo wore his hat even when he went swimming. Boo held his hat against his chest with both hands.

159

The rancher said, "Everybody in Jal knew Troy's daddy as one of the best men at handling stock that the West has ever seen. We knew Troy's mother as one of the sweetest women to ever set foot on this earth. Many of us knew their boy, Troy. He was a top hand. He was a hell of a cowboy. I can say this about Troy—he was as brave as they come. He fought the Nazis in World War Two. And now Troy has returned home to Jal to sleep beside his mama and his daddy and be among his true friends."

"Amen," said Old Elmo.

"Amen."

"Amen."

The lieutenant read a proclamation that Billy could barely understand, for the huge sadness that had suddenly engulfed him, like a cold damp empty space. He finally realized Troy was gone.

The two enlisted men fired eight rounds each into the sky from their M-1 rifles. The noise of the rifle shots blasted through the high plains air and seemed to ricochet into space. The odor of gunpowder covered the cemetery, causing some to cough and blink and all but the already deaf to have a ringing in their ears.

The flag was removed from the coffin and folded and given to Billy by the lieutenant.

Troy's coffin was lowered into the earth.

AFTER THE FUNERAL Billy signed two more government documents for the lieutenant. He accepted condolences from the crowd, most of them returning to their jobs, waved as Boo climbed into the back of the pickup with his dog while his father, mother and sister sat in the front, shook hands with Old Elmo and with Hardy Loudermilk and with the son of the owner of the JAL.

The old black Ford was waiting at the highway intersection.

"Let me drive?" Billy said.

Rather than taking the road east toward Fort Worth, Billy turned the wheels to the west. He drove forty miles, while Bredemus fiddled with the radio, searching for music, before Billy said, "We're not going straight back to Fort Worth, if it's all right."

"So I notice."

"We're going to Albuquerque first."

"That will please her very much," Bredemus said.

The old black Ford ate up the 360 miles from Jal to Albuquerque without a belch from the engine or a bulge from the tires. It was eerie what fine shape this old car was in. Billy had never driven faster in his life over a sustained period. They pulled into the outskirts late in the afternoon. Billy went first to Old Town and showed Bredemus the adobe house that had been his home until recently. Carpenters were working there. The new owner was converting the home into a gift shop. Remembering his childhood years in that house, Billy felt a pang of loss for what could have been.

A stone angel marked Billy's mother's grave in the cemetery. As the sun went down, Sandia Mountain lit up red and purple and gave the impression of looming over them although it was miles away. Billy's shadow fell across her grave as he placed a handful of wildflowers in the arms of the angel. Billy knelt and crossed himself.

He whispered to her.

"Mama, a while ago I got desperate and I prayed to you for help, and I cried like a baby. I apologize for bothering you in heaven. But I'm doing pretty good now. I met a nice man named Mr. Bredemus. We're in his car. I met Ben Hogan, too. I guess you heard daddy got killed. I'm sorry about that. Well, I better get moving now. We're driving back to Fort Worth tonight.

Don't you worry about me. Mama, I love you and I miss you every day."

Billy had tears in his eyes as he crossed himself again and stood up.

"I feel like she heard me," he said.

"I'm sure she heard you," said Bredemus.

A Twenty

AT 2:30 IN THE AFTERNOON Harvey Penick put on a golf clinic at Colonial Country Club for 200 members who paid two dollars each to hear him talk about the golf swing and watch him hit trick shots for an hour on the practice range.

Penick did not teach group lessons, nor did he often leave his home at Austin Country Club. But he enjoyed doing exhibitions, and this was a benefit for the Texas PGA. He chose a left-handed club and hit it right-handed, and then a right-handed club that he hit left-handed. He turned the clubhead upside down and hit shots by spinning the club so fast in his fingers during the swing that the crowd could not see the clubhead squaring up to the ball. Penick brought out a steel ball attached to a length of chain that had a golf grip at the other end. He hit 100 yard shots with the steel ball as clubhead.

Using a rubber hose with a grip at one end and a 3-wood head attached to the other, Penick hit a dozen shots. The crowd was applauding. He placed one ball atop another with a bit of chewing gum. With his 7-iron, Penick hit the bottom ball 125 yards while the top ball popped up and fell into his hand.

At the end of an hour Penick explained what would be his final, climactic trick shot.

He placed two balls side by side.

"I will hit these two balls with one swing," Penick told the audience. "They will cross in midair, one hooking and one slicing."

"Oh yeah?" a voice yelled.

Ben Hogan staggered out of the crowd. His cap was pulled sideways. He had a loopy grin and appeared to be wobbling drunk. A wave of shock went up from the crowd. Muttering began. Hogan did a box step onto the tee. He was using a driver as a cane to keep his balance.

"Nobody can hit that shot. Not even you, Harvey," said Hogan, slurring.

"I've done it before, Ben."

"If you can do it, I can do it better," Hogan said. He tilted to the left as he walked toward the two golf balls. He managed to plant his feet. He waved his driver above the balls, took a big backswing and fell to his knees.

A few in the crowd laughed. The rest were too shocked and intimidated to laugh at Hogan.

"While I'm down here, toss me a ball, would you, Harvey?"

Penick dropped a golf ball in front of the kneeling Hogan. Blinking and wiping his eyes, as though finding the ball hard to see, Hogan twisted his cap again until the bill was over his right ear. He stuck out his tongue, clamped his lips on it and crossed his eyes.

Then from his knees Hogan swung his driver and hit the ball off the turf about 240 yards.

The crowd shouted and applauded. Hogan rose to his feet, pulled his cap around correctly and smiled. The crowd realized with vast relief that he was not drunk. He was pretending. This was an act Hogan had put on at exhibitions when he was younger, before he became a star. Today he did it to benefit the Texas PGA. The crowd laughed and cheered and clapped.

Hogan held up a hand to stop the applause.

"If you think that was a good shot, watch what Harvey does," Hogan said.

The slender Penick addressed the two golf balls.

Gesturing toward Penick's thin arms, Hogan said, "You will

notice, ladies and gentlemen, that this shot requires great skill but no biceps whatsoever."

While the crowd was laughing, Penick swung his 7-iron and the two balls crossed in midair as he had said they would. The laughter turned into cheering and wilder applause. Hogan and Penick both took off their flat cotton golf caps and bowed.

"You got time to watch me hit balls, Harvey?" Hogan said.

Elvis Spaatz dispatched Chili McWillie and Ham T out to the range to act as security, keeping the crowd away from Hogan. Penick stood on one leg, leaning on his 7-iron, while Hogan began working his way through the bag, starting with his wedge. Elvis sent a canvas chair out to Penick after an hour, when Hogan was into his midirons. Penick sat in the chair and crossed his thin legs, showing his argyle socks and his new alligator golf shoes. Occasionally Penick would say a few words that the crowd could not hear at a distance. But mostly the great teacher watched in silence as the champion pounded golf balls down the range at Colonial. Hogan had often said he dug his golf game out of the earth, just as the old Scottish golf pros had said golf is a game of digging holes.

It was toward sundown when Hogan finished. It was that magical hour that falls across a golf course, when there is silence and peace and beauty and the shadows are reflections of another, better world that the golfer can feel the existence of. Hogan invited Penick to accompany him to the men's grill for a drink and a sandwich. "Ben, I try to stay out of the men's grill at my own club," Penick said. "The men's grill is where the booze flows and opinions are stated and arguments start. It's a bad place for a club pro to be."

"The hell with em," Hogan said. "They're not going to start any arguments with me. Come on, I'd like to talk to you."

The champion and the teacher entered the men's grill and caused a brief hush in the room. There were card games being played at three tables. At other tables men added up their score-cards. Black waiters hustled through the room with trays of cock-tails and beers.

At the round table in the middle of the room sat the Sand-paster foursome. They had been off the course for an hour and had downed several glasses of whiskey. Only Sonny Stonekiller was totally sober, as he sat with his glass of 7-Up over ice—the club champion, the all-district quarterback, handsome enough to be a magazine model. Chester Stonekiller, usually jovial, was in a dark mood, his big brown face like a sandstorm. Chester was drinking martinis. Mr. Titus, looking primly satisfied as he sipped his bourbon neat, had done all the arithmetic for their game. Dr. Sandpaster was relaxing with a tall scotch topped by a slice of lime. His purple glasses lay on the table, wisps of hair hung down to his eyes, his fingernails were growing long and clicked on the glass. Ira had come in with an 84. He was pleased because 84 had proved good enough to win a large amount of money from the Indian oaf, who had become entertainingly furious. But Ira was a little distressed about Sonny. Three times Ira had seen Sonny fudge an inch when he marked his ball on the green. The first time, Ira wasn't sure he had seen it. The second time, Ira shrugged it off as excessive casualness. But the third time? Could it be?

Everyone at the Sandpaster table said, "Hi, Ben," except for Chester, who said, "What say, Hogan?"

"Fellas," Hogan said. He glanced sideways at Chester. Hogan looked across the table at Sonny but did not acknowledge him. Sonny sat back, sulking, and sipped his soft drink. A waiter showed Hogan and Penick to a table for two against the wall. The champion and the teacher ordered ice teas and club sandwiches.

Hogan was chewing his sandwich and drawing on a napkin his strategies for defending his championship in the upcoming U.S. Open in Detroit at Oakland Hills with its sixty-six new bunkers and added length. Newspapers were calling the course The Monster. Penick was eating and listening, nodding now and then, impressed by the champion's confidence in a plan that called for many imaginative shots.

"Hey, Hogan," Chester said loudly.

Hogan ignored him and continued talking to Penick.

"Hey, Hogan," Chester said again. The room grew silent. Chester stood up, his prosperous belly filling his golf shirt, a martini in one strong brown hand and a cigar in the other.

"Chester, sit down," said Ira Sandpaster.

"Shut up, paleface," Chester said.

Chester took two steps forward, put both hands beside his mouth to amplify and shouted, "Hey! Hogan!"

"I hear you, Chester," Hogan said, and suddenly there was not even the tinkle of an ice cube.

"How come you won't ever play golf with my boy? You think you're too good for him?"

"Your boy doesn't play golf," Hogan said. "He just tries to see how far he can hit it."

"My boy Sonny can beat your ass, Hogan," said Chester.

"Your boy can't beat that kid Billy who caddied for me the other day," Hogan said.

"Sonny can't beat Billy at what? You don't mean at golf?"

Hogan raised a finger and beckoned to Elvis Spaatz, who was in the doorway.

"Where's that kid Billy?" Hogan said.

"He just come back into the yard, Mr. Hogan," said Elvis.

"Well, go get him. Bring him in here."

"Billy can't come in here. Caddies are not permitted in this room," said Ira Sandpaster.

"Call a board meeting about it, Ira," Hogan said. "Get going, Elvis. Bring that boy here."

Billy had to run to keep up with Elvis as they went up the hill toward the clubhouse. Billy had caddied thirty-six holes that day, as he had done regularly since returning from Troy's funeral. Without Sandra Sandpaster to date, Billy had been saving his money, going with John Bredemus to the cafeteria at night and returning to his room to read books the older man passed along to him. Billy missed Sandra. He longed to kiss her. But he worked hard all day and fell asleep early with a book on his chest. When Billy arrived at the door of the men's grill beside Elvis, he first saw past the quarreling rabble at the Sandpaster table. His glance found Ben Hogan, whose head was tilted to the left and his eyes closed, as if listening to music. It flashed into Billy's mind that Hogan was conversing with Hennie Bogan.

Hogan smiled like Gary Cooper and nodded and opened his eyes.

"Come over here, Billy," Hogan said.

Billy heard anger from the Sandpaster table as he passed it, and he smelled whisky and cigar and cigarette smoke. He wondered what was happening. For a moment he thought of Bredemus, but he didn't know why. Billy walked over and stood beside the table where Penick sat with Hogan.

Hogan stood up, and it seemed the whole room took a step backward, forced back by the zone around him.

"Here's my proposition, Chester," said Hogan. "Your boy can't beat my boy."

"You're crazy as hell, Hogan," Chester said.

"They play four holes. Fifteen, sixteen, seventeen and eighteen. Stroke play. Your boy hits off the back tees and always drives first. My boy hits off the regular tees. I say your boy does not beat my boy."

"When?" said Chester.

"Tomorrow morning at ten," Hogan said.

"How much do we play for?" asked Chester.

"Chester, you're so rich, money means nothing to you," Hogan said. "Let's play for something real."

168   "Anything. You name it."

"If I win the bet, you and your boy both resign from this club at once and move to River Crest," Hogan said. He tilted his head to the left, listened and grinned. "You never come to Colonial again for any reason."

"But what will you lose when you lose?" asked Chester.

"If I should lose, I will resign from Colonial," Hogan said. "I'll never come here again, not even for the tournament."

"Ben . . . Ben . . . You can't do that, Ben . . ." voices pleaded.

"And to sweeten the pot, we'll play for ten thousand dollars," said Hogan.

"Make it twenty-five thousand," Chester said.

Hogan turned to Billy, who stood beside him, their eyes at just about the same level.

"First I better ask how you feel about this, Billy," Hogan said.

"Sir," Billy said, "I need to know what's in it for me if I win the bet?"

"You'll get a piece," said Hogan.

"What I want," Billy said, "is Sonny's junior membership with dues paid for a year."

Hogan laughed. "Good," he said.

"I'm the one says if it's good," Chester shouted. "And I don't believe in gambling against somebody who has got nothing to lose. If you want Sonny's membership, what will you bet against it, kid?"

Billy said, "I have six hundred dollars in cash I will put up. Every penny I have in the world." He looked at Sonny. "If I lose the bet, I swear I will leave Fort Worth and never set foot in this town again, and I will be out of your hair forever, Sonny."

"Like you matter. Don't flatter yourself," said Sonny.

"How about it, Sonny? Do we make the bet twenty-five big ones?" Chester said.

"Hell, yes," said Sonny.

"Ten thousand is mine," Hogan said.

Ira Sandpaster had been feeling disappointed in Sonny, on the basis of very little evidence, actually, but it was a feeling he had. A person who would even casually mismark his ball could never guide Ira to a 79, no matter how sweet his tempo. God would not allow it. Ira had not thought of Billy as being any kind of golfer—well, there were those shots he hit with Hogan and that notion that Hogan had taught him a secret—but if Ben Hogan thought the boy could play, Ira was inclined to think so. And there was the thrilling possibility of Chester Stonekiller resigning from the club. "I'll bet five thousand on Billy," Ira said.

Sonny looked at Dr. Sandpaster as if he had been betrayed.

"I'll cover another five grand," cried a fat man from the bar.

"Two thousand on Sonny," shouted someone from a card game.

"I got your two thousand," cried a card player from another table.

As the betting frenzy bounded back and forth in the room, Hogan said, "Will you stay over and referee the match, Harvey?"

"I'll be delighted," said Penick.

"I'll go with my boy and pull clubs for him," Hogan said to Chester. "I may read the greens for him."

"Who cares?" said Chester. "Sonny can beat that kid with one hand."

"He's got to prove it," Billy said.

"I can't wait to see you walking back to New Mexico, you country dumbass," said Sonny. "Me and Sandra will drive along behind you in her convertible and honk."

With Elvis Spaatz blocking for them, Hogan and Penick and Billy made their way through the room of agitated members, many waving wads of cash, shouting, some starting to push others. At the door to the pro shop, Hogan said to Billy, "You still have that 7-iron that belonged to John Bredemus?"

"Yes sir."

"You hit that club real well. I'll pick you a set of clubs that match it close as I can," said Hogan.

"I can get a set of clubs," Billy said, thinking of Bredemus.

"All right." Hogan tilted his head, this time to his right shoulder, listening for a moment, and then he looked back at Billy. "You're going to remember tomorrow all your life, Billy."

"Yes sir. I believe it."

Hogan turned to go. "Can I give you a ride back to your hotel, Harvey?"

"Appreciate it," said Penick.

"Mr. Penick," Billy said.

"I'm Mr. Penick's son, Harvey."

"Sir, I can't make myself call you Harvey."

"I'll have the car brought around," Hogan said. He walked out the door of the pro shop, past a number of caddies who were staring through the window.

"What is it, son?" asked Penick.

"Speaking of Mr. Bredemus . . ."

"Yes?"

"Could you tell me how he died?"

"Why, yes, I can," Penick said. "John had come through Austin and visited with me in May of 1946. He left in his new Ford and went to Big Spring, where he was remodeling the Pine Forest Country Club, doing new dirt work and planting. And he was suddenly struck down by a heart attack. A coronary occlusion. They said it was like he was hit with a hammer. He went down and was gone at the age of sixty."

Thoughts were racing through Billy's mind faster than he could review them. "You saw his body?"

"Yes, I saw his body. What is it, son? Are you some relative of John's?"

"No sir. I had heard a lot about him and admired him and didn't know he is dead, that's all."

"Play well tomorrow, Billy," Penick said and went to find Hogan.

The lights were on now in the growing darkness. Inside the men's grill the arguments were leading to violence. In the main dining room as the help set the tables and updated the menus, they were talking about the golf match, and one waiter made Sonny a ten to one favorite and began taking two-dollar bets.

Billy walked down the driveway in front of the clubhouse and saw the old black Ford waiting for him with a man in a tweed cap at the wheel. Cars were coming and going as people left after golf or arrived for dinner, but nobody seemed to notice the black Ford.

"Exciting day, Billy Boy?" said Bredemus.

Billy leaned down and looked into the large ruddy face with the broken nose and clear eyes and furrowed brow.

Billy said, "There's not a doubt in my mind that John Bredemus is dead. But there's not a doubt in my mind that you are John Bredemus. What are you? What is going on?"

"I'm hungry," said Bredemus. "Let's go to the Piccadilly."

J Twenty-one

OHN BREDEMUS turned up the volume on the car radio and refused to speak to Billy, who sat in the passenger seat staring at him, until they had passed along the magnificent food line at the Piccadilly and the older man had eaten his fill. Billy was eating hot apple pie and ice cream when Bredemus returned to the table with a fresh cup of coffee.

"How does a ghost eat real food?" Billy said.

"I wish you wouldn't call me a ghost. That word has the air of being unwanted."

"So what are you? His twin brother?"

"Would you find it impossible to believe that I am an angel?"

"Is that what you are?" Billy said.

"Do you believe in angels?"

"My mother believed in angels. She saw an angel in the street in Santa Fe and pointed him out to me. He looked like a hobo. She went to church every Sunday. Angels used to visit her. She said she never knew where or when an angel might appear. When she started getting really sick, angels came to her room constantly. I believed her, but I couldn't see them."

"You can see me, though," said Bredemus.

"You seem as real as I am. If I wasn't convinced that you are John Bredemus and John Bredemus is dead, I would think you are the weirdest con man in history."

Bredemus was wearing his elegant blue and white striped shirt such as a Princeton man would wear. He leaned his right elbow on the table to lift the coffee cup to his mouth, and Billy saw the muscles working in the arm, like the muscles work for a living person. Billy was remembering things about Bredemus that had struck him as odd from the beginning. From the moment Billy had found the lucky 7-iron in the weeds and the old black Ford had approached, there had been peculiar things like the need for secrecy, the false death.

"You lied to me," Billy said. "I was brought up to believe angels don't lie."

"It is frowned on, yes."

Billy asked, "Are you invisible to other people, the way angels sometimes are in the movies? Do the people in this cafeteria think I am talking to myself?"

Bredemus laughed, a booming roar that caused people to look around from other tables.

"You are a funny lad," he said. "Of course they can see me and hear me. If I want them to."

"What if you decide you want to be invisible?"

Suddenly Bredemus was no longer there. Coffee cooled in his cup, food was half eaten on his plates, his chair was as close to the table as when he had been sitting in it an instant ago, but Bredemus was gone.

"Hey . . ." Billy muttered. "Are you there? Please don't do this to me." Billy looked around to see if anyone was watching him. "If you're here, please let me know so they won't think I'm crazy. Send me a sign."

A plump woman in a white uniform with green trim, carrying several plastic trays, bent and picked up a piece of paper she handed to Billy.

"It's your ticket. It just fell on the floor."

"It's been paid," Billy said.

"I said it just now flew off your table and fell on the floor," the woman said.

"Thank you, ma'am. I'm sorry." Billy ate the last bite of his
174 pie with ice cream and walked out to the sidewalk in front of the

Piccadilly. The night had become cloudy, blotting out the stars and the moon, an unusually velvety dark. The old black Ford was waiting at the curb with Bredemus behind the wheel.

"All right. If you're an angel, you don't need to make me look stupid to prove it," Billy said as he got into the passenger seat.

"Sometimes it helps," said Bredemus.

The Ford turned right on Berry Street. The street lamp at the corner had burned out. Lights glowed in the windows of the frame and yellow brick houses along the street, modest homes occupied by faculty and students from Texas Christian University, a block north.

"Why me?" Billy said.

"You asked for help," said Bredemus.

"I was doing all right."

"That's not what I heard," Bredemus said. "I'm always making rounds of golf courses, and I was told to look after you."

"When?"

"At the bridge," said Bredemus.

"Did you set this whole thing up? This match with Sonny?"

"I couldn't have done it without Hennie Bogan. Or without you, Billy Boy. If you had lost heart at the proposition, it would not have happened."

Bredemus glanced out the window as he drove past a dark clubhouse that sat as the citadel for a vast black open space. "This is Worth Hills, a municipal course. I built it," Bredemus said.

"Were you an angel back then building golf courses?"

"You're like a three-year-old child with all the questions," said Bredemus.

"What do you expect?" Billy said. "There's lots of things I want to know. I want to know about my mother. I want to know about Troy. I want to know if you were an angel when you finished second to Jim Thorpe."

Bredemus turned a corner and stopped the car at the curb. The golf course lay at their feet when they got out. The night seemed very black to Billy, and there were no lights on the golf course for a long distance to the east. Billy could hardly get his bearings. He dodged the trees that grew between the car and the sidewalk.

"Is hell a real place?" asked Billy.

"Billy, I can't explain things to you," Bredemus said. "You'll have to learn for yourself. That's how it works." Bredemus opened the trunk and took out his canvas bag with seven clubs in it.

"It seems like you being an angel, you would want to open my eyes to everything," said Billy as they walked onto the dark golf course. Billy couldn't make out his own tennis shoes in the darkness, but he felt the grass on the hard earth beneath his feet.

"Sling this bag on your shoulder. These are the clubs you'll use tomorrow."

"There's only seven clubs in here."

"That's all the clubs you need to play golf."

It was so dark Billy couldn't read the numbers on the clubs, but he knew they were the driver, 4-wood, sand wedge, putter, 5-iron, 9-iron and the lucky 7-iron. He had looked in Bredemus's golf bag several times and practiced gripping and swinging the clubs.

"I balanced and matched them carefully in Harvey Penick's shop in Austin. The wooden clubs are hand-carved and weighted persimmon, the finest. I polished them in Harvey's shop, too, the day before I left for Big Spring."

"Is Big Spring where you became an angel?"

"Think of it as going from one room to another," Bredemus said.

"I don't understand."

"Billy Boy, you should always follow an angel's advice

whether you understand it or not," Bredemus said. Billy stumbled over a wooden peg in the darkness and realized they were standing on a tee box. "This is the third hole, a straightaway par four. Never mind how long it is. Just do what I tell you."

"All right."

"I have teed up a ball. I want you to take the driver and hit a shot that hugs the right edge near the street but hooks eight yards and lands far down the fairway."

"How could I do that? To start with, I can't see the ball."

"I can do it."

"Sure, you can do it. You're an angel."

"Swing the club, Billy."

"I told you I can't see the ball."

"Most golfers look at the ball without seeing it. I want you to see the ball without looking at it."

Billy made several practice swings with the driver. The club felt warm in his hands. His fingers melted into the leather grips. He could feel the clubhead and the whip of the shaft. He thought of Ted Williams. He looked down into the darkness and swung the club. To his surprise he felt the ball leave the clubface, but he knew it was a glancing hit.

They heard a window shatter in the old Ford.

"Sorry," Billy said.

"Put your mind to it, Billy Boy. Do you understand what I am asking of you?"

"To hit a trick shot blindfolded?"

Bredemus knelt and teed up another ball.

"This is nerve. It can't be taught. It has to be in you already. Your father, the captain, lost his nerve for golf. But you haven't lost yours. Yours is waiting to break forth. Your muscles know how to hit a drive that hooks eight yards back into the middle. Don't get in their way. Let them do it."

Billy felt himself relaxing at the tone of Bredemus's voice, and pleased, the sort of feeling he would have had as a child with a glass of milk and two chocolate chip cookies on the kitchen table in front of him.

He didn't know why, but he felt very confident. He swung the driver and hit a long ball that he couldn't see. It was not an eight-yard hook, Bredemus pointed out while they walked to the ball in the utter darkness, but it was a nervy hook.

They played the third and fourth holes, long par fours with hard dry fairways, with Bredemus calling the shots and Billy hitting them in the blackness. On the greens, Billy putted toward the sound of Bredemus's voice. He felt himself in what he imagined a hypnotic state might be. In the total darkness, he could see the ball without looking at it.

The fifth hole was a par three. Billy teed up his own ball. He couldn't see his feet, but he knew where the ball was, where his swing would find it. The green was lost somewhere before him in the dark.

"It's 136 yards," Bredemus said. "Take that lucky 7-iron and hit a fade that comes down three feet left and rolls into the cup."

Billy felt as if there had been no ball on the tee, but he knew there had been, and he realized he had struck it purely.

"Let's go home," Bredemus said.

"I think that shot might have gone into the hole."

"I think you're right."

"Well, let's go see," said Billy.

"No, let's go home. Leave the ball in the hole."

They walked back to the Ford and got in. The right rear window glass had showered the back seat, and a golf ball sat on the armrest. When Bredemus turned on the headlights, Billy was startled at their brightness. He had become accustomed to the dark.

Bredemus drove to the YMCA and double-parked near the front door.

"Take my golf clubs inside. They will do well for you to-morrow."

"Where are you going?"

"Now that you know my secret, I don't really need a room in the conventional sense, do I?"

"But I need you," Billy said. "It's a long night ahead."

"Walter Hagen says you should think about what you are worrying about less than anything else you think about. That makes it easy to get a good night's sleep."

"When will I see you again?"

"When you need me, I will be with you. Until then, what is it the hepcats say? 'Dig you later, alligator'?"

The old black Ford vanished and left Billy standing on the sidewalk with a canvas bag of seven clubs.

T Twenty-two

ROY HAD TOLD HIS SON it was good to be nervous the night before a big money match, but it was very bad to be scared. "If you're scared of losing, don't play," Troy had said.

In his room at the YMCA, Billy sat at the window looking at downtown Fort Worth, as he had sat at his window in Albuquerque and looked at Sandia Mountain. He realized he might be back in New Mexico by this time tomorrow night with all this behind him—Colonial Country Club, Ben Hogan, Sandra Sandpaster. Maybe the angel, John Bredemus, would leave as mysteriously as he came. Billy had bet everything, his whole poke, on four holes of golf. How like Troy that was, Billy thought. Troy had bet everything he and his son owned at the gambling tables at the 2222 Club and had lost it all. Billy noticed his cowboy boots and his hat on the floor beside his bed. If the worst happens tomorrow, I'll still have my boots and hat, he thought. I can hitchhike back to the JAL and run the fence lines with Boo.

Billy was so nervous that his stomach felt queasy, but he wasn't scared. He wished the match could start immediately. Billy wanted to win the money that was at stake—$600 of his own, plus whatever Hogan would give him—but most of all he wanted to win Sonny Stonekiller's junior membership to Colonial. There would be a satisfaction in becoming a junior member of Colonial, particularly at Sonny's expense, that was too powerful to put into words. Becoming a member of Colonial could open future doors for Billy in ways he could hardly conceive.

At last he fell asleep in the narrow bed with the lucky Bobby Jones 7-iron clutched to his breast. He awoke once with the hamstring cramping in his left leg, a sign that he was more anxious than he realized. That had happened last year on the night before he ran the mile for Albuquerque High in the state meet, but his mother and Troy had both been there to massage and encourage him. Now he was alone.

Why had Bredemus abandoned him tonight? Was this a test of courage or desire or faith? Billy rubbed the knots in his thigh and felt the muscles relax. He was imagining stepping up to the bar in the young people's grill and ordering a root beer and then sauntering out to the swimming pool and looking at Sandra Sandpaster in her bathing suit and knowing Sonny Stonekiller was banned from the property, a fallen champion. The pain went away and Billy drifted into sleep again.

Billy was up at daylight and was very hungry, which meant that his nerves were under control and his body was ready for action. He put on the white cotton polo shirt he had worn his first day at Colonial, and his jeans and tennis shoes. He washed his face and brushed his teeth and inspected his cheeks for the faint golden fuzz that was all but invisible. Billy shaved once a week whether he needed it or not, but this was not the day.

"Off to caddie at Colonial again?" said the desk clerk as Billy put his room key on the hook.

"No. Today I am playing there," Billy said.

"Sure you are," said the desk clerk, who also taught swimming and boxing. "I'm conducting the Fort Worth Symphony Orchestra today, myself."

Billy expected to find the old black Ford waiting at the curb, but he was wrong.

With the canvas bag carrying seven golf clubs slung across his back, Billy walked out of his way to go to the Paris Coffee shop because he liked the biscuits and gravy there. He intended to linger over breakfast and then spend a couple of dollars taking 181 a taxi to Colonial. A taxi would be a luxury, but why not? In a few hours it wouldn't matter either way.

"Why, here's our culprit right here," a voice said.

Burgin and Boyle sat down at Billy's table. Their pistols and nightsticks clanked against their chairs. Their badges glistened. Burgin's fifty-mission crush cap was pushed back on his head, but the creases in his shirt were sharp enough to spread butter, Billy thought. Boyle curled his lip above the gap in his teeth. Billy recognized the expression as a friendly smile. Each cop had a cup of coffee in one hand.

"Good morning, sirs," Billy said. "What have I done?"

"The Police Department got a number of complaints last night about a ruckus out at Colonial. Some furniture was broken, a window was smashed, six people were treated at emergency rooms and released. No telling how many got treated at home. I hear there are some divorces being filed today as a result of this." Boyle twirled the ashtray in his fingers. "And you're at the bottom of it, son."

"I wasn't there last night," Billy said.

"Large sums of money are being bet because of you. Violence has been committed because of you. Some say you are trying to overthrow the system and bring on socialism. Did you really go into the men's grill yesterday?"

"Yes sir. But I didn't see any violence."

Burgin said, "Hey, Billy, don't be worried. We don't care how many of those rich bastards pound each other or how many windows they break or how much they gamble. We were coming out to Colonial this morning to look at Ben Hogan and to watch you play Sonny Stonekiller for the big bucks. We know all about it."

"Car Seven is signed out today for crowd control," said Boyle.

"By the way, that day we poured your old man on the bus

for Fort Sill, he was one sick drunk," Burgin said. "I hope he got there okay."

"Yes sir, he got there just fine," said Billy.

"Eat up, boy," Burgin said. "Car Seven is taking you to Colonial this morning. If you want, we can turn on the siren. Scares the hell out of those rich bastards."

On the way to Colonial, Car Seven stopped at a field in Forest Park, and Burgin fetched his shag bag of practice balls from the trunk, where it lay on top of a twelve-gauge shotgun and a set of manacles. Burgin walked down range with the bag to shag for Billy, who hit five warm-up shots with each club except the putter. At first Billy thought about Troy and Hogan and Ted Williams and Bredemus, but after a few swings he was thinking about nothing except his target. As he had read in Captain Tanaka's *haiku,* Billy's eyes were seeing the divot before he was aware of the ball flying. He saved the driver for last. Billy called his shots, as Bredemus had done last night at Worth Hills. *Down the right edge with six yards of draw, now a ball that fades five yards, now a high ball, now a liner that rolls a long way, now a home run over the centerfield fence.* Burgin had to trot backwards a few yards for that one. Billy's drives were forty or fifty yards short of what Sonny's would be, but the distance between the back tees and the regular tees would make up for much of that.

"You got a good swing," Boyle said as they waited for Burgin to return to Car Seven with the shag bag. "Where did you learn it?"

"My daddy, mostly."

"Hogan taught you something, too."

"Yes sir. But I can't say what."

"You mean Burgin is right? Hogan has got a secret?"

"I don't know if it's a secret, but I can't tell it," Billy said.

"If you can't tell it, that makes it a secret," said Boyle.

．　．　．

BURGIN SWITCHED ON THE SIREN as Car Seven cruised the last few blocks on Mockingbird Lane, which ran south of Colonial parallel with the fifteenth fairway, separated from the course by hedges. Burgin knew there would be complaints, and the captain would chew him out, but he also knew that Ben Hogan would hear Car Seven coming, bringing his boy to the big match.

Hogan himself was coming up the fifteenth fairway driving a three-wheel golf buggy with Elvis Spaatz and Chili McWillie trotting on either side of it like bodyguards at a presidential motorcade. Hogan's legs had never stopped hurting from the bus crash. Every day he soaked and wrapped them and used them only for playing and practicing golf. By driving the buggy, he was conserving his strength for the United States Open in Detroit. Hogan was looking forward to this morning's match. Hennie Bogan had put him up to it, but Hennie was a smart little fellow who could be full of fun. Riding beside the champion was the great teacher, Harvey Penick, a stylish dresser, who wore new tan gabardine slacks and alligator shoes, a white golf shirt and a straw Panama hat. Penick was curious to see how this boy, Billy, who had shown such interest in John Bredemus, would hold up. Penick had seen Sonny Stonekiller play. It wouldn't appear to be a fair contest, but in four holes of golf anything could happen.

Between Hogan and Penick on the seat was a box inside a paper bag.

The crowd was growing around the fifteenth tee and down the fairway and onto the hill behind the green. There's 700 people here already, Burgin was estimating as he and Boyle shouldered through the crowd and led Billy to the tee box. Couldn't all be Colonial members. Word must have got out around town. Burgin saw a dozen of Sonny's football teammates in a bunch under the trees, and he saw a like number of caddies—led by the little pest Foxy Lerner and the big black Ham T—lurking in the far left of the bend in the fairway.

Then Burgin saw Hogan. For a moment Burgin was awestruck, like a child who first sees Santa Claus.

Hogan said to the two cops, "Hi, fellas. Is my boy in trouble?"

This must be how it is with my teenage daughter and Frank Sinatra, Burgin thought, trembling as he never would in the face of an armed hoodlum.

"We're looking after Billy, Mr. Hogan," Boyle said.

"Come here, Billy," Hogan said.

Hogan handed Billy the package. "Try them on," he said.

From the box Billy pulled a new pair of golf shoes made in London of brown leather.

"I think we're the same size," Hogan said. "I had an extra spike put in each of these shoes, not just the right. You'll get a firm grip on the ground with them."

Billy put on the shoes. The fit was perfect. He felt the power of the earth coming up through his feet. These shoes were so fine that "thank you" was inadequate.

"Where's Chester and his boy?" Hogan asked.

"They were at the range banging balls," said Chili.

Hogan looked at his watch. "If they're not here in five minutes, they forfeit the match."

Stepping around on the tee box, feeling his toes in his new shoes, Billy noticed Sandra Sandpaster slipping along the outer ring of the crowd. Her crazy grandfather was loping beside her, his huge yellow dentures like the teeth of a donkey, his purple glasses askew, his stringy hair stuck to his forehead with sweat. Billy wondered who Sandra would be rooting for.

Billy picked up his canvas bag and took out two clubs to make some warmup swings.

Penick slid off of his buggy seat and walked over to Billy's bag and began removing the clubs one by one, inspecting them, glancing at Billy.

"This is John Bredemus's last set of clubs. These are the very clubs he put in this very bag the day he left Austin," Penick said.

Hogan walked over, limping slightly this morning, and hefted the driver.

"Where'd you get these clubs, Billy?" Hogan said.

"I found them in the weeds beside the road in the park," said Billy.

"That's where you said you found that 7-iron," Penick said.

"Well, I went back later and found the rest of them," said Billy.

Penick was still examining Bredemus's clubs.

"Exactly the same," said Penick. "I remember the little nick he put in the head of his 4-wood—see, right here? He did it in my shop hours before he left Austin. He loved this 4-wood. Look at the oiled grips and the shiny shafts and heads. I feel like I saw these clubs yesterday."

"This is how they were when I found them," Billy said.

"Why were you asking about John Bredemus? Where did you hear of him?" said Penick.

"Dr. Sandpaster talked on and on about Mr. Bredemus the first day I was at Colonial," Billy said.

"Hadn't you rather have a complete set of clubs?" asked Hogan.

"I'm comfortable with these."

Where had Bredemus gone? Why had the angel left him to face this?

"All right, Hogan. Let's tee it up."

Chester Stonekiller emerged from the crowd. He wore a blue and white Hawaiian shirt that covered his round belly but left his brown arms free to hold a cigar and a glass that was either orange juice or orange juice with vodka. Behind him came

Sonny, darkly handsome, black hair shining, a sneer on his face. Trailing Sonny was a waiter carrying a thermos for Chester.

"Take over, Harvey," said Hogan.

Penick held a coin on his right thumb covered by his left hand.

"You call it," he said to Sonny.

"Heads."

"Heads it is. It's your honor. Hit away."

"We already decided. It's Sonny's honor on every hole," said Chester.

B Twenty-three

ILLY WAS STANDING in the light rough on the left edge of the fifteenth fairway, looking down at his new handmade shoes from London and at his ball that sat up in an inch of grass. The new shoes had given Billy such an unexpectedly strong grip on the earth that he had swung too hard and hooked his drive about 220 yards. Sonny had cracked his opening drive 290 yards. Even with the difference in the back tees and the regular tees on this hole, Sonny was thirty yards in front of Billy and in perfect position at the slight dogleg.

Chili McWillie and Elvis Spaatz were in the middle of the fairway, holding back the crowd. Billy saw people lining the fairway on the left side and surrounding the green. There must be a thousand of them, he thought. Burgin and Boyle kept the crowd from getting too close to the golf buggy bearing Hogan and Penick. Hogan got out of the buggy and stood beside Billy. Hogan scratched his chin and lit a cigarette and studied Billy's shot.

"It's 168 to the middle, pin is back left so add 10, slight rise, all carry, make it 181," Hogan said. "Hit the 5-iron."

Billy wanted to hit the 4-wood.

"Sir."

"The ball is going to jump out of that lie," Hogan said.

"Yes sir," said Billy.

Billy was doubting the 5-iron was the correct club when he struck the ball in its middle and cut an ugly smile in its cover. The ball spun and wobbled and careened like a Mexican jumping bean and rolled to a stop six feet behind where Sonny stood waiting, leaning against his canvas bag, showing the expression of disdain that girls said made him look dangerous.

Billy looked at Hogan, feeling humiliated. He heard the crowd laughing.

"Slash, slash, chop, chop," Hogan said.

Billy walked thirty yards to his ball and bent over and looked at the gash in it. Hogan and Penick drove over in the golf buggy. Chester Stonekiller was walking with his boy. Chester had another orange drink with plenty of ice in a tall glass.

"We want to take this ball out of play," Hogan said.

"When the hole is finished," said Chester, "you can change it."

"Harvey?" Hogan said. "We need a ruling, please."

Penick looked at the damaged ball and said, "Billy may replace his ball if his opponent agrees. Otherwise, he replaces this ball at the end of the hole."

"Play it as it lays," said Chester.

"Aw, let him have it," Sonny said. "He's dead meat."

Hogan tossed a new ball onto the fairway. Billy was still away. Hogan stood beside him, a forefinger to his chin, studying the situation. Billy looked closely at each of Hogan's shoulders but could see no evidence of a guardian angel riding there.

"I make it 141 plus 10, plus the rise, call it 155," Hogan said. "Use that 7-iron and bring it in there left to right."

Billy wanted to hit the 5-iron. He felt the distance was too great for his 7-iron. He could hit a 7-iron that far if he had to do it, but it felt wrong this time. His swing was out of rhythm, his mind distracted—the name *Ted Williams* winked inside his head like a neon sign—and his club caught the turf behind the ball. Billy's shot came down in the swale ten yards short of the green.

"You're just homesick, country boy. You want to go back to the wild west with the sagebrush and the jackasses," Sonny said, standing behind his ball to line up his shot.

Sonny hit a 9-iron shot onto the green twenty feet from the cup. He spun the club in his hands, lightly, in control, and then settled it into his bag and walked toward the applause, his collar flipped up so that his black hair tufted over it.

"Hogan, you are about to get screwed like a tied-up goat," said Chester.

Billy was reaching for the 9-iron to pitch the ball up and onto the green when he heard Hogan say, "Take your 5-iron and run it up there." Billy used the 5-iron and hit a pitch-and-run shot that stopped forty feet short of the pin. Hogan limped out of the cart and squatted to line up Billy's putt. Billy had lined up this same putt twice while caddying yesterday. It was uphill, into the grain and dead straight. Hogan rose, his knees creaking. "Four inches to the right, and give it a rap," Hogan said.

Aiming the putt four inches to the right, Billy realized this was the correct line for Hogan but not the correct line for Billy. The difference was in how hard each one would hit the ball— straight worked for one, a four-inch break worked for the other. Same with the rest of the clubs. Hogan's concept of distance was uniquely Hogan's, just as Billy's concept of distance was uniquely his own. But as Billy was understanding this, he swung his putter and left the ball ten feet short of the cup. Laying five. Sonny was ten feet farther from the cup and lay two.

While Sonny studied his putt, Billy's eyes swept the crowd, looking for Sandra Sandpaster. He saw the crazy old doctor behind the green with his cronies, but Sandra appeared not to be with them. Billy's eyes roamed farther left, along rows of faces he recognized from caddying and of faces that did truly belong to caddies.

He saw John Bredemus leaning against the wall that protected the fifteenth green from the creek that flowed behind it. He wore his tweed cap and was in shirtsleeves but carried a suit jacket. He gave Billy a little wave and a nod.

Sonny putted to within a foot of the cup. He casually rapped in the next putt for a par four.

Billy was looking at Bredemus, trying to determine whether the angel was visible to those around him.

"Are you listening to me?" Hogan said, having lined up the ten-foot putt.

"Yes sir. I've got it," Billy said.

Billy hadn't heard what Hogan had said, but he did know this putt.

The ball made a satisfying rattle as it fell into the cup, and some in the crowd applauded. But the putt was for a double bogey six. Billy was two shots behind already. Billy quickly plucked the ball out of the cup and walked across the green and pushed through the crowd—he heard Dr. Ira Sandpaster telling his colleagues that Billy was proof Hogan had no secret—until he stood facing Bredemus.

"In my original design of this hole, I put this green across the creek back behind me," Bredemus said. "Made the hole a severe test. Marvin Leonard—that's him in the straw fedora—who put up the money to build Colonial, asked me to change it. Marvin said a long approach over water is too difficult for most golfers. I agree. Golf courses should be fun for everyone. But if I had put the green back there across the creek, I could have built a tee up there and made the sixteenth a long downhill par three over water, a type of hole I love."

Billy heard voices around him.

"What is he doing? Why is he staring at that wall?"

"Is he going to jump in the water?"

"He is sucking in universal waves." That, he knew, was Sandpaster.

"Is he sick?"

"Is he quitting?"

"Maybe the boy has got to pee." That was Dr. Kemp.

So Bredemus was invisible. Only Billy could see and hear him. The crowd around Billy thought the boy was in a mental condition. Billy chose carefully what he would ask. At least two dozen people were bending close to look at him and would hear what he said.

"You see the problem I am having," Billy said.

Voices began answering at once. "Hell yes, you're looking up . . . Your grip is too weak . . . The problem is you're not worth a damn . . . Who do you think you are? . . . You're out of your class . . . Your backswing is too long." Nearly everyone within hearing had an answer to what was wrong with Billy. But he waited and let them talk while Bredemus looked him in the eye and smiled and nodded.

"You know what to do about it," Bredemus said.

Billy turned and started toward the sixteenth tee. He saw Burgin and Boyle guarding the bridge across the creek, urging Billy forward.

"One thing, Billy," called Bredemus.

Billy looked back, but Bredemus was gone. Instead, Billy heard his voice say, *Above all, be cheerful.*

G
Twenty-four

UARDED BY BURGIN AND BOYLE, Hogan stood with Penick in the front row of the crowd behind the championship tee box of the sixteenth hole, a par three with a pond in front. Sonny saw them as he stretched an arm toward his golf bag to select a club. Sonny also saw Sandra Sandpaster, her trim brown legs, her tight body in shorts and a low cut blouse. Beside her was her grandfather, the rich old fool. Sonny had become a frequent member of the Sandpaster foursome because he wanted the idiot's endorsement with Sandra, not to help him shoot his age. Sonny believed the old man would never shoot his age. Sonny would be happier if Sandpaster would go ahead and die.

"We saw Mr. Hogan hit a 7-iron from here the other day," Sonny said loudly. "I guess it's a solid 8-iron for me."

"Sonny, that's close to 200 yards back to that pin," Chester said.

"You think I can't hit an 8-iron 200 yards?"

"I'm sure you can, but there's no reason to prove it here," said Chester. "Cuddle it up there with a 5- or 6-iron."

"No, this is a 7-iron for Mr. Hogan and me."

"You hit a 4-iron from here last time," Chester said.

"Watch this."

Sonny's 7-iron shot carried short of the middle of the green and spun backwards down the slope until it stopped in the fringe, leaving him a curling uphill putt of ninety feet.

Hogan cocked his head to the left and muttered, "He swallowed the bait." Penick looked around, not sure he had heard

Hogan's voice in the noise of the crowd that jostled toward the regular tee box where Billy waited.

Billy watched Hogan walking toward him but looking toward the green. Billy was frightened by the enormous thing he was about to do, but the boy breathed deeply and summoned his courage. Before Hogan could describe the shot and name a club to hit, Billy spoke.

"Mr. Hogan, sir, I have bet all my money and my future on this match. I want to choose my own clubs and read my own putts."

The hawk eyes pierced him for an uncomfortable moment but then began to soften, and Hogan gave Billy a tight little Gary Cooper grin.

"All right," Hogan said. "Go get him, Billy."

Hogan walked off the tee and motioned for Penick to follow him to the golf buggy.

"I'm the referee, Ben. I have to see this shot," Penick said. "What did the boy say to you?"

"He wants to choose his own clubs."

"Well, that's what you would have done if you were in his place," said Penick.

"Yeah." Hogan lit a cigarette. "I would. That kid has nerve. Let's settle back and watch some golf, Harvey. I want to see how this comes out."

John Bredemus strolled onto the tee box and said, "Nicely done, Billy Boy. Now what do you have in mind for this shot?"

Billy did not answer. He was not going to be seen talking to thin air by this crowd, which was growing larger. Billy caught a glimpse of Sandra Sandpaster among the people who gathered in a many-colored semicircle around the green, but then she ducked out of sight again. Billy looked at the pin on a shelf at the rear of the green. It was 169 yards from where Billy stood to the middle of the green, and another thirty feet back to the pin. Call it 180 yards. He felt he could hit the middle of the green with the 5-iron, but the ball might roll back down near Sonny's. There was no advantage to that. A 3-iron would have been Billy's club of choice, but Bredemus's bag did not contain a 3-iron. Billy had learned from Hogan that distance is in large part mental. If he felt the shot was right, it was right. If it felt wrong, don't hit it.

Voices muttered, "He's reaching for a wooden club . . . That's what I hit, too . . . Yeah, but you've got arthritis . . ."

He pulled out the 4-wood and set the ball on a low tee. Billy gripped down an inch on the club. He held the shaft up at a forty-five-degree angle to get the feeling of the clubhead and the touch of his grip pressure. He made a practice swing. He looked at the flag. He set his spikes in the earth, waggled the club and hit the shot exactly as he had pictured it—a high fading ball that seemed to disappear against the white clouds in the pale blue sky and then reappeared and dropped onto the shelf at the rear of the green, bounced once, struck the fringe and rebounded to stop fifteen feet from the cup.

The shouts and applause washed over Billy and thrilled him.

"Don't get caught up in the roar of the crowd," Bredemus said. "Your next shot is the only important one now."

Chili McWillie fell in beside Billy to escort him to the green. Bredemus walked on the other side of Billy. He had one of the toughest guys in Fort Worth at one shoulder and an invisible angel at the other. "Lay the lumber to his ass, Billy. The yard is pulling for you," Chili said. Bredemus was whistling, "The White Cliffs of Dover," an old World War Two tune that Billy had heard on the radio when he was a child. The tune did have a calming and cheering effect on Billy but not on the surging mob who couldn't hear it. Chili pushed people out of their way. "Hot stuff! Coming through!" Chili kept saying.

Sonny's first putt rolled up to the edge of the rear shelf,

seemed to hesitate, then trickled onto the plateau and stopped twenty feet short of the cup.

"You're still away," Billy said.

Sonny glared at him and missed his next putt by one foot.

"Pick it up," Billy said, giving Sonny the bogey four.

"Can't pick it up. This is stroke play," said Penick.

Sonny sank the putt and then said, "Let's see you gag on this one, country boy."

Billy looked at the fifteen-foot putt from both sides of the hole, as Troy had taught him. The grain was running toward the hole. It was a very fast putt. If Billy hit it too hard, the ball could go over the edge and roll all the way down to the front of the green.

Billy read the putt as breaking three inches to the left. That's how he would have read it for the golfers who hired him to caddie, and it looked correct for him as a player.

As Billy started to address the ball, Bredemus said, "No, no. Over here."

Billy looked up. Bredemus was standing six inches short of the cup and six inches to the right of it. Bredemus put his heels together and spread out his feet. "Stroke the ball as if the cup is right between my heels."

Billy shook his head.

"Billy Boy, I built this green with my own hands. Stroke your ball between my heels, into the triangle."

Billy looked around at the crowd. The faces were a blur, and they had become silent. They were intent on Billy's every move. They couldn't see Bredemus standing in front of and beside the hole, marking off a six-inch break and a spot far enough in front of the cup that Billy would not hit his ball over the edge. Billy changed his aim. He lined up his putt to go between those two massive calves. Billy stroked the ball and watched it roll into its target. Billy wasn't sure but it seemed to him that Bredemus might have flinched one heel a bit and deflected the ball ever so slightly.

The ball rolled into the cup for a birdie two, and the crowd exploded with applause and with shouts of surprise.

The match was even.

B
Twenty-five

REDEMUS WAS LOOKING down the fairway as they waited for Sonny to hit his tee ball on the par-four seventeenth hole that measured 383 yards from the back tees and 364 from the regular tees that Billy was using.

"Every time I see Big Annie, I remember the day I decided to remove it," Bredemus said, pointing to the towering pecan tree beside the distant green. "It's a beautiful tree, and I love trees, but hot and humid as it gets here in the summer, that green needs air circulation to keep it healthy. A golf course is a living organism that must breathe, the way a person must breathe to stay alive and well. A growth that hampers breathing should be cut away. I had a crew of men and mules digging at the roots of Big Annie when Marvin Leonard and Ira Sandpaster rushed out there, and Marvin told me to stop. He was the boss, so I stopped. There's a story that I quit and walked off the job. But I wouldn't do that. It was Marvin's money I was spending. He wanted Big Annie to stay, and there it is."

They heard the smack of Sonny hitting a 1-iron off the tee and saw the ball come down in the left rough. The crowd pressed forward. Chili McWillie took Billy by the arm and pushed their way onto the regular tee box. Bredemus followed them, floating through the crowd as easily as a puff of gas.

As he placed his ball on a tee, Billy said, "That putt on the last hole feels kind of like cheating."

"Angels don't cheat at golf. I was giving you guidance," said Bredemus.

"He's talking to himself again," said a voice in the gallery.

"You didn't kick it in?" Billy said.

"The ball hit a spike mark," said Chili McWillie. "How could I have kicked it?"

"I want to beat this guy on my own," Billy said.

"On the fifteenth tee you were wondering where I was, so I made my appearance, and now you are telling me you don't want me?" said Bredemus.

"I appreciate all you've done for me, but I need to do this thing for myself," Billy said.

"Is he praying?" asked a voice in the gallery.

"He might be a half wit."

"Did he say he cheated on that last putt?"

"How could he cheat? We were watching."

"Who the hell is he talking to?"

Billy pulled the driver out of the bag and glanced around to read the expression on Bredemus's face, looking for approval.

But the angel had vanished again.

"Hey, Billy, you sure a driver ain't too much?" asked Chili McWillie.

"I'm going to knock it up there in front of the green and birdie this sucker," Billy said.

"Don't hit it into that ditch," said Chili.

"Go ahead and put it in the ditch," a gallery voice said.

"Skull it," another voice said.

"You people shut up," said Chili McWillie.

Billy took aim at Big Annie and waggled the driver. He intended to hit a fade that would leave him 120 yards short of the green with an open shot to the pin. Billy felt he hit the driver hard, and it flew 240 yards. But the ball paused in the air at the end, as though it had struck a disturbance of some kind, like a gust of wind, and hooked into the deep rough farther left than Sonny's ball.

Both players' approaches to the green were blocked by Big Annie.

Striding along the fairway, with Chili McWillie protecting him from the crowd that fell in at his heels and poured onto the course, jostling, shouting, Billy passed Sonny, who stood beside his bag in the rough.

"You don't suppose Sonny would improve his lie in front of all these people, do you?" Billy said.

"I heard that," said Sonny.

"I'll save him from temptation," said Chili, who dropped off to watch Sonny's shot.

"Are you saying you don't trust me, Chili? I thought you liked your job," Sonny said.

"I love my job, Sonny. But in two more holes you won't have any say-so about it."

"You're as good as fired right now," said Sonny.

"I might point out that if I don't work here, you ain't got no more free pass from a butt kicking, and that goes for your whole football team," Chili said.

"What's got into you?" said Sonny. "You've never talked to me like that. We're friends."

"Shows you how wrong a body can be," Chili said.

Sonny was 143 yards from the green. He could hook the ball around Big Annie, but it would not be likely to stay on the putting surface. For a player of his skill, Sonny could hit it over a tree even as tall as Big Annie, and let it fall in a left-to-right fade and stick on the green, if he hit a perfect shot.

"Damn you, Sandpaster," Chester yelled at the scientist whose long feet were slashing through the grass. "We should have cut Big Annie down years ago. You and Marvin should have left John Bredemus alone."

"You redskins should have burned Christopher Columbus at the stake," said Ira.

200   Billy found his ball in two inches of rough. Being farther left

than Sonny, Billy's shot made him look at Big Annie as if the tree were a goalie protecting the net. Billy was 124 yards from the middle of the green. He felt if he could hit the 9-iron high enough to clear the tree it would not go far enough to reach the green. He remembered Ben Hogan hitting the 128 yard 7-iron on the tenth hole, but that was from the fairway and required a talent that in Billy was undeveloped.

Three dozen people pressed around him, trampling the grass, breathing on him, stretching their necks to see what club he would choose. Billy heard them whispering, "Stick a fork in him . . . I hit that damn tree on this hole every time no matter where my tee ball is . . . Where is Hogan? He's right over there in his buggy . . . See the two cops? . . . I wish I had a buggy . . . You'll never see buggies on this golf course as a regular thing, I can guarantee you that . . ."

Suddenly Ira Sandpaster loomed above him, grinning with his big yellow dentures, peering at Billy through purple glasses. Mr. Titus, who watched the money, was mashed against Sandpaster by the gallery but kept his cigarette in his lips.

"I have bet five thousand dollars on you, Billy," Ira said. "But don't let that make you nervous. I tell you this to show you what faith I have in you, to pump up your confidence."

"I won't even think about it," Billy said, thinking about it.

"I know this shot well," said Ira. "Big Annie has adored me since I saved her life. Waves of universal energy flow from pecans and pecan tree bark . . ."

"Please, sir," Billy said, "would you be quiet?"

"I'm saying a tree is more than ninety percent air."

They heard the whack of Sonny's shot, saw the ball rising above Big Annie's grasp, only to nick a tiny limb at the very top and be tossed down into the sand trap at the left of the green.

"It's okay, Sonny," Chester said. "Up and down for four. The kid is hopeless over there." Chester yelled, "Hey, Sandpaster! Your beloved tree is about to cost you five grand."

"Ignore that fool," Sandpaster said to Billy. "He'll stoop to anything to impede you."

"Dr. Sandpaster, you are standing directly in my way," said Billy.

"Oh. Sorry."

Billy had never truly made up his mind what shot he wanted to hit, but he used the 7-iron and hoped it would carry over Big Annie but not over the green.

His ball struck Big Annie in the center of her trunk and bounded to the right, into the fairway, leaving him seventy yards short of the green.

"I would have played it farther to the right and higher," said Ira.

Billy slammed the 7-iron into the canvas bag. He knew what he had done wrong. He had hit a shot he was not committed to. He had hit it and hoped. The confidence he had felt on the sixteenth hole had never truly returned. His hooked drive on seventeen was early proof of that. Now he had struck his second shot straight into a tree. Well, how was he supposed to keep his mind on the game, he thought, with all these people crushing around him, with Dr. Sandpaster braying at him, with Sandra watching him from the crowd, with a long, forlorn hitchhike back to Albuquerque staring at him?

Above all, be cheerful.

Where had that come from? Where was Bredemus?

Billy realized he had not hit a good shot since he had told the angel to get lost.

Okay, please come back, Billy thought, walking to his ball while the crowd swirled around him.

But Bredemus did not appear. Billy thought he would try being cheerful. He began to whistle "The White Cliffs of Dover." He heard the voices around him: "He's lost his mind . . . Whistling in the graveyard . . . He's too young to know that song . . . Look, his ball is in a divot with a downhill lie . . ."

Billy pulled the 7-iron out of the bag. He rubbed the shaft and in his mind apologized to the club for treating it roughly. He kept his thoughts light and cheerful. It was an ugly divot his ball had landed in, but he tried to stay positive as he regarded the situation. He pictured the shot like a Kodak portrait in his mind. He would play the ball back toward his right foot and bump it up to the top of the hill and bounce it onto the green and run it close to the cup. He tried not to think of Ben Hogan and Harvey Penick back there watching, of Sandra Sandpaster, of her crazy old grandfather and his five-thousand-dollar wager, of running a fence line with Boo. But in trying not to think of those things, he thought of them. His mind was not pure as it had been when he hit the 4-wood on the previous hole.

His chip shot bounced onto the green but stopped twenty-five feet short of the pin.

"Okay, Sonny, the door is wide open," Chester said. "You slam it shut. Clip about two inches of sand out from under your ball and lay it next to the cup."

"Don't tell me how to hit a bunker shot," said Sonny.

"Well, excuse the hell out of me," Chester said, swigging from his tall orange drink. "There was a time when you would ask your old daddy how to do it."

"That time is long gone," said Sonny.

"Then you better hit it close, smartass," Chester said.

Sonny hit the shot thin and the ball came down on the far edge of the green, a yard off the putting surface. Chester turned his back and lit a cigar to keep from saying anything. Sonny glared at his father, then climbed out of the bunker and picked up his bag.

"I believe we have some dissension in the enemy camp," Hogan said to Harvey Penick.

Burgin, who was standing now between his idol and the great teacher, said, "Our side caught a break that time."

"You're pulling for Billy?" said Hogan.

"Me and my pardner discovered that boy," Burgin said.

Sonny hit his chip more quickly than usual and his ball rolled four feet past the cup. Chester grunted. Sonny smoothed back his long black hair and then marked his ball without looking at his father.

Billy paced the green and looked at the hole from both sides and got down on his knees to read the slope and the growth of the grass. He studied it until he began to feel a stirring in the gallery and heard someone say, "Is he ever gonna hit it?" Billy felt he was sure of the line but not of the speed. He made two practice strokes and then hit the putt and saw the ball die inches short of the cup. It was a bogey five.

It seemed to Chester that his boy was pretty careless with the next putt, showing the arrogant attitude that he had inherited from his mother, Lowatha Bird, like it didn't matter if the ball went into the cup.

But the ball fell into the middle of the cup, and the match was tied heading into the final hole.

Twenty-six

ELVIS SPAATZ helped to clear a path for Sonny and Chester Stonekiller to walk through the crowd to the championship tee of the eighteenth hole.

"I like it here at Colonial Country Club," Chester said. He blew a smoke ring and sipped his orange drink. "They got fruitcakes in the club like Ira Sandpaster, but in general they got a good bunch of guys. And Sandpaster has this cute little granddaughter that we think so much of. I really enjoy my life here at Colonial Country Club, Sonny. Don't you?"

"Yes, dad. I like it here a lot," said Sonny.

"I'm glad to hear that. Coming from the club champion, that has real meaning. You want to keep your membership here so bad, there's no way you could fail to beat a little creep like Billy, is there?"

"No way."

They could see the green 427 yards away with the clump of trees far down on the left side, and beyond the trees lay the blue pond. There were clusters of people all down the right side of the fairway and on up the hill to the clubhouse where the crowd had spread out on the bank above the green. People crowded onto the deck and pressed against the windows on the second floor of the red brick clubhouse. It made Chester shiver to think how fond he was of this place, of the camaraderie, even of the Indian jokes. As long as he was rich these people were good companions. That would not be the case at River Crest, where the members had been rich longer.

Frowning with determination, Sonny stepped up to his tee ball and drove it 280 yards favoring the right side of the fairway. They saw his ball come down on the slope and roll into the middle and settle on a flat sheet of short grass with a clear view to the pin less than 150 yards farther.

"Great drive," said Chester. "That'll make him taste his chili."

"Speaking of chili, I want Chili McWillie fired when we get to the clubhouse," Sonny said.

"Sonny, I can't think of anyone who would walk up to Chili McWillie and tell him he is fired," said Chester.

"Elvis will do it. Or we'll fire Elvis, too."

Chester shook the ice in his tall orange drink and waved to the waiter for more of it.

"Please, son, put your mind on the game," Chester said. "You throw a dart in there and make a three. We'll fire people later."

Twenty-five yards down the fairway, Billy and Chili McWillie stepped out of the crowd and onto the regular tee box. Billy heard rustling, muttering sounds, as if the entire gallery was shifting from foot to foot and discussing Billy's chances. He didn't look for Ben Hogan's golf buggy or for Sandra Sandpaster's brown legs. Billy breathed deeply to calm himself and thought back to the last good shot he had hit. It was the 4-wood off the tee at sixteen. Billy was trying to recapture that feeling. What was the difference between then and now, except that then there had been an angel at his side?

"Remember, boy, never uncock your wrists!" shouted Ira Sandpaster from the crowd.

Billy pulled out the driver, and the notion came to him that he might be squeezing the club too hard. As he had done with the 4-wood, Billy held the driver shaft at a forty-five-degree angle and gripped it loosely. He made a practice swing keeping the pressure light in his hands. From behind the ball, Billy selected a small target—someone wearing red seated on the bank above the fairway. Then he addressed the ball, waggled once and hit the best drive of his young life.

The ball carried 250 yards straight at the person in red. But when it came down in the right edge of the fairway, the ball landed on a Dr Pepper bottle that someone had tossed there. Making a clank, the ball bounced forward and to the left, rolled past Sonny's ball and careened down the slope to stop finally under the limbs of a tree.

"Aw, man, that's an awful break," said Chili McWillie. "You hit that ball dead solid perfect. This game ain't fair."

Billy remembered Troy used to call that the death song of losers. Billy could hear Troy saying, "What's not fair is that I am better than them, but if they want to blame it on bad luck, it keeps them coming back for more." Walking down the fairway, Billy appraised the situation. The cheerful side was that Billy was nearly ten yards closer to the green than Sonny was. On the other hand, Billy had the tree to deal with.

"How about that? Sonny is the short knocker," Chili said as he and Billy drew near Sonny and Chester.

"I was kidding back there, Chili," Sonny said, feeling at ease with his position in the match and in a forgiving mood. The country boy had a tough shot from down there under the tree with the flag in the front part of the green and the blue pond yawning beside the bunker. "You can stay. You're a good first caddie."

Chester smiled at this and puffed his cigar. Chester didn't want anybody fired. Chester wanted to resume his normal life of spending six days a week at Colonial Country Club and one at his office. Also Chester wanted the satisfaction of collecting ten thousand dollars from the great Ben Hogan in front of his colleagues. Chester figured Hogan was not serious about resigning from Colonial if he lost the bet. That was just so much mouth. Why, this was Hogan's home course. Marvin Leonard wouldn't let him quit. But if Hogan did quit, the hell with him. Chester took a gulp of his orange drink. Sonny was the best player at this club, anyhow. If the others got mad about Hogan quitting and blamed it on Chester, the hell with them, too. They'd just have to get over it. Chester was far too wealthy for anyone to stay mad at him for long.

Chili's voice broke Chester's reverie.

Chili said, "Maybe you'll put in a good word for me when you move over to River Crest."

Chester moaned at the thought. He watched Chili join Billy under the tree on the other side of the fairway. "Don't worry," Sonny said. "We're staying right here, dad. Imagine how mad mother would be if we resigned from Colonial?"

Chester shut his eyes. He considered the fury of Lowatha Bird if she was barred from her bridge games.

He heard the strike of Sonny's ball and opened his eyes to see it come down on the green about fifteen feet past the flag.

"Great shot," Chester said.

"You knew I could do it."

"Never had a doubt," said Chester.

Beneath the tree, Billy squatted and studied his shot. He had seen Sonny's ball land near the cup. Troy had told him to expect your opponent to hit a good shot. Hoping for a bad shot and being surprised by a good one was damaging to the spirit, Troy would say.

What would Billy answer if Ben Hogan asked him how far it was to the pin?

Billy was estimating the range at 142 yards when John Bredemus stepped out from behind the tree.

"Would you do me a favor, Chili? Would you ask those people to move back? I can hear them talking," Billy said.

When Chili had gone, Billy looked up at Bredemus and said, trying not to move his lips, "What should I do?"

"Use the 7-iron and hit it low."

"I was thinking about running the 5-iron up there."

Bredemus removed his tweed cap and wiped his furrowed forehead. Billy had never before wondered if angels sweat. Somewhere Bredemus had discarded his suit coat. He had rolled up his trousers several turns, exposing the tapering of his muscular calves into his drooping socks. Bredemus's shoes were spattered with mud, as though he might have jumped across the pond and not quite made it.

"Billy Boy, I know more about this golf course than anyone living or, uh, otherwise," Bredemus said. "I am your guardian angel and am offering you guidance. And that is a very lucky 7-iron. You say you want to do this on your own. But nobody does anything by themselves, Billy. Will you accept my guidance?"

"All right," Billy said. "I accept it."

Billy gripped down two inches on the 7-iron and played the ball back in his stance to keep the shot low. He glanced at the tree branch that partly hid the green from his view. The 7-iron shaft would hit that branch on the follow through. But Billy thought only of a spot at the front of the green. That spot appeared in his mind as if painted gold.

Billy waggled and then swung through the ball, the lucky 7-iron shaft stopping as it touched the branch. Billy couldn't see where the ball had gone, but it had felt right. He heard shouts and applause from around the green.

"You bounced on and rolled up ten feet short of the cup," Bredemus said. "Hennie Bogan tells me Ben is already celebrating. If Sonny misses, as I believe he will, you have two putts and you win your bet."

"But Sonny will make a four," Billy said.

"There he goes again, jabbering to nobody," cried someone in the gallery.

"Hell of a shot, Billy," Chili said.

"The bet is that Sonny has to beat you, not tie you. Two putts for each of you. Two fours, and you win," said Bredemus.

"That's wrong," Billy said. "I should have to beat Sonny, not tie him."

"You didn't invent this bet—you're just playing the game. It's not for you to change the rules at the end," said Bredemus. "If you could see Chester now, you would believe you have won. Chester has realized he may have lost the thing he holds most dear next to money, which is Colonial Country Club. Why, I believe Chester just said a prayer."

"This doesn't feel right," Billy said as they walked toward the green.

"Something bothering you?" said Chili.

"I should have to make my putt," said Billy.

"Hey, man, don't pull against yourself," Chili said.

Billy stepped onto the green and marked his ball. He saw Ben Hogan up on the hill beside the clubhouse, guarded by two blue uniforms, with his arms folded and a cigarette in his mouth. Harvey Penick walked out of the crowd and onto the green. As referee, Penick was watching the final putts. Billy avoided looking at the crowd again. He watched Bredemus walk over to crouch down beside Sonny, who was lining up his putt. Bredemus shook his head. "He is missing it on the low side," Bredemus said in a voice only Billy could hear. Chester knelt at the edge of the green so people could see over him. He put a hand inside his Hawaiian shirt and felt the pounding of his heart. Great Spirit, please come and help my boy, Chester thought. And since he belonged to the Disciples of Christ, Chester added pleas to God and Jesus and the Mother Mary. Chester promised he would reform. He would go to the University Christian Church on Sundays before golf. He would sponsor a missionary to China.

Sonny propped his putter against one knee as he stood up and smoothed his long black hair with both hands. Sonny flashed his white smile. He stroked the putt. The ball dropped into the center of the cup. The crowd erupted with cheers. Chester cried out to all the gods, "Thank you! Thank you!" Sonny had made a birdie three.

As he plucked his ball out of the cup, Sonny looked at Billy and gently rubbed his throat, as though he had sore glands, but everyone realized he was making the choking sign.

"You asked for it," Chili said to Billy. "Now you got to make it."

Billy looked at his ten-foot putt from below the hole. Then he walked above the hole and studied it. Bredemus stood beside him and watched. Billy returned to the ball and pictured its path toward the cup. Bredemus said, "Do you still have faith in my guidance, Billy boy?"

Billy nodded.

Bredemus planted himself twelve inches past the hole and three inches left of it from Billy's point of view. Bredemus placed his heels together and spread the toes of his shoes to make a triangle, as he had done on the sixteenth.

"The rest is up to you," Bredemus said. "You must stroke it yourself."

Billy rolled the ball between Bredemus's heels and it toppled into the cup for a birdie three.

"Like a mouse going home!" yelled Chili McWillie, pounding Billy on the back and almost knocking him to his knees. Sonny stared at the hole in shock. As Billy lifted his ball from the cup, he heard the crowd screaming and realized how silent they had been—or how he had closed them out. "Well done," said Bredemus.

"Thank you," Billy said. He was speaking to Bredemus, but he appeared to be addressing the crowd.

"You take it from here, Billy Boy," said Bredemus. "I have to keep making my rounds."

Bredemus disappeared. Looking at where Bredemus had been, Billy saw across the blue pond to the forest that hid the caddie yard.

Harvey Penick shook Billy's hand and said, "Well played." Up in the crowd on the terrace, Billy saw Ben Hogan take off his cap and wave, as did Burgin and Boyle.

Chester Stonekiller straightened his spine and pulled forth his dignity.

He walked to Billy and shook his hand.

"That was a brave putt, kid. Congratulations. I'm not gonna hand you six hundred dollars with everybody looking on, but I will leave it for you with Elvis in the pro shop. My lawyer will write up the transfer of Sonny's junior membership to you, starting this afternoon, with one year's dues paid. I hope you enjoy it. I really do. But let me warn you of the facts. You're just a caddie who had a lucky day. You can't even afford to eat dinner here."

BURGIN AND BOYLE drove Billy back to the YMCA in Car Seven. Billy sat in the back seat with a Colonial Country Club towel— one of the big ones from the men's locker room—covering his shoulders. His blond hair was flat and dripping. In the celebration, Chili McWillie and the guys from the yard had carried Billy around on their shoulders and then, the ultimate tribute, had thrown him into the pond.

Billy was on his way to his room for a change of clothes. It seemed this day had lasted forever, but it was only noon.

"When you made that putt back there on sixteen, I was telling Ben you had won him the bet," Burgin said.

"Did you get Ben's autograph?" asked Boyle.

"Hell, yes."

"Me, too."

Car Seven stopped in front of the YMCA and Billy got out.

"Thanks for the ride," Billy said.

"You call us any time, kid," said Burgin. "Tell Ben to do the same."

As he entered the lobby of the YMCA, Billy heard the desk clerk calling his name.

"That's him. Right there," the desk clerk said.

A postman had a thick brown envelope.

"Certified mail. Sign here," said the postman.

Billy looked at the return address: Department of the Army.

"Where'd you play golf at, in a swamp? Somebody has got to mop up this water," the desk clerk said.

But Billy was tearing open the envelope as he walked toward the elevator. Riding up to his floor, he began reading the document. His mouth dropped open. He was stunned. He finished reading the legal language by the time he reached his door. He turned the envelope upside down and shook it.

Two government checks fluttered to the floor.

M Y POKE

Twenty-seven

Billy wrote those words at the top of a sheet of paper on his desk in his room.

> $77,723.50—Troy's life insurance policy
> $3,000—my cut from Hogan
> $600—winning from Stonekiller
> $600—my savings
> Total—$81,923.50.

He added the numbers again. Then he picked up the second government check and wrote down the sum he was to receive in regular installments from Social Security and the Army as Troy's surviving son.

> $419.36—per month until age 21

Billy multiplied by 12 and arrived at:

> $5,032.32 per year

He put down his pencil and stared out the window. His mother had been paid thirty-six hundred dollars per year for teaching at the University of New Mexico. He had heard her daydreaming outloud about her chances of ever being paid the lordly sum of one hundred dollars per week. To his mother, an income of five thousand dollars per year would have seemed like enough to live on easy street.

Billy changed into his boots and clean jeans and shirt. He put on his cowboy hat. He stuffed the rest of his clothes, including the wet ones, into his satchel, picked up Bredemus's golf clubs and went down to the lobby.

"Checking out?" asked the desk clerk.

"Yeah. Time to be moving on," Billy said.

Billy walked several blocks to the First National Bank and went inside and asked for a trust officer. They steered him instead to an assistant who sat at a mahogany desk beside a potted plant.

The assistant was a young man wearing a starched white shirt and a black knit tie. He looked at Billy and glanced at his watch as if about to say he had an important meeting to attend. Then Billy showed him the two checks and forty-two hundred in cash.

Billy opened a savings account with seventy-five thousand dollars at five-percent interest. With the rest, except for six twenty dollar bills that he kept for himself, he opened a checking account. As a minor with no adult guardian, Billy needed a vice president to co-sign his deposits. For the sum involved, a tall, portly man in a gray three-piece suit came out of his office and shook Billy's hand and signed the papers.

"Would you call me a taxi, please?" Billy said.

The vice president and the assistant gazed with curiosity at the young cowboy who sauntered out of the building carrying a canvas bag with seven golf clubs in it.

"You think he stuck up a bank?" asked the assistant.

"As long as he deposits his money with us, who cares?" the vice president said, and they laughed.

Billy bought a *Star-Telegram* for a nickel from the rack on the sidewalk before he opened the taxi's rear door and said, "Take me to a Chevrolet dealership."

"You mean used cars?"

"New ones," Billy said.

Within an hour Billy drove a 1951 Chevrolet Bel Air, black and yellow, with leather seats, off the dealer's lot. The new car smell was intoxicating. He stopped at The Griddle on Eighth Avenue and ate two cheeseburgers and an order of fries and drank a chocolate milk shake while he read the classifieds.

After lunch Billy drove to the Park Hill Apartments, a pink two-story building on the hill that rose out of Forest Park roughly halfway between Colonial Country Club and Texas Christian University. He rented a one-bedroom furnished apartment. The landlady phoned the bank to be sure Billy's check for his first two months' rent was cashable.

Since he had no telephone in the apartment yet, Billy walked down the hill and across University Drive to the drugstore on the corner. He dropped a nickel into the pay phone and dialed the private number of Sandra Sandpaster. If she was not in her room, he would page her at Colonial. But Sandra answered the phone.

"Hello."

"It's Billy."

"I watched you today," she said.

"I saw you."

"Congratulations. You made my grandfather very happy."

Billy said, "I need to talk to you."

"We're talking."

"I mean I need to see you."

She paused. "Well. I guess so. Shall I come downtown and pick you up?"

"Just wait where you are," Billy said. "I'll be at your house in five minutes."

• • •

Dr. Ira Sandpaster was looking through the window into his front yard when the black and yellow Bel Air turned into his driveway. Ira saw the driver was someone wearing a cowboy hat and thought of hitting the security alarm. But Ira was sipping scotch and feeling mellow, and he kept his hand off the button. He recognized the driver as Billy. What was Billy doing dressed like a cowboy? No matter. This was a good boy. Ira had picked him out as a good boy right at the beginning. Ira had told Titus, "As a scientist I don't take anything for true right off the bat. I run experiments before I make up my mind." The horrible day of the four shanked shots had thrown Ira off the track, but the scientist in him now saw that the four shanked shots were an anomaly. Ira's original judgment had been proved. This boy had rid Colonial of the Indian lout. Now there was one more thing Ira wanted Billy to do.

Sandra opened the front door and came outside as Billy switched off the ignition and stepped out of his car. She wore white shorts, white sneakers, a white polo shirt and carried a tennis racquet in a head cover under her right arm. Her skin was very tan against the white costume, and her short hair was artfully mussed. When she smiled and turned her brown eyes toward his face, he wanted to grab her and kiss her.

"Nice car," she said.

"Thanks."

"Did you win it today?"

"Yeah. You want to go for a ride?"

"I have a tennis lesson."

"Oh."

"Let me see inside." She bent her head through the window, her shorts drawing tight. "Oh, I love that smell." She straightened up again. "It's nice, really."

"It's cute, too," he said.

"I don't use that word any more. Thanks for stopping by, Billy. You were really great today. But I'm in a hurry."

"Wait a second," he said. "I want to ask you. Are you still going steady with Sonny?"

"I gave him back his little gold football this afternoon."

Billy lifted his hat and let out a cowboy yell.

"Sonny yelled when I told him, but it was a different kind of yell," Sandra said. "I told him it is impossible for me to go steady with a boy who doesn't belong to Colonial."

"How about it then?" said Billy. "There's a French movie with subtitles at the Seventh Street. We'll go to the Triple X Root Beer afterwards, and then . . ."

"There'll be a bad scene at the Triple X," Sandra said.

"I don't think so. The McWillie brothers put the Triple X off-limits to the Arlington Heights football team."

"Well, good. What else were you going to say?"

"About after the Triple X?"

"You don't need to say that. I mean, what time will you pick me up?"

They heard Ira's voice crying, "Billy! Billy! A word!" The old man came at them through the doorway, tall and gaunt with purple glasses and long toes with long yellow nails sticking out of the straps in his sandals. He listed toward his glass of scotch.

"Be nice to him, Billy. Please," Sandra said. "I'm gone to tennis now. Pick me up at 6:30." She waved. "Bye, paw paw!"

"Have a good tennis," Ira said. "Love you, doodlebug."

"Love you more," said Sandra, running for her car.

Ira gasped for breath. He had jumped down the steps too fast. But he was excited. Ira turned his purple gaze onto Billy. Despite the cowboy outfit, this was a good lad, Ira felt.

Billy had done a great service for Ira, but he wasn't through yet.

"A place has suddenly opened in my regular foursome," Ira said. "You will join my foursome tomorrow. Balls in the air at 10 A.M."

O *Twenty-eight*

N THE THURSDAY IN JUNE that Ben Hogan teed off to defend his U.S. Open championship at The Monster in Detroit, an event of vastly greater magnitude, in the view of Dr. Ira Sandpaster, was taking place on the eighteenth green at Colonial Country Club.

Ira's ball lay thirty feet from the cup. In the fairway he had asked for the opinion of Billy and had taken the advice of his former caddie and used the club Billy suggested. Billy had told him to lighten his grip. That extra bit of advice was almost crossing the line, but Ira had been playing well in his days since Billy became a member of his foursome. His colleagues noticed that Ira had been in a better humor than usual. So Ira did what Billy said in the fairway, and he hit a rocket.

Now he could three-putt for his 79.

It would be weeks, or is it months, before he turned eighty, and the way he felt now he could break 80 any day he wished.

"How would you read this one?" Ira asked.

Foxy Lerner, who was carrying the Sandpaster bag, said, "He's talking to you, Billy."

Billy was sitting on the canvas bag of seven clubs that John Bredemus had left him, wearing the spiked shoes given him by Ben Hogan. "How do you read it, Foxy?"

"It'll break four feet to the left, but it's got to have enough speed to clear that ridge."

"Foxy is the best out here at reading greens," Billy said.

"Then you would concur with this rat-faced boy?"

"Foxy is right, Dr. Sandpaster."

Ira rapped the ball with his blade putter and watched it roll across the green, climbing over the ridge and then gaining speed as it turned left and rolled toward the cup. Ira felt transported. He was in a land of magic. His ball had a will of its own. It was going straight into the cup as surely as if it were steering itself.

The ball fell into the cup for a 77. Ira had beaten his age by two strokes.

Ira shook hands and accepted the congratulations of Mr. Titus and Dr. Kemp and their caddies, Ham T and Roland. He patted Foxy on the back. He ambled over to Billy, grinning and clicking his big yellow dentures, and embraced the boy. Billy felt Ira's fingernails digging into his back.

"You have been very helpful to me, Billy," Ira said. Holding the boy at arm's length and staring into his face, Ira said, "I want you to go to work for me. Find me some oil. Find me a sea of oil. You've got the luck and the nose and the nerve to be a great oil man. Get him an office with a window, Titus."

"Thank you, sir," Billy said. "But I have one more year of high school. Then I have the draft and college. I can't go to work for you."

Ira wobbled a bit, losing his balance in the giddiness of his joy.

"I'll take care of the draft board. I'll get you in a good college," said Ira.

A baseball bat hit Ira in the chest. He staggered backwards and fell to his knees. He looked around at the faces that were becoming foggy before him. "Why, this is easy," he said.

Dr. Kemp pronounced Ira dead of what appeared to be a massive coronary.

DR. IRA SANDPASTER's funeral was sparsely attended. Billy sat alone in the back row of the University Christian Church. He counted thirty people at the ceremony. Sandra sat on the front row with her mother and a dozen relatives who had arrived from around the world. On the second row were Mr. Titus, Dr. Kemp and a few others Billy recognized from Colonial. He guessed the rest might be employees of Sandpaster Oil & Gas.

Billy wore his boots and jeans and sat with his hat in his lap as he listened to the preacher. Mr. Titus wept while doing his eulogy. Billy had not seen Sandra since the day her grandfather died. She had been busy with family and guests and her mother. She said her mother was eating up her time, demanding things of her constantly. She would get with Billy later, when this was over.

In his new Bel Air, Billy joined the procession to the cemetery. He stood apart from the others at the graveside. The men were wearing suits and ties. Sandra wore high heels and a black dress.

When Ira's coffin had been planted and the others were returning to their limousines, Sandra summoned Billy with a wave.

"Mom, I want you to meet Billy," she said.

Sandra's mother was tall and thin. She lifted her veil and smiled at Billy. He saw that she was beautiful.

"How cute you are," said Sandra's mother. She did not offer a hand. "Sandra has told me how adorable you are and how nice you were to daddy at the end. I don't know how I can ever thank you." She glanced at the motor procession. "Come along now, dear. There's so much packing to do. We'll miss our ride. We wouldn't want to be stranded in a cemetery, would we?"

"I'll be right behind you," Sandra said as her mother walked away.

"Your mother is great looking," Billy said.

"She's a pain."

"When can I see you again?" said Billy.

"Mom and I are leaving tonight."

"You going to New York with her?"

Sandra bit her lip before she answered.

She said, "Paw paw's will says if he dies before I graduate from high school, my mom becomes my guardian and I go to a boarding school in Switzerland to prepare for going to Stanford. I don't know when I'll see you again."

"You're really going away?" Billy said. "How about us?"

"I know what." She smiled. "You make good grades and we'll meet again next year at Stanford. You can play on their golf team."

She kissed him on the lips and turned and followed her mother.

BILLY HADN'T LOCKED THE DOOR of his apartment since he had moved in. People in Fort Worth didn't lock their doors. He turned the knob and stepped inside. Light shone from the lamp in the living room, but the bedroom and the kitchen were dark. Billy heard someone moving. He guessed it was Foxy or one of the boys from the yard. They had visited him a few times. But if it was Foxy, the phonograph would be playing.

He saw a figure sitting on the couch at the edge of the lamplight. The feet and lower legs were in the light, and Billy recognized the muscular calves and drooping socks.

"Hello, Billy Boy," said John Bredemus. "I came to fetch my clubs. I feel like playing some golf."

"They're in the closet," Billy said, opening the door in his entryway. He picked up the canvas bag of seven clubs and carried it to Bredemus, whose eyes sparkled as he reached for them.

"When you go away, where do you go?" Billy asked.

"I've told you, I have rounds to make. Many golf courses to watch over. Sometimes I whisper into a golfer's ear." Bredemus picked up a familiar cigar box from the couch and handed it to Billy.

Billy opened the box and saw the velvet pouch that contained Jim Thorpe's medals.

"Keep these safe for me, will you? I'll be back to get them someday soon. Polish them until they shine brightly again. I want you to absorb their spirit," Bredemus said. "The more you polish them, the stronger you will become." Bredemus hefted his canvas bag onto his shoulder and pulled his tweed cap at an angle toward his right ear. "But first, take a look in the bedroom."

Billy knew he had left the bedroom door open, but it was closed now.

He walked over and opened the door, and it was like looking into a mirror. Troy stood there, wearing his boots and jeans and hat and rodeo buckle, his shoulders wide and straight, the smoky blue eyes studying Billy.

"Nice place here," said Troy.

"I have a new Bel Air, too."

"Great car."

"You gave all of this to me," Billy said.

"Truth is, I didn't set out to blow myself up. But it happened. I'm glad to help you have a better life. Improve on what I did with mine, will you?"

"I'm sorry I called you a jerk," Billy said.

"You forgive me?"

"I love you, daddy."

"Then things are straight between you and me?" asked Troy.

Billy stepped forward with his arms spread to hug and kiss his father, but he embraced a mist.

Troy was gone.

Billy rushed into the living room. "Please, call him back," Billy said.

"Not in this lifetime," said Bredemus. "Remember this when you become a father, Billy Boy."

Carrying his golf clubs, Bredemus walked to the door that led into the hall.

Bredemus said, "I'll see you soon. *Above all, be cheerful.*"
The angel dissolved and passed through the closed door.
Billy felt a surge of happiness.

He sat down in his chair beside the lamp and looked out the window at the darkening sky and the roof of trees that covered Forest Park and the road to Colonial Country Club.

First thing he would need tomorrow is a new set of golf clubs.

About the Author

BUD SHRAKE is a novelist, screenwriter and coauthor of *Harvey Penick's Little Red Book,* the best selling sports book of all time. He lives in Austin, Texas.

For advice on the games of golf and life, look for these Harvey Penick books, all co-authored by Bud Shrake.

HARVEY PENICK'S
LITTLE RED BOOK
Lessons and Teachings
from a Lifetime in Golf

0-684-85924-6 • $10.00

HARVEY PENICK
with Bud Shrake
And If You Play
Golf, You're My
Friend
THE NATIONAL BESTSELLER
FURTHER REFLECTIONS OF A GROWN CADDIE

0-684-86773-8 • $10.00

HARVEY PENICK
with Bud Shrake
The Game for
a Lifetime
MORE LESSONS
AND TEACHINGS

0-684-86735-4 • $11.00

The
WISDOM OF
HARVEY PENICK
Lessons
AND
Thoughts
FROM THE
Collected
Writings
OF Golf's
Best-Loved
Teacher
HARVEY PENICK
with Bud Shrake

0-684-84508-3 • $26.00

HARVEY PENICK
with Bud Shrake
FOR ALL WHO
LOVE THE GAME
Lessons and Teachings
for Women

0-684-86734-6 • $10.00

FIRESIDE
A Division of Simon & Schuster
SIMON & SCHUSTER
A VIACOM COMPANY
SOURCE